ANCIENT
FLAME
ARLETA RAE

ANCIENT FLAME

CHILDREN FROM SACRIFICE
BOOK THREE

ARLETA RAE

BOOKS BY ARLETA RAE

Children From Sacrifice

Rising Ember

Dark Inferno

Ancient Flame

Find author made playlists for all books at msha.ke/arletarae

For you, reader.
Make that leap into the unknown and trust your gut.

CONTENTS

CHAPTER ONE

THEA

Underneath the cracks of souls are all the people and circumstances that have either helped create them or tried to mend them. In life, those cracks are inevitable. We all receive them in some form or another, but it's how we respond to them that determines their depths. Some people try and ignore them. Others lash out, gripping the anger that serves as a shield.

I've come to learn that those cracks shape who we are. They are never asked for, but yet they happen.

After years of refusing to truly acknowledge what the death of my loved ones had on me, I gave in to the primal emotions. It wasn't just the grief and anger that I locked away in that gilded cage, but also the unconditional love they held for me. That kind of emotion could never leave me, even if the person who provided them did.

But as the dimension I am tethered to crumbles, and I lie here dying, was it worth it? Yes, I think so. I try not to regret things in life, but it is hard not to wish that I nurtured those emotions instead of shoving them away like unwanted gifts.

"Thea, just hold a little longer," an unfamiliar voice says tenderly into the waves of pain wracking my body.

My limbs are screaming like they are on fire, or like someone is trying to rip them off. Each torrent of agony ripples in both me and the dimension as it breaks. I can feel the cracks in the ground and in the sky just as I feel the ones in my body.

"Cole is trying to fix this," that voice says again. Actually, I know that voice. It resonates with memories of the past, though I don't know their origin.

Mica. He holds me firmly against his chest as he carries me through the dimension. I can feel the wind as he moves swiftly away from that clearing in the woods where we failed at defeating Morwen, the King of the Brais. My brown hair swishes in the movement, jarring despite his secure grip on my back and behind my knees.

"He left," I cry. The garbled voice that spills from my mouth doesn't sound like mine. There is a brokenness in it that I haven't recognized in so many years.

Cole left me. We fought for each other. And when I was lying on the cold grass in this unnatural dimension dying, he left. The symbol on my collarbone that binds me to this dimension as the anchor burns against my skin just as another wave of rolling sharp pains wrack my body. At the same time, a jagged fissure tears into the ground somewhere along the southern edge of the dimension. The destruction flashes through my mind like it were playing on a movie screen.

"Thea, please."

With blurry vision, I look up and see Mica, his emerald gaze fixed forward as we move. His pale hair is a stark contrast to the charcoal-colored clouds above our heads. Heavy drops of rain fall from the sky, drenching the false nature of this magically conjured dimension around us. "We lost," I whisper as a tear falls from of the corner of my eye.

Mica tightens his hold on me as we dart faster through the forest. There are no sounds of insects or wind-rustled leaves. Thunder cracks above, echoing against the sound of Mica's quick footsteps and the erratic heartbeat in my chest. "The war isn't over yet, Thea. Just hold on a little longer, please."

I roll my head to the side, away from his body and see we are moving closer to the Brais' castle. Closer to the spot where Morwen transferred the anchor mark from herself to me. Nausea roils inside me with each step forward. Despite the gnawing pain, I push a weak palm against his rain-soaked shirt. "Don't. I don't want to go back."

Mica looks down at me without missing a beat in his strides. "We will be safer in there. I promise."

Somehow, my body relaxes at his words.

There is a reprieve from the unrelenting fury of the rainstorm as we cross the threshold into the castle. Mica kicks the large doors open and they slam against the wall, echoing down the empty halls. The air is warmer inside, though there is still a chill that sits on my skin.

Mica lays me down gently on a soft, plush sofa. We are in the grand entrance room. When the castle was full of Brais vampires, this gigantic room seemed ancient and lifeless, but with only the two of us, it seems like a relic lost to time.

I will love you for as long as stars shine over your head and Earth sits beneath your feet. Cole's words ring in my ears as the weight of what happened crashes against my skull. We fought the King of the Brais and lost. Now, Morwen is out in the real world where she can wreak havoc on the innocents. She seeks revenge on those who have wronged her. The humans and witches. And, for some reason, Cole and I are at the center of the hatred she bears.

The lives of so many people may be at risk and all my selfish mind is concerned about is that Cole left me here.

I swallow and wince at the dryness of my throat. To my right, Mica sits on the coffee table with his head in his palms. I reach a shaking hand and place it on his knee. "Where did Cole go?"

Mica stills at my touch before running his hands over his

head. "He's trying to save you. To stop the dimension from being destroyed."

I open my mouth, but whatever words were about to come out are replaced with a scream. As if someone were dragging a knife through my insides, I crumble into a fetal position, my body shaking uncontrollably.

Mica is over me in an instant, his hands trying to soothe me as they rub my arms. "I'm sorry." He repeats those words over and over. His hands stop when the screaming does.

The sharpness of the magic connecting me to the dimension tears at my body, at my soul. It fades away at an agonizing crawl. Panting, I unfurl and stare up at the ceiling. "How?" I manage to ask. My throat is hoarse and my voice comes out rough.

Mica tilts his head, his gaze surveying. "How what?"

"Cole," I answer.

Mica must understand the question because he takes a deep breath and shakes his head. "I'm not sure how he plans to stop it." He looks to the vaulted ceiling, to where an ornate candle-lit chandelier hangs. "But he seemed quite determined and confident in what he needed to do. To save you, Thea. If this dimension falls, so do you."

"I know," I whisper, my throat hoarse. My chest tightens at the thought of Cole leaving me behind. Then again, if this dimension is crumbling, I would rather Cole be as far away from here as possible. Morwen said if the dimension would be destroyed, anyone inside would be as well. Was that a truth from her lips or just something she would hope I would relay to my allies? "You should go," I rasp.

Mica knits his brows together in defiance. "I'm staying."

Sharp pains explode in my head and I gasp, clutching the material of the couch. An image of a tree splitting in two flashes in my mind as a sharp, splintering pain cuts through my shoulder. The intense pain fades as quickly as it came, though its ghostly touch lingers. "I'm okay," I assure, faltering on the words.

Mica and I sit in silence for a beat, listening to the weather as it batters the castle. When I turn my head to him, he is looking at me, his green eyes holding some eternal emotion I can't pinpoint. "Why?" I ask.

A corner of Mica's lips turn up. "You've never been very good at asking questions, Thea. Why what? Why am I staying?"

I shake my head, though consider that question as well. Days ago, when Mica caught me in that room I was using to spy on a Brais General, I noticed something about him. For some reason, when we were alone then, staring into his gaze pulled me into a vision. All visions I have experienced thus far have been of the past. "Why are you with the Brais?"

He glances down at his hands, clasped over his knees. When he looks back up, there is a trench of sadness in those emerald eyes that lurches at my heart. "Not long after I was turned, I fell in love."

With that short sentence, I know what he is going to say next. Grief tightens around my heart and my hand moves to his in comfort. If I had any ounce of strength left, I would use energy manipulation, my beta ability, to send calming emotions into him.

He doesn't move, doesn't return the hold of my hand. He stares at my hand in his, and it seems that his sadness grows deeper. "I made a deal with someone who claimed they could help."

"Morwen?" I ask gently.

He frowns at the question.

Then, my eyes land on that mark along his collarbone, just barely visible underneath his shirt. It looks like a plant, one covered in thorns. And it binds him to the King of the Brais. To Morwen. She showed me she has the same mark. She was the one who informed me the repercussions of receiving it.

Those who bear it cannot speak against the King, nor can they fight against him—*her*—lest they forfeit their lives. No wonder Morwen has been able to stay in power for so long. "I understand," I say for him.

He exhales a long breath. "The King wanted my magic, and all I wanted was to save the woman I loved from the fate life dealt her. I didn't give any thought into the words that were used to bind me." He squeezes his eyes shut, his breathing ragged. "All I could do was watch while the person I loved suffered a horrible death."

Even with my slumbering beta ability, the grief Mica holds is palpable. I squeeze his hand. "I'm sorry," I offer. No sooner that the words leave my lips does another round of pain ravage my body. Blinding agony ripples through me and I convulse under its waves. I see the cliffs to the east. My mind travels there without my body, as if I were an apparition gazing down on them. Rocks and debris crash into the raging sea that surrounds the dimension as a trench forms alongside the cliffs. The pain is so intense that it stifles my voice. Unable to scream, I just shake silently on the couch that now feels like cement as my body tears from the inside out.

Mica whispers soothing words, though I don't hear them. His voice is soft and calms the ravaging storm within my mind. He runs a hand along my arm as the torrent of pain slows. He glances to the large window at the back of the room just as a blinding flash of lightning strikes a nearby tree, the accompanying thunder rattling the castle and my bones.

The tree shatters from the strike, my mind splintering with it. Hot tears sting my eyes. My body convulses with each round slashing through me. I am grateful for Mica, who remains quiet as he runs his hand over my arms in comfort. I don't know how long I remain curled on the couch, riding out this tsunami of agony, but when it finally slows, my body is stiff.

"Thea?" Mica asks, worry laced in every letter of my name.

I swallow and keep my eyes pinned shut, my jaw tight. The familiar sensation of hunger returns, chasing away any lingering shadows of distress. This time, I welcome that uncomfortable gnaw in my stomach. Compared to what I was just feeling, the hunger is like a paper cut.

I hear Mica shift on the table, and I open my eyes. "I'm okay at the moment." With a swallow, I slowly rise to my elbows, waiting for more waves of pain, and glance around the grand sitting room of the castle. The enormous room feels haunted with the lack of vampires sitting and conversing on the various couches. I am reminded of the time I walked down the stairs and found Mica and Morwen sitting beside each other. I turn and look at the green-eyed vampire and the mark underneath his shirt. "If you have the curse on your collarbone, how was it that you spoke Morwen's name when I was new here?" Both he and Commander Kael had uttered her name before.

Mica sighs and rubs his neck. "The King created that curse. It is an active spell and he has the power to alter it." His brows crease in regret. "I was ordered to use the King's name while I was around you so that you wouldn't become too suspicious, too quickly." His fingers tap with an irregular beat on his knees. "The curse is active again, ever since I threw my magic at the King back in the clearing. I'm sorry for helping deceive you."

"There is no need for apologies. You helped me despite your own trials. For that, I am thankful." A sharp, needlelike pain shoots across my forehead and I brace for more. I wince, but it disappears. "I'm okay," I say quietly.

The fireplace behind Mica and me is crackling, the scent of its smoke soothing. I notice that the fireplace on the far side of the room, the one beside a giant wall of windows, is cold.

Candles in the elegant chandelier above us are casting a glow on the vaulted ceiling.

Mica opens his mouth to say something, but the double-arched front doors groan as someone from outside pushes them open. Mica jumps to his feet, the temperature in the room plummeting as his ice magic whirrs around him, taking the shape of ice daggers that hover at his fingertips.

I motion to stand as well, but my body feels so weak and nausea still fights with the hunger. My magic hums in my veins, coating my body in a thin, protective barrier. Protection from whoever opened the doors and from Mica's ice. Puffs of breath cloud in front of my mouth.

A tall, dark-skinned vampire enters the castle. He holds a dagger in his right hand, though it is not poised to strike, only to defend. His deep brown eyes are crinkled with worry as he scans our faces, then the foyer beyond. His leather armor is wet and slathered with mud. Rainwater drips from his fully stocked bandolier strapped across his chest.

Mica lets out a breath. His hands flex at his sides as the iciness of his magic simmers away, letting the warmth from the fireplace snake over my body again. Mica sits back down on the table, though with a bit more distance between us. He runs a hand through his pale blond hair as he looks to the vampire closing the doors. "Oba. Good to see that you're still alive. I feared the worst when I didn't see you with Cole."

This vampire came here with Cole? Could he be another member of the vampire faction that Cole and I belong to, the Essites? The ones who stand in the way of the Brais—who stand in the way of Morwen's desire for destruction and power.

Oba takes more steps into the foyer. His eyes scan the room quickly before they land on me for a beat then return to Mica. "That dark-haired vampire broke my neck when Cole and I ran into her. Where is he?" There is a mixture of worry and trepidation in the towering vampire's voice. He seems to trust Mica, though there is a wariness in his stiff body language.

Mica rolls his head, as if to chase away an ache, then narrows his eyes at Oba. "He's fine. Did you know the Minuit Coven were planning to destroy this dimension while we were in it?"

I flinch under Mica's words, the movement sending a ripple of pain lancing down my spine. I brace for another bout of sharpness, but what comes is more bearable. It slices down my neck and into my arms, all the way to my fingertips, the sensation reminiscent to a cat scratch.

There is no way that Sarah would plan to destroy this place if she knew I had become the anchor that tethered it. Her plan must have been to give us time to flee Morwen while it was crumbling. But why did the coven never try and destroy the dimension before? I don't know much about how spells and other witch magics work, but perhaps they were missing necessary pieces.

"Cole figured that the coven leader was planning to do something like that," Oba answers. He takes a deep breath and runs a finger along the inside of his bandolier. A dagger and wooden stakes sit snuggly in their sheathes attached to the leather. "It is why our plan consisted of getting in and getting *you* out," he adds, jerking his chin toward me.

I furrow my brows. "What about everyone else who was still inside? If the dimension was destroyed, they would have been killed." The moment I finished the sentence, I realize that I'm not even sure if there are any other beings in this dimension. Though, I know of at least one other vampire in here who would have perished…

"*You* were the only one Cole and Sarah had their mind on," Oba says.

"We didn't matter," Mica adds, as if he could read my

thoughts. His head is tipped down, and he glances at his clasped hands. He turns and lifts his gaze to me. "The King wants you dead because you are a threat. It can't be a coincidence that you are the first and only vampire who survived the anchor transfer spell." His words evoke the memories of Morwen's horrendous spell from only a few hours ago. Of the pain and agony it caused. Of the symbol that stains my skin, marking me as the anchor.

I shake my head before pinning my own lethal gaze on the water wielder. "The lives of those who would stand against the Brais *matters*. They all matter."

Mica stares, unblinking, as a plethora of emotions streak across his face. The intense color of his eyes threaten to pull my soul away from the present like before. Snippets of a memory flash in my mind, coated in a haze: a cool breeze on my skin and a warm, golden beam of sunlight.

I break his stare and run my hands over my face. "How am I supposed to fight her when I'm stuck in here now?"

"Who even is she?" Oba asks.

Mica begins to say something, but a sharp pain slices through my body causing me to scream. The bones in my arm break and I double over, my vision blurring from the agony. I see rocks cracking and becoming dust, trees uprooted and crashing to the ground, and I see the pond to the north shriveling.

Oba and Mica are talking, but I can't hear them. Not over this pain. It's too much. A metallic tang coats my tongue and I feel someone trying to comfort me by rubbing their hand on my back.

My bones stop breaking, my magic humming as it heals them. I take in a shaky breath, not daring to move when a ripple in my awareness sends shivers down my spine.

I can feel the expansiveness of the dimension as if it were indeed in my mind. And at the very corner, a barrage of odd energy pulses, running its sinister fingers down my soul. My body protests at the unwelcomed sensation, lurching me forward as my magic stirs to protect. With a hoarse voice, I say, "I think something bad is coming through the portal."

CHAPTER TWO

COLE

The brick manor sits well away from the quiet road. Thorny vines climb around the stone wall and creep over the cobbled path. Flower beds grow outside of their oblong-shaped beds. With the coming of autumn, leaves litter the ground, nestling themselves into the long grass. If I didn't know that someone lived here, I would think the place was vacant. That or the occupant cares little for tidiness. Nature is slowly reclaiming this estate.

If Valeria were still alive, I doubt the place would look as chaotic as it does now. The old Minuit Coven leader had always kept things orderly, especially her plants.

String lights are loosely wrapped around the wooden columns of the front porch. The strand looped onto a hook from the ceiling droops too low, as if someone tugged on it. I dart up the first few steps to the porch, intending to duck under the lights, when my body is pushed back from the impact. I stumble backward, tripping on the steps. My limbs prickle with the uninviting magic that protects the house, urging me to turn around. I push my black hair out of my face, tousled from the sudden impact, and bite back a growl.

"Sarah!" I yell, glancing at the windows. There is no

movement, no curtain swaying or lights flickering on. With each second that passes, Thea is in pain and her life in danger because of Sarah's secretive plan to destroy the dimension, and thus destroying the Brais King. It must have been why she was so insistent about getting Thea out as fast as possible, so that she could destroy the dimension the moment we were safe. Why would she have even started the spell without knowing whether we all made it out? If she confided her plans to me, I would have told her how reckless that would have been.

But witches keep secrets. And their trust comes slow. Valeria never trusted me enough, either, even when we were forming an alliance decades ago. Sometimes I wonder if she had trusted me more, maybe I could have understood that there was more to this world than the Brais.

But I can't put that blame on her. In the end, she was right to have doubts about my alignment in the war between vampire factions. I was a Brais then, fighting against the Essites for dominion over the vampire species.

Today, I fight for the Essites. I fight for life and for balance. I fight for Thea. And I'll destroy the Brais for everything they have done.

"Sarah!" I shout again, my nostrils flaring as the wind rustles the leaves on the ground and sways the dangling string of lights. I'm about to throw my air magic at a window when the front door opens, a brown-haired woman stepping onto the threshold, her bright blue eyes full of fury as she scans the yard. Her olive green shirt is tucked into black pants and her arms are crossed at her chest.

"Where the hell is Thea?" Amelia asks, her voice laced with venom. The young werewolf carries a commanding aura that I can only assume an alpha could hold. I figured Sarah would have the wolf shifter guarding the house.

The feral presence that I have associated with a werewolf's energy pricks at me from all sides of my awareness, indicating the other wolves in Amelia's pack are around, but not too close. It is a bit disturbing that I am just now noticing their presence.

The gusting wind doesn't lessen, fueled by my increasing anger. "She is stuck in the castle dimension." I dig my nails into my palm as my voice becomes lethal. "Sarah needs to stop destroying it immediately." I cut the rest of my sentence off before the building rage in my chest unleashes itself on everyone within the estate.

Amelia's lips part at the news, the only indication that she is surprised, but she schools her features quickly. She doesn't move, doesn't rush to whatever room Sarah and the other witches are in. She remains fixed in the doorway, letting Thea suffer with each breath.

I feel my vampiric features shift under the growing silence within my mind. If I release most of my magic at once, a blast of wind like that could destroy whatever protection magic the witches used to keep vampires out. It would also demolish the house with everyone inside. Sarah, Thea's best friend, and the other Minuit witches, along with the alpha in front of me… Could I justify killing them to keep Thea safe? Something inside my mind snarls its approval.

Amelia's gaze flicks to the trees around the property before she takes a step back into the house. The movement pushes that predator instinct inside me to chase. Since I can't follow her into the house, my magic stirs under my veins, ready to go where my body cannot.

The wolf inside must have realized this, too. Amelia's gaze, though turned up in worry, is fierce. A *warning*. From one predator to another. "Wait here," she says before turning around, all traces of venom leaving her tone.

Despite the chaos that whirs in my blood, I listen to the wolf, my teeth grinding together. Taking a deep breath, I tilt my head back and glance at the ceiling of the porch. There are faded sigils written in some sort of aging ink. Even though the drawings look chipped, the spell holds.

Movement to my right catches my eye, and I turn my head. A large wolf stands just beyond the property line. It is smaller than the one I believed to have been Amelia at the battle against Amaund, solidifying the theory that Amelia is, indeed, the alpha. This wolf is sandy colored with a white ear and matching paws. It just stands by a large oak tree, its golden gaze locked on me.

I exhale another long breath and return my attention on the empty threshold. Just in time to see a furry little cat run out the door and stop at my feet. Helios stares up at me and lets out a loud, happy meow. I reach down to pet Thea's orange cat who we stashed here for safety. We weren't sure if the Brais were keeping scouts stationed at my cabin, so we figured here would be safer for the feline.

Helios meows again and weaves through my legs before plopping his butt down on the sidewalk as if to command me to hurry and get back to Thea.

Only a minute passes before Amelia returns, though it feels like an eternity. Sarah follows behind her companion, an expression of concern etched into her soft features. Her light brown eyes are flecked with a mix of emotions, and it looks like there is charcoal or ash smeared on her dark skin. The smell of woodsmoke drifts to my nose, making me believe it to be the latter. It lingers in the space between us, mixing with the scent of herbs I can't identify.

"What happened?" Sarah asks, her gaze searching behind me as Amelia's did before, as if Thea could appear out of nowhere. Her eyes widen a fraction when they take in the blood on my shirt. "Where is Thea?" Her voice trembles as she says the name of her best friend.

I cross my arms. Oba said that witches and vampires will never get along, and I disagreed with him. For the sake of ending this war with our lives, I hope he is still wrong. But every time I thought our alliance was genuine and trusting, the witches kept vital information from us. I've learned that Sarah, like all other Demoix witches in the past, has been cursed into silence, unable to speak about the King of the Brais. Her family did something to the King, causing a retaliation. Whatever it was that they did, I haven't figured out yet.

"Like I told her," I jerk my chin at Amelia but keep my eyes on the witch. "She is stuck in the dimension you are trying to destroy."

Sarah blinks at me for a moment before narrowing her eyes at me. "One of my witches saw Thea leave the dimension. We started the ritual immediately upon confirmation." There is a flicker of doubt that flashes across her smooth features.

Before my anger can call her witch a liar, I take a breath. Frustration will not help this precarious situation. "She didn't." Sarah's eyes widen, like she was realizing the ramifications of her spell, as I continue, "Only the King did." I drop my hands to my sides and take the next step, standing just outside the barrier. Out of the corner of my vision, I notice the wolf on the outskirts moving slowly closer to the house. Amelia inches closer to Sarah as well. I clench my teeth before saying, "Please tell me that the spell has stopped."

She bows her head. "It stopped the moment I heard you yell my name. Thea…" She swallows, the movement in her throat catching my attention. "How? Why is she still there?"

I force myself to stop looking at her throat. At the increasing pulse pounding against her skin, and the blood beneath. The guilt and sadness in her expression doesn't make my anger disappear. "The King." I shake my head. "No, that wo—"

"Don't say the King's name," Sarah hisses as she takes a step in front of Amelia.

With another shake of my head, I say, "The King made

Thea the anchor. And you almost killed your friend because of that." I point a finger at her.

Sarah brings a shaky hand to her mouth, the other clutching her stomach as if she might get sick. She closes her eyes tightly. Behind her, Amelia places a gentle hand on the witch's shoulder, her ice blue eyes landing on mine. "We didn't know."

Relief mingles in my chest, pushing against the anger still lingering. "Stop keeping information from us then." The vampire side of me wants to break free, to shift and take control. To let both my wind and psychic magic destroy everything. I shove it down when it urges to rip into everyone's neck. "How can we fight this war together when you are keeping secrets, Sarah? We are on the same team."

The witch hangs her head, Amelia silent in the background. The sand-colored wolf to my right has stopped advancing and remains halfway between the house and the trees. A light breeze sways through the porch, rustling the string lights and my hair. I take a breath and watch as Sarah steps across the threshold of her home.

"You're right, Cole." She slides her hand over the bare skin of her arm. "This was something that I should have shared with the Essites. With *you*." She turns to Amelia. "Gather the wolves and the witches."

Amelia nods without hesitation before darting into the house. I don't miss the reassuring squeeze of her hand on Sarah's shoulder.

"So then, Thea is the anchor and the King has escaped?" Sarah asks, her voice steadying. Her back straightens as she reclaims the composure of a powerful witch and coven leader.

"Yes."

She glances to the sigils written on the roof of the porch as if making sure they can't be easily erased. "Tell me every-thing," Sarah says, not in a commanding way, but in the way a friend would ask another. The kind of tone that promised harm to their enemies.

"I can't," I respond, taking the few steps down to reach the stone path that will take me back to the portal. The only way to use the portals to and from the Brais dimension is with an offering of their blood. I hope that Mica gave me enough of his for a two-way trip. "I need to get back to Thea."

"Then tell me on the way," she says.

CHAPTER THREE

THEA

The portal to the dimension hums, its song echoing through my mind as intruders walk through it. Their presence is jagged and undeniably dangerous. It is like an itch in the back of my throat that I cannot scratch. The sensations skittering into my mind as they walk through the portal are uncomfortable.

I stand from the couch in the castle foyer, wincing as I prepare for another wave of agony. Nothing happens. The pain and the nausea scurry away like rodents. The ghost of the discomfort lingers, like the bad taste of something on my tongue. My chest moves in heavy breaths as I stand there, blinking and waiting.

But hunger is now the only discomfort I feel in my body. And in my mind, I see the pond returning to its usual size, the cliffs no longer breaking apart, and new trees sprouting where the others splintered.

"Are you okay?" Mica asks, his hands outstretched as if he were preparing to catch me should I fall.

"Yes, I think so." I take a deep breath and roll my shoulders. I can't help the sliver of gratitude that spikes through my chest. Despite the fear from those who are coming through the portal, I am thankful that the pain has stopped. That the dimension is stitching itself back together and not crumbling on our heads.

My magic sizzles under my skin, readying to fight. "Let's go," I say.

"What came through the portal?" Oba asks as the three of us make our way to the only portal left in the dimension. In hopes of trapping the King in this dimension, I destroyed the other one. I had no idea until afterward that the portals are tethered to the anchor. Tethered to *me*. Destroying the smaller one felt like someone dragged a sword through my mind.

I chew on my lip, reaching into that part of myself that is connected to the dimension. "Vampires I think. I'm not sure how many. A few maybe." I flex my hand at my side, grappling for something that isn't there. "Where is Vitamors?" The sword of all swords, the Brais Commander called it. It came to me when I summoned it. A sword made of metal that can kill a vampire. The *only* sword that I am aware of that can kill a vampire. It can also heal its wielder.

Mica keeps his gaze forward. "I left it in the clearing. I didn't think we would need it if we were all going to die."

I test my magic, calling the flames that flow through my veins. It seems that I have regained enough strength to at least conjure something. My palms heat, a glorious sensation that somehow feels different than it usually does. Does it have something to do with my parents visiting me when I was dying after saving Cole? My entire body burst into flames when I awoke.

"Can you try and keep the clouds covering the sun?" Mica asks, shifting his steps so that he is traveling in the shade of the trees. Indeed, the sun is slowly making a rare appearance. Most days that I have been here, it was either overcast or rainy.

"Oh, that reminds me," Oba says as he reaches in a pocket of his pants. He pulls out a silver chain necklace with a pyramidal, amber pendulum. Oba tosses it to Mica, who catches it just as the clouds break apart. There is a moment of the skin on his hand burning before it mends itself back together again.

More clouds part and the sunlight touches Mica's face as he loops the jewelry around his neck. "You had my sun totem this whole time?" His green eyes shimmer in the bright daylight.

Oba shrugs. "Yeah, sorry."

"I'm still stuck on you asking *me* to keep the sun hidden. I can wield fire, not the sun," I interrupt, glancing at the necklace Mica holds gently in his palm. The amber appears to have yellow, fossilized flowers inside. As we round a fallen tree, I hear the distant sound of crashing waves.

"Technically, he asked you to keep the clouds overhead. Not to keep the sun from shining," Oba chimes in.

Mica and I cut him a glare, but he only laughs. "As the anchor, you can control the nature of this place," Mica says, dropping the totem under his white shirt.

I open my mouth to tell him that he's insane when I remember the lightning and thunder during those wrenching moments I thought Cole was dying. The sky seemed to weep with me. And the lightning pointed me not only where he was bleeding out but where Morwen was running to.

"That's wild," I reply, thinking back to all the times the weather spontaneously got better when Morwen wanted to train outside with me.

We reach the beach, stopping just at the edge of the tree line. My jaw drops at the number of vampires who have entered through the portal. A part of me wants to dip below the tall grasses at our feet, but it is highly likely that they have already spotted us. Even with the expansive beach between us, it would be hard for vampires to miss oncoming enemies. This dimension has always been too quiet.

It only felt like a few came through.

"There has to be at least two dozen vampires here," Oba hisses, snatching one of his wooden stakes from the bandolier across his chest. He rolls his broad shoulders, loosening his body for a fight.

I test my own magic. Both the flames and energy manipulation stir at my call, ready to be unleashed. I've come a long way with both abilities. My flames burn so hot that they'll ignite things close enough to feel their heat. And with my energy manipulation, I can heal an ally or force an enemy to feel paralyzing fear. Of course, healing with my beta ability would be a lot better if I had Vitamors with me. Since healing like that transfers the injury to myself, I risk impairment to my own body. But Vitamors heals me, a complementary ability that makes me wonder if it was made for me.

Though, it did belong to the first vampire before. To Morwen. We have the same abilities, and yet, she is exponentially stronger than I am. What good is being immune to her silence curse—being the only one able to truly fight her—if I can't keep up with her?

"Considering that they have not moved from the beach and returned to the castle, they probably know that the King is not here. They were likely given the order to fight us, knowing we would be weak and outnumbered," Mica says.

The temperature around us declines, and my breath puffs in front of me. Glancing to him on my left, I see tiny shards of ice forming around his body. Like a thousand daggers, they create a shield and an array of deadly weapons. Water is pulled from the grasses beneath our feet, rising to him like rain climbing toward the sky. The plants that he pulls the droplets from are turning brown, dying and shriveling from the lack of hydration.

Fire isn't the only element that can maim.

"Unfortunately for them, we aren't as weak as they assume." Flames lick up my right arm, swirling from my palm to my fingertips, up my wrist and to my elbow. I keep my left hand free, not wanting to melt Mica's ice blockade.

The pinprick of an ancient magic pokes at my side. Something far to my right hums, tugging at my awareness. It doesn't feel like Morwen or another enemy, so I ignore it and focus again on those in front of us.

"No, we are not," Mica agrees. And then he starts running.

Oba and I jump into a sprint after him. My flames dance in the wind, flowing behind me like a cape. With Mica out of range, they emerge from my left palm and swallow the rest of that arm. Soon, my entire back is consumed in fire.

The Brais vampires in the front line prepare for our attacks and ignite their own magic, all of which is fire. A couple of them take a few steps toward us as we continue to charge forward. I notice one who stands in my line of sight, his limbs trembling slightly as he plucks a stake from his belt. His brown eyes widen as he takes in the growing cloak of flames behind me.

Mica releases the shards of ice hovering in front of him as he pushes on. I hardly see them move before a handful of Brais drop to the ground. One must have been struck in the neck by many ice daggers, because his head severs from his body by the time it hits the sand, dangling by just a few arteries. Their blood soaks into the beach, staining the air with a fowl stench.

Using those shards left Mica's front vulnerable. There must be less water in the sand than in the grass because the ice that forms now is considerably thinner than what he had before.

I'll gift him with water then.

Within seconds of the thought, clouds form above. Dark and threatening. None of the Brais seem to take notice of the storm brewing above them, all attention fixed on us. Light rain showers around us, hissing as it hits the hot beach.

"Hold," I say. Both Oba and Mica heed my word and come to an abrupt stop. They look to me, but I am looking at the sky—at the clouds that swirl overhead, so dark that they almost paint the world black.

The dimension seems to pause, silence rippling through the beach like a suffocating tidal wave. Even the rain hits the trees and sand in a quiet beat.

A few of the Brais vampires take this as a chance to advance.

I hear some of them call their allies back.

Lightning strikes the sand as a deafening crack of thunder roars through the air. There's screaming. Then the smell of burnt flesh.

By my side, Oba lets out a string of curses.

My fire sputters as a surge of dizziness roves over me. I connect my mind to the dimension again, to create another bolt of lightning that will take out the back of the Brais' army, but a sharpness cracks through my skull and I wince, grasping at my head. I return my focus on my own magic and the forces in front of us, and the pain relinquishes some of its hold. The lightning is only something I can occasionally call upon, then. Perhaps if I wasn't still worn out from fighting Morwen, I could control it more.

Instead of a raging thunderstorm, we get a violent rainstorm. The clouds open and rain pours down on us, heavier than before. I turn my head and find Mica already stealing the rainwater to replenish his shield of ice. "Don't say I never gave you anything," I jest.

He snorts, a corner of his lips pulling up. "You're too kind." He starts running again, but I catch the last word he says. "Kindria."

I growl and run after him. Raindrops sizzle as they meet the heat of my flame, evaporating before they even touch my skin. Ahead, four charred bodies lie on the sand, their skin still engulfed in fire. Another drum of thunder echoes above and some of the Brais flinch. Enraged by the death of their comrades—and probably the misinformation of our weakness—they charge forward, weapons and magic aimed to kill.

"That was insane," Oba says as he catches up to me. He holds a wooden stake in one hand while the other is held out in front of him. It appears that there is nothing in his hand, but I can feel…something. An invisible force stirs in that palm.

"I was hoping to get more," I admit. Small gusts of wind, circular in rotation, hit me only on the side where he is running. It brushes against my head before sliding to my feet, my flames moving with it. I want to reach out to it, to see if the wind is something I can manipulate as well. But the threat of a mind splitting headache keeps my curiosity at bay.

He curses again. "No wonder Cole chose you. You both have the same fighting spirit."

A lump forms in my throat at the mention of Cole. Wherever he is, I hope he is okay. "You have air magic. Like him."

He nods, a toothy grin cutting across his face. "That's not all I can do."

Before I can ask what he means, he breaks away, running faster toward our enemies who are quickly closing the distance. A green substance bubbles from his palm. It mixes with the air that whirls around his arm before it flies forward. The Brais who get hit crumble to the ground, their screams rivaling the storm and waves. Their clothes and skin sizzle and melt.

Acid. His beta ability allows him to secrete a highly lethal acidic substance.

I turn away from the dissolving vampires, not allowing myself to feel sorrow for them. For any of them. They have come here to kill us, and we must defend ourselves.

There are other ways to disable a vampire other than killing, Morwen's words spill uninvited into my head just as one of the Brais reaches me.

He swings a flame-engulfed stake at my chest. I side-step

out of his path and grab his weapon arm, shoving his body so it continues in the same trajectory. His steps become unsteady, and I push forcefully on his back so he falls to the ground. The sand devours his flames, putting them out on contact. He sneers as he swivels, plunging the stake at my heart.

Flames burst from my body and leap on his before he lands the blow. He jumps away from me, dropping his weapon as he tries to wipe away the fire devouring him.

I don't wait to see him burn before turning away.

Morwen is a liar. She has only ever been a liar.

She preached about not killing other vampires when all she has done since revealing herself as the King is try and kill me. And I am fairly certain that she was the one who almost killed Cole.

Someone behind me grabs the back of my neck and I tense, panic rising through me. My flames are snuffed out. I try to call for them, but they don't come. Fear takes root in my mind, and I thrash against the one who holds me like a help-less victim. Another Brais charges at me, a wooden stake in her hand and a snarl on her face. Wavy, pale hair blows in the wind as she runs, her ruby eyes promising death.

She looks familiar, but I can't seem to remember. Her dark skin is caked in dirt, her clothes covered in splatters of blood.

Fear. I am frozen in place from fear.

Fire won't heed my call, but I feel the stir of something else in my veins. I let the fear take over, let it flood my body, my entire being. I let it become me. It manifests into the outside world as a wall of terror. It explodes, first slamming into the vampire who holds me and then into the woman barreling at me. Her ruby eyes, just previously contorted with rage, now shift with horror. They dull to a brown, like blood that has dried.

The vampire holding me trembles, allowing me to shake loose. A veil that doused my flames releases as my captor lets go. I half turn and grab him, noting his expression that is a mixture of both shock and fear. With all my vampiric strength, I pull and throw him into the woman. They collapse on top of each other, their bodies still stiff from the horror I placed in their minds. I consider leaving them to the crippling emotions when I notice it already washing away. The woman's brows furrow in anger as she moves to shove her companion off from her.

She hardly has time to register natural fear as my flames hurdle toward her.

Leaving them, I run to the remaining Brais. Oba and Mica have taken a considerable number down, though there still seems to be a lot. A large group moves on Mica, so I head his direction with fury in my blood.

I watch as vampire after vampire drop, their bodies full of daggerlike ice shards. When I catch Mica's eye, I almost trip. Someone managed to get him in the shoulder with a stake. Blood pours from the wound, mixing with the rain that drenches his light-colored shirt. One of the vampires in front of him stiffens like a statue, his skin turning blue. Mica opens a palm at the vampire's shoulder, and the vampire falls to the ground like a log, shattering on impact. I fight the queasiness in my stomach at the sight.

Someone to my left throws a punch at me. I dodge the first blow but am hit in the jaw with the second. White hot pain shoots into my skull, my vision becoming blurry. I look up and see three attackers instead of the one, all moving quickly and simultaneously, their fists aimed for another strike. I bring my hand up to block, pulling my fire to help defend. But I'm moving at a snail's pace compared to them. They break through my defense and something cracks in my hand. Their fists hit me on the bridge of my nose. No, not three fists. Just the one. My head snaps back and I hit the sand.

My head throbs and my hand feels like it is bathing in a tub of broken glass. A metallic liquid coats my tongue. The male vampire stands over me as I gasp for breath. His image trails in my vision, creating multiples of him.

Move. I need to move.

He lifts a fist, a wooden dagger in his grasp. Words spill from his mouth, but something reminiscent to a raging waterfall is roaring in my head. Rain pelts me in the face, in the eyes.

Then something slams into the Brais, knocking him onto his back. I scramble clumsily to my feet in time to see Mica strike the Brais in the face with a bloody fist. The vampire's face shatters, pieces mixing with the coarse sand.

"Are you okay?" Mica asks, concern flooding his expression. His words sound muffled even though he is only a few feet away from me. The stake in his shoulder has been removed, and the wound doesn't appear to be bleeding anymore. His ice shield is gone and he is breathing heavily. I can't tell if that is sweat or rain dripping down his forehead.

I clutch my hand as it slowly heals, the sharp pains still incredible. I nod and immediately regret it. A headache blooms and my jaw aches. My body is trying to heal, but there is too much to attend to at once.

Then, my eyes catch a vampire materializing out of thin air. Almost ten feet behind Mica, a stake in his hand aiming right for his back. If the tip reaches his heart, he'll be killed.

CHAPTER FOUR

THEA

*D*read floods my body, and I scramble to find my voice. Time moves exponentially slower as I watch the vampire behind Mica aim his wooden stake at a lethal spot. I am acutely aware of the remaining vampires that entered through the portal. They are not moving, not charging at us. Whether they are waiting for something or unable to fight, it doesn't matter. None of them matter right now.

Mica's emerald eyes, still locked on mine, widen. If it is a reaction to my sudden fear, or if he can sense the vampire who is about to end his life, I don't know.

My legs won't move, and my magic shudders under the horror that sizzles through my blood. My voice stirs, the only part of me not frozen. "Mica!" His name is the only warning my mind can conjure.

Water droplets stop in midair around the beach as I call out to him, making it seem as if he could control time itself. The vampire behind him doesn't falter under Mica's display of power. In fact, it appears that his movement becomes swifter. Perhaps he knows that if Mica were to get just a moment of advance, it would be all over.

There is no way I can run over there to save him in time. Aside from my legs refusing to move, the distance is too great. And I would have to maneuver around Mica to get to his assailant. My magic could likely reach them first, but it, too, has refused to surface in this moment. The fear for my ally's life nestles into the magic of my blood.

That emotion is a weapon. Like the times before, I let it latch onto my beta ability. I conjure it as a manifestation and aim in the direction that Mica and the other vampire stand. I will gladly let my magic swallow Mica whole if it saves him in the end.

The thought is all my magic needs to roar to life.

I watch as the vampire closes the gap between him and Mica, the stake in his hand leveled perfectly to his heart. The droplets in the air slowly freeze solid as they move like tiny missiles toward his attacker.

Neither of us will make it. The wave of my magic is moving fast, but that vampire is already so close. Mica's ice will likely strike before the stake does, but there aren't enough shards to stop the attacker.

He's going to die. Right in front of me. My friend is going to be killed and I can't do anything to stop it.

I latch on to the dimension's magic. To the strand that connects me to the weather. Pain lances through my mind as I conjure a bolt of lightning to strike Mica's attacker down. I bite down a cry of pain as the ache in my skull intensifies with each rallying electron above.

Still, they move too slowly.

I hear the ghostly wail of a woman somewhere far, far away.

But then something made of shadow emerges from behind the Brais attacker, engulfing him whole. Bones crunch and he screams before dropping to the ground, limbs twisted in all the wrong ways.

I scramble to call my magic back before it reaches Mica. It

retreats gladly as if it, too, didn't want to be let loose on him. The darkening clouds above stop swirling as I release my tether to them, the ache in my head lessening.

Mica looks to me for a moment, his expression assessing, then he turns around. Snatching the wooden stake that almost killed him, he plunges it through the chest of the Brais vampire.

"I'll admit, I'm a little surprised," Mica calls out as he rises from the already-decaying vampire. The skin on the Brais pales to a sickening white, his cheeks already sunken in.

I'm about to ask him to clarify when someone steps out of the shadow withdrawing from the dead Brais. Alec. His skin is paler than I remember it, and his short, dusty brown hair is longer. He worked alongside Mica when I was captured by Amaund, a Brais General, and brought to this dimension. He has never shown any sort of kindness to me. Nor has he ever offered his aid like Mica has.

Despite him just saving Mica, I tense and prepare for him to attack us. My defensive movement catches his attention, and he flicks his light blue eyes at me, though his words aren't meant for me. "If I were to be completely honest, I was a bit surprised to end up here as well."

"Then why? I thought you sided with the King?" Mica asks. His breaths come in heavy, and I can't help but assume that he is running low on his ability to use magic. It makes me wonder how Oba is doing on the other side of the Brais group. I hear fighting in the distance and am anxious about joining Cole's friend in battle.

Alec doesn't get a chance to respond, nor do any of us have a second to brace ourselves. I feel the tinge of magic before anything happens, telling me just how strong this magic wielder must be. Then, a wall of sand rises from the ground, swallowing us.

I cover my face with my arms, unable to do anything else. The sand stings as it grinds against my body, filling my clothes and shoes. Some grains lodge into my nose and I struggle to breathe.

The sound of the ocean waves is lost in the rumbling of falling granules. I can't hear my comrades and hope that they were able to take cover somehow from this barrage of magicked earth. A part of me worries that this was to separate us, and the wielder is making a path to take us out one at a time.

But the sand falls back to the ground in a cacophony that sounds strangely like marbles hitting wood. My comrades— Alec, too—are standing, unharmed. The remaining Brais are crouched low, save for one who stands in the center. This vampire holds his arms out straight, his back to the portal. His eyes are a menacing garnet, and they are glued to mine.

"Get down!" Alec roars. But his warning comes too late.

The Brais vampire unleashes his magic and a silver light explodes from his palms. It speeds forward in a flat wave, over the crouched Brais, and right for each of us. I try to dodge the blast by dropping to the ground, but as it moves closer, it expands. Once it clears the huddled vampires, it stretches and touches the ground as it moves. There is no way to avoid being hit.

I fling my beta ability in front of me, hoping that it may act as a barrier of some sort.

The moment the Brais magic touches my own, panic settles into my body. My magic retreats just as the wave hits. And I drop to the ground, unable to move. It feels as though there are invisible bindings tightly woven around my body with something massive pressing down on top. I can only breathe and stare at the single spot in the clouds that my eyes landed on as I fell.

My heart thumps in my chest, rivaling the roar of the ocean. Then, I hear the soft crunch of boots on sand as someone makes their way leisurely over to me. I try to call on my fire, but it feels stifled. Almost like whatever is keeping me from moving has layered itself over my magic as well. My magic recoiled at the touch of it.

Someone moves into my frozen gaze. The female Brais from earlier. Her clothing is charred and torn, blood stains her cheeks, and her blonde hair is matted to her face from the rain and something foul smelling. There is an endless pit of anger behind her ruby irises. She takes another step so her face is directly in my line of sight. She hovers over me, her feet on either side of my body.

The corner of her thin, cracked lips tug upward in a snarl. "Do you know what happened to me when I returned to this dimension without you all those months ago?" She reaches behind her and pulls out a wooden stake, both ends sharpened to a point. The side of the stake facing her is already stained with someone's blood.

A silence roars into my head. Did she kill the others with that weapon before coming to me? Then her words register. She was one of the vampires who tried to recruit me to the Brais before Amaund found me. She might have been the one who destroyed my apartment. When I denied her invitation, she attacked. But Sarah was there and protected me, driving the Brais vampire away.

She leans in, the stake poised in line with my chest. "The King tore out my organs," she seethes. Her grip on the stake tightens and loosens as she talks, and I'm surprised the wood doesn't break against her strength. "One by one. I was left bleeding in the dungeons like some *human*." The point of the stake is only a foot away from me. "And when my body finally healed and I came to…" Her irises grow a frightening shade darker. "The King did it again."

She lowers the stake from my frozen view, and I feel it poking my stomach. "Maybe I will do that to you, too. Then, when you are in unbearable agony and pleading for death, I'll drive this through your heart." Her breath is hot on my face as she leans in.

My finger twitches as I try to break this paralyzing magic. The movement catches her eye, and she rises with a snarl. Still staring at the clouds above, I see her at the edge of my vision. Dread floods my body as I feel the pressure of more vampires entering through the portal. More Brais to kill us off.

The stake retracts as she looks over her shoulder. She lets out a grunt before she gets to her feet and falls out of view. Nerves prick at my skin, and I push harder against the magic keeping me still. The clouds above, though not producing rain anymore, swirl angrily. There are screams beyond her, short but painful.

"Thea?" someone shouts frantically, their voice blanketed by the cacophony of noises. "Thea?" the voice yells again, this time clearer. And more worried.

Cole. And my allies. My friends.

I try to lift an arm to signal where I am, but my limb is nonexistent to my mind. The paralyzing magic sits on me like a suffocating weight. I push against the hard, unbending wall of it. My beta ability slowly stirs and crashes against the foreign magic, seeking to break it. Sweat beads on my forehead with each clash of magic. My tired body protests at the exertion, wanting instead to fall asleep. But I fight the exhaustion, forcing my weakening beta ability to keep going as it pushes harder against the foreign magic. And just when I feel my magic wither, it finds a weak spot. My energy manipulation punctures a hole in the paralytic and slithers to cover my fingers. I dig a fingernail into the coarse sands and flick some of the grains.

"Thea!" Cole exclaims as he drops to my side, his dark hair falling across his forehead. He hesitates for a moment before scooting closer, scrunching the sand between our legs. His black shirt is torn and stained with his dried blood. The hole from where the stake had been plunged into his chest now reveals unblemished skin beneath. Grief blooms in his expression like an unwanted flower in a garden. To him, I probably look dead. He places a hand on my cheek and searches my face. "Thea, please." He hovers over me, water rimming his gray eyes.

The sight of them tear at my heart and I try harder to fight against the magic. My own sizzles in my veins, fighting to burn away the Brais'. One of Cole's fingers brushes just below my ear. In the dream sanctuary, I could touch him, but not feel him. This invigorating touch ignites my fire. I've longed to feel him since I was taken here. Every meeting in the dream sanctuary solidified how I feel about him, how I missed him. *Needed* him.

I not only fought to free the world of the King and the Brais, but to see and touch Cole again. To see those beautiful eyes in the real light. Many things didn't turn out how I envisioned them, but him being here safe is enough to cure all the hurt in my heart. His presence fuels my fire and it ignites against the paralyzing magic, pushing it back and lessening the hold it has. My arm slides across the harsh sand, my hand connecting to his knee in a light grasp.

Cole looks to where I am grabbing him. He lets out a choked noise of relief, a shaky smile reaching his lips.

"Cole..." I whisper, my voice raspy. The strength in my head slowly returns, enough for me to be able to tilt my head slightly and truly look at him. My heart skips, and I am acutely aware of his hands. One is still placed just beneath my ear and the other is resting on my side. I swallow, my throat having gone dry. "I'm... okay. It's hard...to move."

He slides his arms under my back and pulls me in to his chest. I nestle my chin into the crook of his neck, breathing in his scent of cedar. Everything about him seems to chip away at the lingering magic in my veins. The foreign magic breaks under my own and my desire to hold Cole. I wrap my arms around him and hold on.

I lift my head and we release each other, still resting in the sand. "You're here," is all I can say.

The corner of his lips quirk up, crinkling his eye. "I told you, didn't I? That you would never have to be alone." And I never was, not really. Even though we were separated by a portal, Cole still managed a way to get to me. When distance separated us, he created a sanctuary where our minds could meet.

"Thank you," I say, fighting the hot tears that threaten to form.

"Thea!"

I turn my head and see Sarah step over a fallen Brais vampire and run toward us, a silver cloak billowing behind her. Her honey-brown eyes are wide, but there is a tiredness in them. The tears become harder to fight as I try to get to my feet to see my best friend. Cole notices my wobbliness and helps me stand. My legs still feel a bit fuzzy from the magic, so I let him be my crutch.

Sarah slams into me with a fierce hug that I return in kind. Salty water drips down my cheeks and onto her shoulder. I let myself drown in her love. We might not be related, but we are certainly family. It is easy to sense that in the weeks I have not seen her, she has become stronger. Whether it is because of her status as Minuit Coven leader or because of training, I'm not sure. Both most likely. Her energy, though intense, is also comforting. Like the waves crashing to shore before the hurricane.

Through the bleary tears, I see a woman I don't know coming slowly toward us. Is she a Brais? Where did the rest of them go? The fire inside me hums at the stranger. I tense and release Sarah, who turns and notices the cause for my concern. "Thea, it's okay." She places a hand on my arm. "This is Amelia. She's—" Sarah pauses and the stranger's gaze flicks to my best friend. "She's my girlfriend."

Amelia smiles shyly, her cobalt eyes sparkling. She turns her attention to me, her expression hardening a bit, but still kind. "It is nice to meet you, Thea. I've heard so many good things about you."

My heart warms for her. Sarah squeezes my hand before making her way to Amelia. "It's nice to meet you as well. And I look forward to hearing about you."

Amelia beams at my words as she laces her fingers with Sarah.

A group of young women, about the same age as Sarah and me, approach behind the two of them. They all wear the same cloak as Sarah. Her coven, then. I nod my thanks to them, linking eyes with each face.

The last witch, a tall, ivory-skinned woman with black hair, gives me a slight, familiar smile. She is the only one who I recognize. She went to school with Sarah and me. We never had many in depth conversations, but she was always kind.

"I'm glad that you are okay, Thea," she replies in a soft voice. Her smile reaches her brown eyes, crinkling the small birthmark underneath her left one.

"Thank you for your help, Alain."

"We are recovering fine, thanks for all the concern," Mica says dryly as he walks over to us, Alec following. Oba is making his way over to us as well. He is rolling his broad shoulders, washing away the remnants of what paralyzed us.

"Nothing can keep you down, Mica," Cole jests, his shoulders dropping in relief.

I step up to Cole, my arm brushing against his. The contact sends electricity into my body that amplifies the heat pooling in my chest. Mica's gaze flicks between us, an expression I can't name crossing his features, before he looks back to Cole.

"Leave it to Cole to forget to check on his friends," Oba chimes in as he steps past Alec.

Cole chuckles. "I could never forget about you." They clasp wrists, both laughing. "I'm glad you're okay."

"Aye, me too mate." Oba jerks his head at Cole as they

step away from each other. "I take it you defeated that psycho vampire woman."

Cole returns to the space next to me, his jaw tightening as he rubs his chest with a palm. "No."

"We should go inside," Sarah interrupts. "For now, some of the witches will keep watch over the portal. We need to discuss our next moves."

CHAPTER FIVE

THEA

We walk back to the castle, leaving the dead Brais on the beach, most of which have already decomposed into the sand, their bodies merging with nature. The face of that first vampire who tried to bring me to the King all those months ago flashes in my mind. Of how Cole killed him to save me. Cole has saved me so many times now, I don't know if I will ever be able to fully repay him. Thinking back to when Morwen trained me in the garden, I am ashamed to admit that I listened to her and questioned Cole's good intentions.

I glance to him, walking on my right. Our arms occasionally brush against each other as we make our way through the winding dirt path. He is speaking to Oba about something regarding daggers and throwing techniques.

I want to hold his hand, but Helios is sitting contentedly in my arms and I could never disrupt his bliss. His joyful purring vibrates my entire body. I kiss the top of his furry head, happy that Cole was able to bring him from Sarah's house. One of the witches held on to him during the fighting, though from what I heard, he wasn't thrilled with it.

In front of me, Sarah and Amelia walk hand in hand,

laughter filling their steps. I smile at them, happy that Sarah has found someone to share her love with.

Someone nudges my left shoulder and I turn to see Mica. He leans in as we continue walking, and says, "It is strange, isn't it?"

I furrow my brows. "Now who isn't very good at asking questions?"

He chuckles, the sound making my body relax just a bit. "Not having to look over your shoulder for someone trying to manipulate or stab you."

That may have been my life these past few weeks, but Mica has been living with Morwen a lot longer. Something squeezes my heart at the thought. He won't ever truly be free of her, not with that mark on his collarbone. And I have little doubt that we won't see her again.

In fact, I look forward to it. To the day that I can bring justice to all those she has killed.

Mica nudges my arm again. "Didn't mean to upset you."

I look at him, my brow quirked up, when a single, cold raindrop hits my nose. Though it has been overcast, I have managed to keep the rain at bay. It must be reacting to my emotions. I shake my head and wipe the rainwater from my face. "I'm sorry you have been shackled to her for so long."

At that, Mica looks to the ground, the slight smile vanishing from his lips. After a moment, he says, "Not as long as others have." Though his voice is quiet, there is a trace of lethal venom coated on each word. I wonder, if Morwen never gave Mica that mark, would he have killed her already? His ice magic is powerful, even against her fire. In the clearing, he likely could have. Despite activating the mark to kill him in the process, he almost succeeded in freezing her. If the mark did not hinder his attack, maybe he could have pulled it off then.

We all walk in silence for a while. The spires of the castle poke through the canopy of trees, its dark stone a vestige of gloom. With some dedication, the castle could become a thing of beauty. But I doubt there is anyone who would want to transform it, considering what evil lurked within. The horrors of everything Morwen stands for has corrupted every brick, every piece of furniture, and pane of glass.

Reaching the drawbridge, I hear a couple gasps from those who have never seen the castle before. The enormous stained-glass mural of angry flames rests vibrantly over the open double doors. I'm surprised that Morwen never had them painted black to resemble her own magic. Just the thought of her menacing fire sends a shiver down my spine. Witnessing them is like bringing forth all the memories that thread through the fear in my mind. Even the most tempered veteran might freeze from freight at their likeness.

"Home sweet home," Mica says dryly.

"This is probably a stupid question, but is there anything to drink in there? I used too much energy fighting those damn Brais." Oba crosses his arms as he takes his unimpressed gaze away from the castle and looks to Mica and me.

"There are blood bags to drink," Mica says. He turns to me and says, "We need to free the humans in the cellars."

Free the humans. My heart hammers in my chest at the thoughts racing through my mind. Everyone starts walking toward the doors. Cole and Mica are the only ones who notice that I haven't moved. My eyes are wide as I stare at the wooden bridge and run through all that has happened recently.

"Thea, what's wrong?" Cole asks, his voice carrying concern. At his question, I see Sarah stop and turn around.

"Please tell me no one is coming through the portal," Oba says as he grips the hilt of a dagger, his dark eyes flashing behind us.

Cole steps forward, closer to me, but it is Mica who I look at. His green gaze swirls with so many emotions. "I asked Morwen to free the humans." Bile rises in my throat.

But what if she didn't? At the image of vibrant red hair and beautiful brown eyes, my heartbeat staggers, my hand flying to my mouth. Riley. Where did Morwen really send Riley that day? I just know Morwen didn't set her free like she had said. My stomach roils at the thought of participating in Riley's demise. All because I trusted Morwen.

Maybe when I confronted Commander Kael, she didn't go down to the cellars when I asked. Perhaps she just shadowed me, waiting to see what the Commander would do when I showed up to challenge him.

My gut is telling me that something horrible is waiting for us in the cellars of the castle.

Mica and I move at the same time, our feet pounding against the drawbridge as we dart into the castle. I hear Oba ask who Morwen is, but I don't think anyone responds. Not that I can hear anything over the intense roaring in my ears. Whatever happened, it was my fault. I sent her down there. If I had never told her to free those people, would she have left them alone?

The sweet iron scent hits my nose before we even make it to the landing that leads to the closed-off hallway. It is strange, to be pulled by the aroma, almost as if hypnotized, but also to recoil at it. My heart pounds in my chest, awoken by the surge of fear coursing through my body.

Mica's jaw is tight as he twists the knob and pushes the door open. The smell that hits us is even greater now, almost knocking me to the ground. I suck in a gasp at the sight.

Human bodies are scattered out on the stone floor as if it were a battlefield. Their faces are forever set in waves of terror. There is blood, so much of it. Like someone took a brush and painted the floor crimson, not caring that they splattered the walls as well. My stomach roils with both hunger and horror.

Mica curses under his breath as he takes slow steps into the hall, careful not to step on anyone. "It is like she let them try and escape." The door set in the middle of the wall, the iron one that leads to the dungeon where the humans were kept, is propped open with a crumbling brick. She wanted them to think she was there to free them.

So that they would try to run. And she could chase.

It doesn't even look like she drank from any of them, given how much blood pools around each of their lifeless bodies.

My lips quiver, anger and sorrow rising in my throat. My magic thrums in my veins, my palms heating. It wants to let loose. To consume. When we enter the doorway to the dungeon, I do all I can to not explode.

The scent of stale blood mixes with other unpleasant smells in this room. Just thinking about how the people were forced to live down here would be enough to set my magic ablaze. My hands clench into fists at my side. I wish Morwen was in front of me. I would incinerate her, leaving only ashes behind.

I hear two sets of footsteps echoing down the stairs. "Gods," Oba hisses from the hallway. "They were massacred."

I force myself to look at each of the dead. Each victim. In this room, there are eleven. The six in the hallway make seventeen. Seventeen humans, dead. For sport. Because she is vile and relishes in killing.

The humans, even the witches, deserve nothing but torment for what they did to me. Morwen's words, again. Her hatred for humans was so strong when she uttered that sentence to me in the clearing by the old portal. She hates humans because they wronged her. Whatever occurred in her past, it was something that happened centuries ago.

Centuries. She has held that grudge for so long, never willing to seek peace for herself.

Most of these humans were too afraid to even leave their cell, their bodies forever silent on the cold floor by the cots, throats slashed or torn out. My eyes fall on the person who had been in the cell farthest from the door, or what is left of them. My nails dig so hard into my palm that I feel blood trickle from them. It drips to the floor and mixes with that of the humans. Morwen didn't just kill the person who was in that last cell. She destroyed them. Their head must have been slammed against the wall because one side of the skull is cracked and bloody. Their arms and legs are broken and twisted in odd directions. And in the center of the person's chest, a gaping hole.

The temperature in the room drops quickly and I glance at Mica. His skin has blanched, as if his ice was freezing his own body. "Did you know that person?" I ask as gently as my rage allows, resisting the urge to touch his arm and comfort the storm of emotions that swirl around him.

He jolts to my voice, his gaze drifting to the corners of his eyes. His jaw clenches and loosens before he says, "No." And then he brushes past me and exits the bloody room.

I feel Cole as he takes a step next to me. Anger and something else radiate from him. "It isn't your fault, Thea."

"It is," I breathe. The mixture of scents in the room fills my nose and I almost vomit. There is more than the blood and urine and dirt. The emotions swirl around the particles, filling in the gaps. I can smell the hatred that Morwen undoubtedly had coursing through her as she tore into these innocents. But above that, I can smell their fear. The absolute terror that still clings to their clothes and skin—that is still etched onto their faces.

We should bury them. But would they want the magically crafted dirt of this dimension—their living nightmare—be the place of their eternal rest?

Fire can heal as much as it can destroy. My father's words are a beacon of strength in my heart. I can't heal these people, but I can perhaps cleanse their souls and help them move on from this place.

In answer, flames emerge from my palms, tender and pure. My magic awakens, fueled by the fury and grief at what was done. Cole places his hand on my back, his calming touch a reassurance. I stand there as I hear him and Oba leave the dungeon and the hallway beyond.

In the silence of the cellar, I stand, my body becoming a gentle inferno. Water stings in my eyes, but I shove the sorrow down. When this is all over, I will shed those tears. Whether I defeat Morwen or if I fall to her. Until then I will keep the emotions inside and let them be my fuel. I'll take the fear that these innocents felt and store it inside my body.

I close my eyes as my heated magic slithers past my shoulders, covering my torso, my neck and legs. When I am a living blaze, I open my palms. My heart shudders at the flood of alien emotions, all familiar but none of it mine. I've felt them all. In emotions, we are all the same. More or less.

I open my eyes, my vision coated in dancing flame and shadows. And I touch each and every person who died here, my fire spreading gently. "I'm sorry," I whisper to them all as their bodies sigh with the flames.

CHAPTER SIX

THEA

*D*espite wanting to be nothing like Morwen, I can't help the rain that falls consistently over the dimension, pounding against the slender windowpanes in the stairwell. Even when I focus on the sun, the clouds remain, drenching the castle and land with their tears. Under Morwen's control, this place was forever coated with gloom. I want nothing to do with how she lives and commands, but right now, the rain is freeing. The sky sheds the emotions that I keep clutched to my heart.

My body feels heavy as I finally reach the top of the stairwell landing. I can hear the others rambling in the grand sitting room down the hall. It sounds like Sarah and Oba are butting heads on some plan. I don't bother reaching out with my hearing. I'm too tired to handle anything at the moment.

The candles that line the circular stairs flicker against the usual breeze that whistles through the timeworn windows. I lean against the doorway, watching the small fires dance when a long sigh wracks my body. Where would I be if I had never decided to come back home two months ago? A part of me imagines that I would be in some grand state forest, creating more art with Helios by my side, purring away at the sun on his orange fur.

A louder part of me knows that I would most likely be in this same situation, if not dead already, regardless of coming home that day in late summer to see Sarah and Valeria. The Brais wanted me. *Morwen* wanted me, and the magic that would develop in my body once I became a vampire. One that would be strong enough take on the mantel of anchor for this dimension. So that she could finally be free of it.

If Cole never found me, someone else most likely would have. Perhaps Morwen planned to have a Brais turn me. I would have been in her clutches from the beginning, then. I wonder how that would have played out.

"Thea? Are you all right?" Cole's soft voice sends shivers down my spine, erasing the disgruntling thoughts that emerged from the deep corners within my mind. I turn my head and see him standing a few feet away. His obsidian hair is tousled, like he was constantly dragging his hands through it. The talking in the room down the hall hasn't lessened, though I now hear Amelia and Oba arguing instead.

My eyes dip to Cole's mouth. They part slightly, and I drag my gaze back to his incredibly gorgeous gray eyes. His heartbeat sings to my own. We stand like that, silently staring at each other, for a few breaths. I have to force myself to remember that he asked a question.

I swallow, his eyes catching the movement in my throat. My toes curl in my sneakers, tight enough to pull me from drowning in his presence. "What did you say?" My voice comes out a little dryer than I intended it to.

Cole chuckles, the sound dragging me back into his intoxicating aura. He takes a step closer, a half-smile on his chiseled features. He is still in that bloodied, black t-shirt from all the fighting. The muscles in his arms flex as he takes his hands out of the pockets of his dark jeans. "I asked if you are all right." The huskiness in his voice threatens to melt my body into a puddle. I've missed him. I knew I did, but I didn't know just how much.

I give in to that invisible magnet that always seems to tug us together and move closer. "Yes."

"Liar," he says, taking another step. There is only a foot of space left between us. His cedar scent fills my nose and I can feel my entire body release a bit of the tension it has been gripping onto. His fingers twitch at his side and I reach out to grab them.

"Thea!" Sarah yells from down the hall, her melodic voice swaying in the still air.

Cole and I hold our breath, as if moving would break the addictive buzzing between us. We hold each other's gazes. I wish we could teleport away from everyone. From everything.

I hear Sarah's footsteps before she comes into view at the edges of my vision, past Cole's broad shoulders. "Thea. Cole. We need your opinions on some things."

Her voice breaks the heat between us, and I close my eyes momentarily before stepping away from the wall. Before I can respond, Cole turns to face her. "I listened in on most of what was being said back there, Sarah. All of it can wait. Thea is exhausted."

It's true. I feel like I have been running marathons for weeks with no sleep. Or food. My stomach rumbles in response to my thoughts. And all that blood downstairs triggered a desperate hunger.

A hint of irritation seeps into Sarah's expression, her honey-colored eyes narrowing at him. I take a step forward, my arm brushing against Cole's. The touch, though brief, sends jolts to my core. It wipes away some of the tiredness and fog in my mind. Our fingers graze each other's momentarily before I shove my hands in the pockets of my pants.

"It's all right, Cole." I feel his gaze turn to me, his concern flitting through my humming beta ability. There is a sliver of defiance in his emotions. Like he wants to correct me and say that the exhaustion that plagues me is not all right. That may be the right call, but finding and defeating Morwen is all that matters right now. "Let's hear your plans."

"Absolutely not," Mica says as he pushes off the wall beside the fireplace and crosses his arms. His green gaze burns at Sarah, who surprisingly, has kept a level head through all of Mica's and Oba's disagreements. Cole has remained uncharacteristically quiet as he stands next to me behind the long, slate-colored couch.

The handful of Minuit witches are standing behind the white couch opposite Cole and me. Half of them keep their attention fixed on their coven leader while the other half look like they might try and tear into Mica for speaking against Sarah. Alain, to my surprise, stands just behind Sarah, her attention fixed on the conversation. I have mostly only ever seen her shy away from conflicts. It reminds me of a time in school when she silently stood like a guardian behind Sarah when she was yelling at a bully for being rude to me. That was right after my parents died.

I clench my teeth, waiting for the inevitable waves of grief to wash over me at the thought of my parents. But, it doesn't come, not like it used to. Though there still is the deep sorrow over losing them, a tender warmth blooms in my heart with it. The memory of seeing them after healing Cole's deadly wounds stitched my broken heart. They are here, watching over me.

"You all seem to be forgetting that Thea can't leave this dimension," Mica seethes to the witches. His hands flap violently around. "These few vampires, your witches, even with the wolves... None of us have a chance against the King. Only Thea and Cole do. They know who the King is and were not affected by the silence spell. They can fight, we cannot. Even then, the King is infinitely more experienced with magic and fighting than they are."

My eyes catch the dark mark underneath Mica's disheveled white shirt. Beneath the dirt and sweat and rainwater, it sticks out. Like a separate entity ready to report back to Morwen. It must not, given that Mica has not said otherwise. My brain catches on the meaning behind his other sentence.

"Wait, are you implying that the spell affects more than just vampires?" I hold my breath, waiting for an answer.

Sarah and the others cast their gaze downward. Cole steps in, his face hard. "It does."

I can feel my face blanching as a coldness seeps into my bones. "Who here cannot fight the King?" We stand no chance if all of our allies are spelled into submission to the King. I think about the day with Morwen by the tree and the warmth in my heart simmers into a rage. She stood there and watched my emotions rise. Watched as my anger took over after she fed me lies. Lies that I greedily took in. Because I saw her as a friend. Someone who needed protection.

When my eyes meet Oba's he gives a shake of his head. Cole is staring daggers at Sarah, who takes a deep breath, but doesn't shudder under his glare.

"I cannot fight the King directly," Sarah says quietly, her expression regretful. "Not without forfeiting my life."

It feels like the floor has slipped from under my feet and I am falling into an abyss. "How long?" My words come out more bitter than I intended.

Sarah flinches slightly, and I notice Amelia take a half step closer to her. She swallows before saying, "My entire life." I must have a particular disturbed expression because Sarah lifts her chin and says, "It's the curse of the Demoix bloodline. I couldn't say anything, you know this."

Valeria too, then. I grip the cushion on the back of the couch. "You could have done *something*. When I was meeting with Cole, I mentioned Mor—"

"The King," Mica adds swiftly, cutting me off.

I shoot him a grateful look before turning back to my friend. "I mentioned to you both the King's name. You could have given some sort of warning." The rain drums on the windows. I breathe with the wind as it howls through cracks in the castle.

"I wanted to, Thea. Trust me, I wanted to. I will do anything to keep you safe. But…" she grimaces and rubs a hand along her neck. "Witches don't heal like vampires. The damage done by the silence spell could be irreparable to us."

My gaze flicks from her eyes to where the spell marks its victims. Even though what she says makes sense, anger still churns in my blood. It wants out. Out of my body. It is like the vampiric magic that courses through me sees Sarah and her witches as a threat, conditioned by centuries of hatred between the two species. My heart knows she is not a threat. But where there was once an unwavering trust in my heart, this has left it shredded. I've known Sarah my entire life, and there was so much about her she kept hidden from me. The part of me that trusted her broke a little over the past few weeks. And when Morwen deceived me, preyed on that trusting part of me, it tore my heart in pieces.

"Thea." Cole's soft but cautious tone breaks through the roaring in my head. I am brought back to the calming sanctuary that linked our minds while we were apart from each other.

I blink and turn to him, noticing a single spark lifting into the air between us. A small but intense flame swirls along my arm. I quickly put it out, the magic retreating back into my body. There is the feeling of disappointment as it recedes.

"I'm sorry," I say, turning back to Sarah. Outside, I feel the gathering clouds retreating as my emotions return to a calmer state. Sarah's eyes are wide, hands clenched into fists at her sides. A stray beam of sunlight shines through the cracked doorway, illuminating her irises.

Sarah shakes her head, brown curls swishing in the movement. "I'm sorry too, Thea." She sighs through her nose. "I'm sorry for everything that I have kept from you and for everything that has happened. You—" she stifles herself, her voice so subtly changing tone, likely going unnoticed by anyone who doesn't know her well. She is fighting her emotions. Behind her, Amelia places a gentle hand on her back. The witches all bow their heads. "You," she continues, "have always been the better of us.

"When you died and were turned into a vampire, it broke a part of me." Sarah keeps her attention on me, though I can tell she wants to fix a glare onto Cole, who tenses at her words. "How could something like that happen to someone so good? And I hated myself for letting you get hurt—killed." Her nails dig into her palm and I could have sworn something glinted underneath.

"Sarah," I say gently. "It isn't your fault." I want to tell her everything, about the Brais. About how my parents were killed because of them, because of *Morwen*. Her decade long scheme to recreate magic that would be the twin to her own just so she could transfer the anchor spell.

"It is," she counters before I can explain further. "You are my sister, Thea. My family. I lost my mother. I refuse to lose you, too. I will do anything to keep you from any more harm." She shifts her attention to the vampires who opposed her. "My plans have always been to keep her safe." Her palms open, a golden medallion clenched in her left hand. Cole and Mica bristle next to me. "I am sorry. For everything that has happened. And for this."

There is a light, so bright that I feel like my eyes might burn out of my skull. It is followed by a searing pain in my forehead that travels like tendrils of lightning to the base of my head.

Then darkness.

CHAPTER SEVEN

MICA

Consciousness filters in as my eyes fly open, the last of the searing pain in my skull flowing away like a receding tide. I blink away the images that flashed through my brain while I floated in the darkness. Before my mind can comprehend what happened, my body moves, forcing me into a defensive position. Panic rises in my throat when I catch sight of everyone crumpled on the floor. Then, movement outside the large, double doors catches my attention.

A heated fury courses through me at the sight of the witches departing. Water pools in droplets at my fingertips, forming ice-like claws. "Sarah!" I yell, and I swear my voice booms through the entire dimension. Stomping past the furniture and Oba's prone body, I make my way toward the traitors.

Except something stops me. A barrier of some sort. It sits, not visible to my eye, at the threshold to the castle's grand entryway. I glare daggers at the Minuit coven leader, who turns around and stares right back. The rest of her witches continue on while the wolf shifter waits a few feet behind her lover.

Each of them wears a silver cloak. A wind swishes the

fabric back, revealing an array of wooden stakes strapped to leather belts.

A growl rumbles in my throat as I bare my fangs at them. Neither are phased by the anger that ripples through me. "You mean to fight the King alone?" I ask, pressing my ice tipped hand to the invisible wall. Not even my magic can pass through. The ice clinks against seemingly nothing.

Sarah studies me for a moment, her honeyed eyes narrowing into slits. She twists to fully face me. "Everything I do, I do it for her." The witch points to the castle, to where Thea had been standing, right before she spelled us all. It was an invocation that I've known almost every witch to be able to perform. But to have the power to attack the minds of multiple vampires at once? In all my centuries of living, I've never seen that. She truly is the leader of the strongest coven. I still wonder why Amaund never killed her when he had the chance.

"You'd betray her? Us?" I ask, my hand curling into a fist as it rests against that barrier.

The witch lifts her palms, and I instinctively flinch, preparing myself for another mental attack. She only raises them to her hips and shakes her head. "I am not alone." The wolf shifter steps closer as she says that. A declaration of ally-ship. Of protection.

"Do you even know where the King is?" I ask, nostrils flaring.

She takes a breath before answering, the nature around her calming. "I have a better idea than you do."

My fist slams into the invisible wall, the vibrations rippling through me as her witch magic ricochets into my body. "You will die. You said it yourself. You're cursed." I warn. If she weren't cursed like I am, she might stand a chance. "All of you." And what a waste of strong allies that would be. Morwen will slaughter them all. Maybe torture the witch and wolf alpha first, just for fun. "You need us."

She snorts, her face twisting into one of disgust and ire. "You vampires always think you are the only strong force in existence. If I didn't trap you and the others in there, you wouldn't let me walk out of this dimension. Wouldn't let me keep my friend—my sister—safe while finishing what my *family* started so long ago. The coven will be back in twenty-four hours, when everything is right again."

I catch the slight dip of her eyes as she says those words. *The coven will be back.* My hand slides down the barrier and falls to my side. "You intend to sacrifice your life for this." The mark on my collarbone vibrates and I resist the urge to touch it. Sarah is going to fight the King with all that she has, knowing that it will kill her in the process. Behind Sarah, Amelia lifts her chin as if to say she won't let that happen.

Sarah's gaze flicks behind me. With that, she turns and follows her fellow witches down the path to the remaining portal.

I contemplate yelling again, but clearly, she has no desire to talk things out by the way she was still walking away from us. Stepping away from the open doors, I look back to the others. Everyone is still unconscious, even Alec. Out of all of us here, he has been a vampire the longest. He's had longer to develop his magic, offensive and defensive. It is a wonder that he wasn't the first to awake.

Then, I glance to Cole. He lies on the floor next to Thea, their hands almost touching. Like they were reaching for each other as they collapsed. The images that danced in my mind while I was unconscious slip unwanted in front of me again. Flashes of auburn hair and irises the color of sand. Of a smile that would render me speechless. I run a hand through my pale hair, eliciting another image long stashed away. Of gentle fingers tangled in my hair, those same beautiful eyes studying mine so intently. Squeezing my eyes shut, I shake my head and reach for the totem looped around my neck. An ache burns heavy in my chest as I clutch the pointed amber stone.

"I should have said yes," I say quietly to the totem with a long breath. A part of me sometimes wonders if the person who the stone once belonged to can hear the words I whisper to it. Words of sorrow, regret, and longing. But how can they reach those ears when that person's soul never reaches the afterlife?

"Yes to what?" Alec responds with a weary voice as he sits up, his question tugging me from the consuming spiral of thoughts. He rubs his hands over his face before rolling his neck.

I drop my hand to my side and force a smirk. "Welcome back. What took you so long?"

Alec just looks at me, his brown eyes fierce. "That was pleasant," he says after a moment, a smirk tugging at his lips. He gets to his feet and wipes any dust from his trousers. Then, he jerks his head toward me. "Were you talking about that promise again?"

Shoving my hands into the pockets of my pants, I shrug. One stupid night, when I was feeling particularly saddened over my past, I told Alec about how I joined the Brais. How the King tricked me so many years ago. About the promise my lover had made to me. Would she truly have given up the life she knew so we could be happy? If I said yes back then, would she still be alive? A part of me knows that her fate would have ended the same way.

Which is why the second promise I made, the one over her grave, will never be broken.

"Sometimes, Alec," I reply quietly, "I wish I never mentioned my past to you." Not because I don't trust him, nor do I particularly care that he always seems to know when I think about it, but that time in my life was a treasure. A time that I wished I locked away, only to be visited by my own broken mind. Despite that, there was a sense of relief when I confided in him, like the pain in my heart lessened at sharing it with a friend.

Alec scoffs. "I know. You said that when you finished telling me everything that day." He lifts a dusty-colored brow. "Do you remember what I told you?"

I clench my jaw, frowning at my friend. There would never be a time when I would forget his response.

"I said I'd carry that promise—that pain—with you. *For* you if you need me to." A muscle feathers in his cheek as he watches me.

Despite his cold exterior, Alec has always been kind. At least, to me. Granted, there were times when he would show his teeth, but mostly I deserved it. He was protective in that way. He feared the Brais. Mostly, he feared the King. He wasn't tricked into the service of the King like I was. No, he was forced. Like Thea. Hundreds of years ago, the King, though strong in his own right, sought to bolster the vampire faction. He wanted the Brais to be the strongest force to have ever existed. Alec, like so many others, were forced to join the Brais, or watch everyone they loved die. After joining the Brais, the King would share with his new warriors his true identity. The silence spell took effect after that, rendering an uprising impossible. He created an army of soldiers, bound to him by fear and magic.

Most think the army is simply to destroy for him. To carry out his whims and kill those who would oppose his absolute rule. But I know the truth. I know that he is afraid of something from his past. This army of vampires he has created, it wasn't for destruction, but for protection.

I glance to the two newest vampires, still unconscious on the floor. But now, with the two of them impervious to that curse, we could stand a chance against him. Even though Thea and Cole are both strong, the King is infinitely more so. They need all the backup they can get. The Minuit coven leader may think she is helping her friend by doing this on her own, but in truth, it will make things bleaker for us all.

I look back to Alec who still watches me and let out a

breath. Before I can respond, there is a shuffling from the opposite end of the long couch.

"Oye. You two are so loud, y'know that?" Oba says with a groan as he sits up and rubs his temples. "What did that damn witch do? My head is pounding." Getting to his feet, he winces and resumes massaging his head.

"She trapped us here," I say flatly.

"What?" Oba's brown eyes widen with some emotion I can't read. Likely disbelief, but a slice of fear slips into the air. He glances around the room, his shoulders slumping as his gaze lands on Cole. Then his eyes shift to Thea and his brows furrow. "She locked us all in here?"

I shake my head. "As far as Sarah is concerned, this is the safest place for Thea." I blow out a breath between my teeth. "Absurd." Thea might be safe here at the moment, but once the King does whatever it is he is planning, once he kills the Minuit Coven, he'll come back. I look back to the fire wielder still unconscious on the floor, then to the air wielder. The King will be back, for both of them.

Oba follows my gaze. "We are as good as dead in here."

CHAPTER EIGHT

THEA

"*I'm not sorry,*" *Sarah says, planting her feet into the carpet of the living room. Her ringlets fall just below her chin, framing her gentle features. "That bully had it coming."*

"Violence doesn't solve violence, love," Valeria says. Her soft voice lulls like a song in my ears. She kneels so she is eye level with her daughter and glances behind her to where I sit on the floral-printed couch. "Isn't that right, Thea?"

I look to the ground with a shrug, my feet kicking out against the side of the couch. "It made her stop picking on me," I offer, twisting my little finger in a lock of brown hair, soothing the strands that were tugged on earlier in the day. I frown at the memory of the confrontation at school, a sadness sweeping through my heart.

The bully, a beefy girl who was tall for her age of twelve, followed me to my locker during lunch break, her group of antagonizing friends flanking her. "Stupid hair as always, Knight." Her voice always sounded hoarse, like she needed to clear her throat or had a cheese grater lodged in there.

I looked up to see her hands wrap themselves around the small buns on the top of my head. She pulled on them, eliciting a cry from my mouth. I landed on the cold floor of the school's hallway, my hair falling over my eyes. Her friends laughed. She laughed, too, even when I stood, my hands clenched into fists.

Tears stung my eyes at the sound of their hateful laughs, and I closed them, imagining what my fist could do to their mouths.

But then the laughing stopped. It was replaced with a thud and a gurgled sort of sound. I opened my eyes when the others gasped. My bully had her back to the wall, her hand clutching her throat. And instead of tears in my eyes, there were some in hers.

"If I ever catch you bothering Thea again, I will put you in the hospital," Sarah said. She came out of nowhere. My protector.

Valeria smiled and turned back to her daughter, whose honeyed eyes blazed with some sort of courageous spirit that I could not understand. The sun was glistening through the window beside her, shining right into those eyes. It made them look like they were something from an enchanted forest. I was in awe of my best friend—of my sister. "It is important to protect those we love. But never let your fury get the better of you." She tucks a curl behind Sarah's ear. "It is easy to get into the rhythm of depending on violence. But it will change you, the more you rely on it for solving problems."

Sarah's expression shifts, a slight frown curving her lips downward. "But what about being afraid? Is it okay if we use violence if we fear for those we love?" Sarah glances at me, frozen on the couch. "If someone we love is in danger, and we can help, should we?" At her question, I cock my head in confusion, not understanding why she would assume any of us would ever be in that sort of danger.

Valeria's smile turns sad at that question and she seems to contemplate her answer for a moment. "Fury is just a mask fear uses. There will be times in your lives that you must protect each other, no matter the cost, but never let your fear make you choose violence as a first response, okay? It will only lead to more heartache."

Sarah stares into her mother's eyes before nodding.

"Promise me." Valeria runs a hand down her daughter's soft hair.

"I promise."

"Good." Valeria hugs her. When she let's go, Sarah darts up the stairs and Valeria turns her warm gaze at me. I can't help but smile. At *the love that always radiates from this kind woman. She sits on the couch beside me. "Sarah has always had a strong mind and an even fiercer heart." She tilts her head toward me. "But you've known that."*

I nod, hanging my head as my cheeks warm.

She nudges me in the shoulder. "Do you want to know what I think?"

I look back up at her, eager for those words of wisdom, and nod again.

She smiles, her brown eyes crinkling in the corners. "I think that you are just as strong as Sarah. But, sometimes, you put the well-being of others above your own. Even when that other person is not kind." When I look to the floor, Valeria puts a hand on my knee, bringing my attention back to her. "That isn't necessarily a bad habit to have, love. But, sticking up and fighting for our own self is something we owe our souls. Knowing when someone deserves mercy or not is a quality owned by the best of souls." She taps my nose with a gentle finger. "I think you need to trust yourself more. That you can fight for yourself with your friends by your side. Trust yourself to know who deserves your kindness and who does not."

There is an endless strength to her gaze. It radiates to everything that she touches. I can't help but curl my fists in sure conviction. Her words, like always, ring true in my head. "I will."

Her smile widens, the sight making me happy. "Good." She leans back, resting into the couch. Her voice softens, though it doesn't lose any of its potency. "You, and Sarah, are forces to be reckoned with. And together, you two could change the world."

I JOLT AWAKE, rising swiftly to a sitting position and wincing at the sharp ache slicing through my head. Adrenaline courses through my veins, heating my body.

"Thea," Cole's voice rings from behind me. "It's all right."

I hear a sharp breath of air. "That's stretching it."

Mica.

I was in the foyer of the castle. With Cole and Mica and Sarah… I frantically look around the room, my gaze roaming over my allies. Mica, Oba, Alec, and Cole. The witches and Amelia are gone. Sarah is gone.

"What happened?" I demand, turning to see Cole sitting on the couch. My head must have been in his lap, given the position I rose from. Blinking away any thoughts of that, I push down the rising anger. "Where is Sarah?"

Cole shifts in his seat, sighing through his nose. "She left. With the bulk of our allies." There is something in his tone—in the stiffness of his body, that tells me he is trying desperately to keep his own ire down. I contemplate using my beta ability to test whether I am right, but I don't want to know how he is feeling about Sarah.

Not when I don't even know how I am feeling about her.

I stand from the couch. "We need to go after her. She is going to go after the King." Perhaps without the mark, she could do it. Knowing Sarah, she wouldn't hesitate to do as much as she could before the silence spell killed her. It didn't sound like any of her coven, other than herself, have the mark. And if Amelia and her pack are free of it as well…

But all it would take is Morwen declaring herself as the King right in front of those who aren't plagued with the silence spell, and they all would be helpless.

"We can't," Cole replies sadly.

I turn my humming anger toward him. "She's going to die, Cole!" Tears well in my eyes. Despite what she did, I need to help her. She can't do this on her own.

"She made that choice when she locked us in here," Mica adds calmly. His arms are crossed at his chest, his pale hair a ruffled mess.

"What?" The question spills from my lips half in rage and half in disbelief. Cole stands, his arm brushing against mine. A gesture to calm as much as it is for stability.

"She locked us all in here, Thea," he says softly with a grim expression. "If they aren't successful, we are sitting ducks if the King returns."

"What?" I repeat, though it comes out less as a question this time and more of a statement of exasperation.

Mica walks to the door that is already flung open, the gloom of the dimension filtering inside. He places a hand on what appears to be an invisible wall at the crest of the doorway. His ice-like claws dig into that invisible force, as if he could scrape his way out.

"How?" My brain can hardly churn past Sarah locking us in. Was this her plan all along? To go against our enemy alone, in hopes of saving the rest of us?

A sacrifice to save others.

Mica shrugs casually. "The blood of the Minuit coven created this dimension, so the blood of that coven can alter it."

I stitch my brows together in confusion. "The Minuit coven didn't create this dimension." Morwen's name sits on the tip of my tongue and I pause to adjust the sentence. It will be difficult to reign in using her name. Given the times he has corrected me, Mica seems to think that just saying her name with the implication that she is the King will curse others with the silent spell. "The first vampire did." Morwen is the King, the first vampire. She told me she had created this dimension as a safe haven so many centuries ago. The witches anchored her here.

"I don't think—"

"Oye. None of this really matters at the moment, does it?" Oba grumbles, interrupting Mica. He runs a thumb underneath the bandolier strapped across his torso. "We need to prepare. Either the witches and wolves succeed and come back, which is ideal, or they don't." He looks to me, but I school my features into neutrality. "In that case, we might get the King knocking. And I don't know about you lot, but I don't like the odds of fighting him in a place he has lived in for centuries."

"Your witch friend might have sealed our fates here," Alec

chimes in, his brown eyes set on the table in front of him. At first, I wasn't sure if he meant to say that out loud because he continued to stare at that single spot, his chin resting in his hands. "If she fails, the King might just use her to destroy the dimension with us in it."

Silence rings in the air. It seems that is something no one else gave thought to. The lives of everyone in this room is in danger because I couldn't kill Morwen back in that clearing. If I trusted the fear that first sang in my gut at the sight of her, perhaps I could have put the pieces together sooner. She used the same power that runs in my own blood to control me.

We are the same, she said to me. Before turning me into the anchor that holds this dimension together.

"There is no use in dwelling on what has happened," Cole says. He looks to me before scanning the faces of everyone else in the room.

Even without the ability to read emotions, Cole knows what thoughts race through my mind. He must have heard more of that conversation between Morwen and me than I thought.

"We need to find a way out of here and go help our allies." Help Sarah. *Sarah has always had a strong mind and an even fiercer heart.* Ever since we were children, she would put herself in harm's way in order to help someone who needed it. That person was generally me. And a part of me has always let her. "They are not the only ones in this war." The fire in my veins simmers at the declaration. At the unsaid promise to both me and to Valeria.

I will fight for myself, and for the Essites. I will fight for the world.

"Maybe we should wait to see if the witches can actually do it," Alec suggests.

I narrow my eyes at him and reel in the irritation at his absurd comment. "I'm not waiting to find out."

"I agree with Thea," Mica adds, casting a frown at his

comrade. The two exchange a look that seems to convey some sort of meaning only they are aware of. "By then it could be too late to do anything."

Cole sighs a long breath through his nose. "I think it is important to note all of our options, but I don't think we should accept that one without trying others first."

Alec just shrugs. "Like you said," he jerks his chin at Oba before continuing, "the King will likely come here once he finishes whatever it is he wanted to do. We could ambush him."

Cole shifts his weight to his right foot so he is closer to me, offering that grounding brush against my arm again. "We don't know if that is what the King will do. Besides, your assessment about the King using the coven to destroy this dimension could very well be the route he takes." It is so easy for Cole to use Morwen's title instead of her actual name.

"It isn't even an option," I repeat to Alec, this time with more sternness. "I will *not* allow others to risk their lives for me." Not anymore.

I feel the sharp jolt of shock mixed with…anguish? Without even calling upon my beta ability, the emotions pour from Mica like a floodgate opening, stretching across the room. When I look to him, he reels them back in, stifling all feelings. Whatever memory or thought manifested those heavy emotions must have been traumatic. "It could be a good option," he says, his green gaze locked on mine.

Cole snaps his head to Mica as I grit out, "What?"

There is a slight dip of the corner of Mica's lips, gone as quick as it formed. He leans against the wall beside the still open door and says, "The King plays the long game. I doubt he will destroy the dimension. He likes to…" Mica pauses, those jolts of emotion trying to sprinkle from his closed aura again. "He likes to take his time."

"I know," I seethe. As if I needed to be reminded of that.

"I'm going to save them, even if I have to do it alone." My magic swirls beneath my skin as if in agreement.

"You won't be alone," Cole says beside me. I feel those tendrils of electricity fly between his body and mine. Between our arms that are just a few inches away from each other.

I look into his gray eyes and see a fierceness that makes my stomach flip. I've said those words to him before, when I threatened to leave the safety of his cabin alone in order to save Valeria and Sarah. I wonder if he is remembering that moment, too. It feels like so much time has passed since then.

"I'm with you, too," Oba says with a dip of his chin. "I figure, if Cole will be watching your back, somebody's gotta watch his."

I nod, not bothering to tell him that I'll watch Cole's back, too. The more help to keep Cole safe, the more focused I can be. I turn away from them all and move around the couch and down the hall.

"Where are you going?" Cole calls. I hear his feet shuffle around the couch to follow.

Without turning around, I say, "To get a drink. Then to start researching how to get the hell out of here."

CHAPTER NINE

THEA

After our quick meal from the blood bags in storage, Cole, Mica, and I are searching through the library for any information that might help us get out of this dimension. It has been two hours, which means we have a little over twenty before Sarah expected to be back here. My eyes ache from staring so intently at book titles and the small print of most tomes. After snapping at Mica about doing things alone, he has been mostly silent. Still, he offered to help with the research. I'm not sure if his volunteering is because he felt guilty for suggesting we leave Sarah at Morwen's mercy or if he has faith that Morwen is on her way here. Every minute that passes by without my best friend returning creates a wedge of fear in my heart.

How long before the witches march onto Morwen? I wonder how Sarah even knows where to find her.

I grit my teeth and reread the sentence my eyes keep skimming over in this worn tome about curses. The tables in the center of the library are covered in stacks of books, each deemed useless in our quest. I slam the cover shut and dust puffs out from the pages, billowing into the stagnant air. Cole and Mica just look at me, their grim expressions relaying my own fruitless finds. Between the three of us, we have only scratched the surface with what information sits on the shelves. There are hundreds more books in here. It would take hours more, *days* even, to look through each one for any information on how to get free from this barrier. Sarah might not have that time.

Morwen is the first vampire. I saw what she could do with her magic, speed, and strength. And I doubt that I saw *all* that she could do.

With a sigh, I stand from the chair. The golden light of the sun beams through the dome glass ceiling of the library, casting the room in an ethereal glow. Scanning the shelves of taunting books, a heaviness settles in my mind. "Stop," I murmur. My voice comes out unsteady despite my efforts to keep it firm.

"What's wrong?" Cole asks, his voice coated in concern.

I shake my head and open my mouth, but then shut it. In the silence, Mica slides a slender book into place on a wooden shelf. "The King has been trying to get out of this dimension for years." Decades or even centuries. "If there was a book in here that held the secrets on how to escape, she would have found it already. And even if we find the answer, how are we supposed to break Sarah's barrier spell?"

Cole frowns and glances at the open book in front of him. "Perhaps the King found the answer but was unable to use its contents."

"That doesn't make me feel any better," I say flatly.

Cole offers a sad smile. "We will find a way, Thea."

Mica taps his fingers on a dusty shelf. He has forgone his dirty, white button-down shirt for a dark green one. In his usual style, the top set of buttons are undone. "There is another place where the King might have kept his research." He runs a hand through his pale, shoulder-length hair and loosens a long breath. Both Cole and I remain quiet, waiting for him to continue. My own anxious energy mixes with that of Mica's. "The King's chamber. I have never actually set foot inside, but I would imagine important things being stored in there."

Likely important notes that Morwen herself deemed too secretive to keep in this more public space. There could be anything written in the books there. Then, I remember another small, leather-bound tome that caught my eye not too long ago. Right here in this spooky library. I glance to the darkened back corner of the large room. There are enchanted candles flickering behind the rows of shelves, the only source of light in that area. Even with the size of the dome-windowed ceiling, its light doesn't reach.

There was something about that particular book that called to me. If it weren't for discovering it after that horrible vision the statue gave me, I might have plucked it from the shelf then.

"We should check that room out first," I say in answer to Mica's suggestion. Both vampires watch me, waiting for my response. As if they couldn't have gone into that room without my approval. Something twists in my chest at that, and I don't know what it means.

"You two can go first. Get a head start on looking through her personal books." I take a step toward the back of the library. To that isle that has haunted me since the day of the vision. To the faceless statue that still seems to watch me somehow, remnants of flames and sorrow that filled the air around me. A ghostly chill caresses my spine and urges me to that dark corner.

That statue is the first vampire.

It is a depiction of Morwen. And that horrifying vision I endured was of *her* past. Those two corpses at my feet—her feet—were her parents. Or someone who cared deeply enough for her to sacrifice themselves to save her. Using the spell that my own parents cast. I squeeze my eyes closed and see the faint glow of that blue light that pulsed in both my parents' hands and Morwen's parents' hands.

Our magics *are* the same. We were both saved by a sacrifice then turned into vampires. Did that spell somehow affect us as we transitioned?

Our magic may be the same, but that is where our similarities end.

"Are you all right, Thea?" Cole asks, his voice quiet.

I take a deep breath, the ghost of a cedar-kissed wind caressing me. "Yes."

"Is there another section in here that you are going to look at?" he inquires. "I can help. Mica can start in the King's room."

I contemplate that for a moment. Going back to that isle alone, or letting Cole accompany me. Something in me urges to go without him. I'm not sure if it is my nerves and desire to protect Cole, just in case that statue tries to pull him into a horrible vision, too, or if it is the manipulation of whatever is left of Morwen in this place. Like she wants me alone.

Mica clears his throat. "Actually, I think I will need another vampire to help open his door." Both Cole and I look to him. He is standing by a table shrouded in books, all worthless to our research. His fingers lightly tap a book with a red cloth cover. He rubs his neck as he says, "Assuming that the King told me the truth when I inquired about it one day, he informed me that a spell on the door prevents any one vampire from entering."

"So, we can't get in?" I ask, a layer of frustration building in my chest. One roadblock after another.

Mica shakes his head. "The King usually chooses his words carefully. I think the spell guarding the door has something to do with only one person trying to enter at a time."

"You two go and get a head start," I say. "I shouldn't be long." That is, unless any unwanted visions pull me in again.

"We could just wait," Cole offers as he stands from the

chair he was using. The movement shifts the air, causing dust to swirl into the beams of sunlight around him. The sight tugs at an old strand of memory stashed away in my mind. Except I don't remember putting it there. Instead of looking into those smokey eyes in a dust-covered library owned by a terrifying vampire, the memory is of me looking into them underneath a willow tree, surrounded by glistening early morning sun and a quiet lake. Everything but his eyes are blurry. But I would recognize them anywhere.

It was just a flash of a memory. There, and then not, with just a blink.

I turn from Cole and Mica with a shake of my head and swallow. "It's all right." I fight the strain on my voice, hoping that neither of them can hear what emotions roll through my body. In this moment, I am glad they don't have the same beta ability as I do. If they did, they would sense the swell of trepidation. Not just because I fear for Sarah's life or the fact that we are up against possibly the strongest being on the planet. No, my fear has been building with all the pieces that have been slowly coming together over the past few weeks. At the memories and visions that flood my thoughts. At the words spewed by Morwen.

"Meet us in the northern wing when you are done, then," Mica says. I hear him walk up the few steps to the library's entrance. There is a pause before Cole's steps follow.

I don't wait to hear the door close before making my way to the back corridor of towering shelves and books. The painting of Vitamors sits where it was when I first found it. The colors seem duller now, making me wonder if the sword came from the piece of art itself. My hand lifts to trace the amber paint that depicts the stone in the sword's pommel. I pull it back a few inches away, remembering that this, too, plunged me into a vision.

I flex my hand, picturing the sword grasped in my palm.

There is a faint hum of magic swirling underneath my skin, but no sword. It doesn't come to my call.

"Just the book," I order myself and shove my hands in the pockets of my pants. I don't want to touch anything other than what I am seeking. Before I make my way down the aisle, I glance back to the archway between the two bookshelves in front of me.

It was here, in this spot, that I came to the possibility that Kael, the commander of the Brais, could be the King. He matched all the stories and depictions in the art gallery on the castle's first floor. He urged me then, to look for the sword and to be careful. That was the first, and only, moment that he seemed like anything other than an immortal tyrant.

I wonder, if his lover had not been killed by my comrades right after that conversation, would he truly have been an ally? Perhaps an ally against Morwen, then turned on us after. During our fight, he said things that made it seem like he wanted to help. Though he tried to kill me all the same.

With a long breath, I turn down the aisle and make my way to the gloomy corner. The library grows darker as clouds move in overhead, covering the glass ceiling, and I have to remind myself to keep the sun shining. Not that the light reaches the spooky back corridor.

My steps echo into the silence, the sound mimicking my thumping heartbeat. Every moment of that vision the statue gave me is still present in my mind. Just thinking about it sends shivers down my spine. A part of me feels bad that Morwen went through that, regardless of what she has become.

Trust yourself to know who deserves your kindness and who does not.

Valeria's words sing into my mind. My hands curl into fists as I shake my head. Morwen certainly does not deserve my kindness. Not after all that she has done. Still, as that thought slithers into my consciousness, the pity for her glides with it.

Everything quiets as I round the corner and see the statue in its entirety. The headless, graphite-colored stone stands seven feet high in the center of the aisle, its dominant presence is suffocating. The line of wooden shelves that runs parallel to the stone wall feels too close, like they are pressing me to the outstretched hand of the statue. I avert my gaze, making sure to stay away from the circle etched onto its breastplate. The sigil of Morwen's family. The same symbols are carved into the guard of Vitamors.

My shoulder scrapes lightly against the shelves and dust-covered tomes as I continue on. The book I noticed when I was last here wasn't far from the statue. It was tucked between taller books…

There. The single, cloth bound book. It is immaculate compared to its neighbors. The last time I saw its gray cover, it had been sitting on its bottom side, like books usually are upon a shelf. But now it is lying on its spine, the top edge poking in front of the others. My fingers stop their reach.

Did Morwen do this? Did she leave the book like this so that I, or someone else, would find it? My heartbeat drums in my ears, and I take a step back, nervous that the book holds another vision ready to consume me. I didn't want Cole or Mica to be pulled into any of the horrors this library holds, but now that they are gone, I have no one to pull me out if I do.

We will always be here.

A warmth blooms in my heart. I'll never be alone, not truly. The love my parents held for me still lives within. So, I lift my chin and grab the gray book, steeling myself for whatever vision awaits.

CHAPTER TEN

SARAH

I was wrong. Utterly and devastatingly wrong. Every single move was so meticulously considered, but somehow, still, we calculated incorrectly.

It wasn't hard to find the location of the King's old, secluded home. The Demoix family grimoire had everything, even the coordinates. For this place used to be the home of a Minuit witch, a wellspring of old magic that kept this once flourishing haven safe from the outside world. The sketches in the grimoire were never updated. They depicted a beautiful forest with a stream that snaked through the center. But now, it is nothing but a derelict remnant of death.

The moment we stepped foot onto this tainted marshland, we failed. The King had every aspect already countered, before we even acted.

But he is a vampire. Created by that of a witch's magic. The same that runs in our blood. Our magic should be able to overwhelm hers without any trouble.

I was wrong.

And now, Amelia, her wolves, and my sisters of the coven are going to die.

Shakily, I rise to my feet, my breathing heavy as I wipe foul smelling mud from my hands. The bare, scraggly trees that surround this marshy clearing seem to taunt me. It is as if the plants, once vibrant with life, became ill and tainted with vampiric magic from their proximity to the King, and now they cheer him on.

Bringing my gaze upward, I glare down the ancient vampire standing before me. The King's dark hair glints red underneath the sun. It matches the blood splattered on his slender face, his armor, and hands. The blood of my comrades. It matches the color of his eyes. "Stand down," I repeat to him. The grip on the golden medallion nestled in my palm tightens. Its power floods my body, connecting me to nature and to my coven.

It is weaker than it usually is.

The King of the Brais laughs, a hateful horrible sound. "I don't think you're in the position to be making demands like that, little witch." He flicks a lock of his long hair over a shoulder.

Beside me, Amelia limps closer, her hand clutching a bloody wound on her abdomen. Her wolf was gravely injured within the first five minutes of arriving. Now it rests in whatever dimension a shifter's other self goes when dormant. She snarls in warning. The physical aspects of the wolf might be gone, but I can still sense it in her voice and in her fluid movements.

In the lull of fighting, many of the witches stand, most noticeably injured. "We will not stop fighting you." I wipe blood away from my lips that has dribbled down my chin. My insides are on fire from attacking the King. That symbol on my neck that ties my life to hers is like charred metal pressed to my skin.

But I ignore it all. It doesn't matter what happens to me at this point, not if it means destroying this vampire in front of us. I just need to weaken or distract him enough so the others can finish him.

Black flames emerge from the King's fingertips and move upward like a snake twirling around a branch. The smile that curves on his crimson lips is absolutely savage. "I was told that your mother pleaded for your safety."

A numbing hum sings in my ears. It travels from my head to my toes and sinks like roots into the soft, watery earth below. There are bones and rocks and debris cemented into the ground here. That hum slinks around them. It is searching.

Those black flames are up to his elbows now. The King cocks his head, the sun shining on his feral gaze. "She got to her knees and begged Amaund to not harm you." The vampire King takes a half step forward, the strength of his magic pressing in on me. His bloodied, black leather armor devours the sunlight.

"Shut up," I whisper through clenched teeth. The humming attaches to pockets of natural magic stored far underneath the surface of this marshland. My medallion burns in my hands.

The vampire takes another half step, his menacing flames almost to his shoulders. "She struck a bargain with the General. In that bargain, she would give her life freely if it meant you would make it out alive." It is suffocating, the sheer strength of his magic. His flames are the manifestation of fire and fear, combined into one horrific power.

My limbs shake and my stomach roils at his words. The humming merges with those pockets of magic long forgotten by the abomination who has dwelled here for centuries. The well of natural magic pours into those roots and travels to my feet.

It isn't a numbing hum crafted from the pain of his words. It isn't the caring earth trying to comfort a grieving witch whose time is coming to an end.

No, it is raw magic.

And it is mine.

The moment before it strikes, Amelia breaks off from behind me and launches for the vampire, whose magic has increased in intensity. Our minds are one, and she knows—can *feel*—the surge of my own magic.

The King moves his gaze to the wolf shifter charging straight at him. Amelia carries a stake poised for the King's chest, a growl on her lips. The vampire only smirks at the wolf then readies his flame-coated hands for a block.

With all of my own strength, I pull on those underground pools of magic. The coven darts out of the way, not knowing what I plan, but in tune with me enough to be aware that something is coming. Amelia jukes to her right, creating space between her and the vampire. The King's face twists in confusion. He takes a step toward the vanishing Amelia before his attention furiously turns to me.

The King's eyes widen as a flurry of magical aura is hurled at him like a horde of serrated javelins. The magic, sharp and vicious, cuts through the air with ease. It emerges from the ground around my feet and strikes directly for him. The Brais King has milliseconds to decide what to do. Even for a vampire, that is hardly enough time. A swirl of black emerges in front of him like a shield. But my magic hits his body before his defense can fully form.

The sound of skin and clothing being ripped apart fills the droning silence of the marsh. Then, the all-powerful vampire King screams, his blood pouring onto the soggy earth. his shield flickers as it is torn apart by my magic.

I feel the hatred in his shield as my magic spears through it. Like layers of an onion, centuries of fury piled on top of each other. Each layer is pointed toward something else—*someone* else—and tells the story of his life.

The humans, and how they betrayed his village when he was a child. This layer is mixed with his disgust and ripples of grief.

The witches, for how they turned on his family, deeming them too dangerous to let live.

Two nameless and faceless people whose lives are eternally tethered to his. Phantoms whose actions once pushed him to the point of his mortal death.

In the same breath that these fleeting emotions slip around my magic, a searing sharpness erupts from the inside of my body. It shreds everything as it slithers from my neck to my stomach. Iron coats my tongue as I grip my clothing, teeth grinding against the ripples of pain.

The King of the Brais collapses to a knee as his blood pours like rivers from the many wounds created by my magic. With eyes like burning coals, he lifts his head. And despite the holes in his body, and the blood running down his chin, he *smiles*.

Bloodied fangs emerge from underneath his upper lip, reaching well past his bottom lip. I've never seen vampire fangs that long before. The sight chills me to the bone.

The pain caused by the silence spell ignites in my body, ricocheting to every inch. It is too great for me to ignore, and I fall to my knees and hands. The King's smile only grows wilder, like a feral animal who knows its prey made a lethal mistake. Nausea ripples through me, and I fight the shakiness in my limbs. With a wince, my head lifts just in time to see a giant, iridescent, black wolf charging toward the fallen vampire.

Like we planned, as a last-ditch effort if all else failed, Amelia strikes after I unleash all the magic I can. Her lips are pulled back in a snarl, rows of sharp teeth glinting in the light.

The King doesn't flinch, his glowing gaze holding steadily on mine. And then it happens so fast. I didn't even see the vampire move. Amelia yelps and I hear something crack. The growling ceases abruptly and the large black wolf is writhing on the ground. Her body convulses from some unseen force.

Bile rises in my throat, and I am about to roar at the King, trying to show that I am not yet done despite the screaming in my head and in my limbs, when I notice the pull on our coven's shared magic. I feel it like icy claws grasping Amelia's mind, digging and shredding.

Then Alain steps forward, her brows angled in wrath. She holds her hands in front of her, palms out in the motion for spellcasting. For a heartbeat, hope blossoms in my chest. The King doesn't seem to notice her approaching from behind. She could end things now.

Hope shifts to horror as I realize it is Alain whose magic pulls and twists into Amelia's mind. Alain, the soft spoken Minuit witch who has always had my back. Her magic spears into Amelia's mind like an array of daggers. She even has the audacity to use the coven's magic, knowing well that we can all feel her spell.

My magic, fueled by betrayal and my own burning hatred, churns in my chest. The medallion wrapped around my hand warms. I reach for more of that stored well under the ground, greedily taking what little is left.

The earth seems to loosen, allowing my access.

And then the King attacks.

CHAPTER ELEVEN

MICA

"Really? You never tried, not even once?" Cole prods as we turn the corner that leads to the northern wing. The corridors here are narrower than in other parts of the castle and the candle scones are more spread out, drenching us in shadows. Though this particular area of the castle has always been quiet, it is strange walking through the rest of the enormous building with only our voices and footsteps to fill in the stillness. Even the lack of rain pounding against the windows is noticeable. To me, at least. When Cole was a Brais, he never took a step into this dimension. Sometimes I wonder why Morwen never summoned him here.

Then again, maybe she knew that he would end up turning Thea into a vampire one day. She probably orchestrated that, too.

I shake my head as we pass a narrow, walnut accent table. A silver candelabra rests on top, the candles flickering in the dark as they always do. "Nope, not once."

He blows out a breath. "Why?" With a wild gesture of his hands, he says, "This place isn't that great." We pass a section of the stone wall that is severely cracked and he waves a finger at it with an embellished movement.

Shoving my hands into the pockets of my pants, I contemplate ignoring his question. It isn't like I didn't *want* to escape this dull dimension. Or the King for that matter. There hasn't been a day that's gone by without me running scenarios through my head about leaving. Or risking it all to try and end the King's life. But if I tried, and failed, I would be breaking the oath I made so long ago over a silent grave nestled under the sweeping branches of a willow tree.

I think back to that death, the one still haunting my heart. My hands ball into fists in my pockets. "I made a promise," is all I say.

A promise that I've done a horrible job at keeping thus far.

Cole mercifully reads that as an end to the conversation and doesn't press for more. It makes me wonder what, if any, promises he holds in his heart that he will not say. He lets out a long, descending whistle, pulling me from my thoughts.

"What even is going on here?" he asks, his tone shifting in a way that conveys just how tired he is. A trait he hides quite well, I've noticed.

Though I know of what he speaks, I follow his gaze to the wide, hand-carved wooden doors that shimmer from both the torches and the magical seal. Morwen's quarters in this castle have always been off limits for everyone. I've always been intrigued though, like many of the other Brais.

"It feels like a witch's magic," Cole says, his head tilting slightly in observation.

My lips press into a thin line. "Thea said the King was a witch before a vampire."

Cole's brows are furrowed, his gray eyes hard as he watches the iridescent colors move like waves. "It feels faintly familiar." He crosses his arms and leans forward with a tentative curiosity.

The shimmering veil shifts as he inches closer, the colors

swirling like scales of a fish. Or something fiercer, like a dragon. My eyes widen as sparks of wariness flit through my body. In all the times I have peered upon this door, I have never witnessed the magic that shields it react in this way.

"I don't think we should go in there," I whisper. My heart pulses with increasing fear.

Cole's nostrils flare. Not in anger. No, his eyes are turned in both confusion and worry. He can likely scent the fear coursing through me, even though I don't know why I'm feeling this way.

"What is it?" he asks, stepping back from the magic veil.

"I—" images flash through my mind, stifling my voice. Hair that glinted gold in the sun. Eyes of sand. Blood painted on the green grass, staining everything crimson. Not just images, but memories. Ones from so long ago that I stashed away. It feels like these doors are beckoning me inside. But I want nothing to do with them. I never want to be reminded of that day again.

"What are you two doing?" Thea's voice chases away the fear as it bounces softly over the stone walls. I keep my eyes downward, swallowing any lingering images as Cole turns to face the source of that toying voice.

"You were a lot quicker than I thought you'd be." Cole's matching tone brings me wholly back to reality. I turn to see him jerk his chin to the object in her hand. "What is that?"

Thea shrugs and holds up a worn leather book, flipping it to look at both blank covers. "I thought it would show me more."

A vague answer if I've ever heard one.

"What is it?" Cole asks, his repeated question jolting some-thing in me.

Thea lifts her hazel gaze to respond, but something behind us snags her attention and her eyes widen. "What is that?"

Cole and I twist to face the door, the veil shifting more so than it was before. It reminds me of rippling water, similar to when the portal to the dimension is activated. But where the portals are sheets of inky black, this is like an artist's canvas. One that has been layered and layered and layered, worked over the course of years to create an abstract masterpiece. Each color streaking in parallel swirls with the one next to it. They seem to reach out, extending like mountains in some areas and dipping like valleys in others.

I step away, and Cole follows. The veil surges for him as he steps back, though only reaching a foot out before snapping back to the door. We all stand in stunned silence, watching as it vibrates like a living entity.

"What the hell is the King keeping in there?" Cole asks.

They both look to me for answers. Answers that I don't have, so I shake my head. "Something he doesn't want others to know about."

"Well, let's get in there then," Thea declares as the temperature in the corridor rises. She places the book on the accent table as her magic emerges and swallows her hand, molding itself into a ball. "I would take a step back if I were you two."

Cole and I do as she says without hesitation, moving behind her and away from the lethal path.

The heat of Thea's fire is suffocating and my own magic squirms under my skin. I can feel the moisture in the air draining away with each pulse of her flames. I cross my arms, tucking my hands away so they don't call forth water to douse her attack.

Out of the corner of my eye, I see Cole shifting on his feet. I wonder if his air magic is reacting like mine. If he strains against the pull to stop the deadly force that grows just a few feet in front of us.

But something tells me that Thea's magic would devour ours.

There is a wildness to her magic that reminds me of a living beast. When she summons a blaze to her palms, it is like she calls upon the ancient, primal elemental entity itself. The soul of fire answers to her when she wills it.

I find myself holding my breath as she releases it. Violent winds rip through the air as the inferno cuts across the space, her brown hair whipping around her head. The giant orb of conjured flame hurtles toward that still shimmering barrier. The two magics slam against each other in a ferocious surge. Thea's fire roars against the veil, spreading outward in each direction as it searches for a way to break through. If that magical barrier were not there, I think the wooden door beyond would shatter against the force.

Cole and I drop out of the way as the fire expands over our heads, reaching like branches of a tree. And when I think that it will sweep down and engulf us, Thea's outstretched hand forces it away, pressing it against the ceiling. My jaw slackens at the color of her eyes when she glances at us.

Molten. Like that of her magic.

Maybe she doesn't call upon the soul of the element, bending it to her will when she has use of it. Perhaps the soul of it lives within her.

Thea turns her attention back on the warring magics. The flames dwindle as they recede, the barrier forming a whirlpool. It nullifies her magic as if it were nothing.

Thea hisses as she hurls another fireball at the shimmering veil. It is smaller than her first one, though the temperature in the hall remains scorching. The barrier ripples in wait, producing a crater in the center that swallows the fire mote.

Thea is panting, sparks flinging from her hands as she shakes them. Then she curls her fingers and another flame forms, winking in and out with each heavy breath.

"I don't think another will do anything," I offer, straightening and taking a step beside her. My magic pools in my palms, cooling the air around me to a tolerable degree.

The heat pushes against me as her nostrils flare. "I'm getting in that room." She points to the veil that taunts us with its dancing colors, a spark jumping from her fingertip. "Even if I have to destroy this part of the castle to do so."

Her fire crackles like it is readying to explode, but Cole's hand on her arm simmers it down. Her body reacts to his touch with a drop of her shoulders. "Mica, you said this magic prevents any one person from getting in?" Cole gestures to the door, still hiding behind its barrier.

I rub my neck as I say, "That was how I interpreted it."

"Let's test it then." A light wind stirs in the corridor as Cole lifts a hand in front of him. "Thea, throw your magic against the barrier and I'll add mine."

I step back as their magics react to the other's. Thea's flames seem to jump toward Cole. Not in a way they might an enemy, but like the sparks are happy to see him, to see his magic roaring to life beside them. Tendrils of the element curl upward in wisps. If I could see Cole's air magic, I would imagine it doing the same sort of movements. The two elements together in a dance.

Thea and Cole glance at each other, a look filled with such heartfelt emotions.

Their magic slams against the barrier in a silent assault. It buckles against the force, a deep ripple spreading to each corner. A tear forms under the pressure of their power, and I hold my breath in anticipation. But then the barrier starts reforming, thicker than it was before.

So I add my own magic to theirs. Dense ice forms along my fingertips and I hurl it all at the magical veil. Lethal ice shards that could tear through a person's body crash into the wall mixing with Thea's and Cole's magic.

The iridescent veil churns, shifting to a depthless, murky black as it pushes against our combined force. My magic strains against it and sweat beads on my forehead.

Thea grunts, her fingers curling as more flames spit out of her hands. The golden hues of her irises glimmer in the blazing light of her magic.

The pressure around us increases as the barrier darkens. Breathing becomes difficult, but only for a moment. The veil surges forward with a sound similar to a percussion drum. As if it punched a pocket of air, an invisible force slams into us and we all are blasted on our backs.

With a screaming headache, I look to the veil and see its swirling colors dancing like nothing happened.

Thea growls as she gets to her feet. Cole rises behind her and places a hand on her shoulder. "I don't think vampire magic can break that spell," he says.

Thea looks to her right hand, an inquisitive gaze upon her face. Her magic sizzles away as she stares, furling and unfurling her fingers. The air, still buzzing with the intensity of her flames, becomes electrified. My feet back away on their own accord as tendrils of uncertainty tickle down my spine.

Thea brings both of her hands together above her head as she steps toward the door. There is a flash of light, blinding enough that I squint against it. A deafening crack slices through the narrow corridor, and I think for a moment that the castle is collapsing on our heads.

I look up, expecting to see Thea thrown on the floor again for attacking the veil. Instead, she stands, her hands clasped around the hilt of Vitamors. The sword's blade penetrates the barrier, no longer iridescent, but a dull gray, like the life has left it. Fissures snake from the center of the veil to the borders, reminding me of broken glass.

Thea twists the blade before pulling it free. And the veil shatters to the ground, silent as it disintegrates.

We all stand motionless, staring at the ornate door no longer hiding behind a barrier. It is rounded at the top with an intricately carved, iron frame that spreads a foot outward. It makes me think of a security vault door and not so much one that leads to a bedroom.

Thea transfers the sword to her other hand and flexes her

fingers before looking at Cole, then to me. Her irises are back to their golden brown. "Shall we?"

Cole blinks at her for a moment. He shifts his attention to the door and cocks his head as he studies it, his gray eyes narrowing. "Do you think there are traps inside?" The air in the corridor stirs with a light breeze, propelled by Cole's magic.

Shoving my hands in the pockets of my pants, I say, "Its possible, we should certainly stay cautious. But, I don't think there will be." The magic sealing the door was strong, meant to keep anyone who wasn't the King—or a legendary sword apparently—out. Which likely means that the King kept the inside free of other protection spells.

Possibly, anyway.

With my reassurance, Thea moves toward the door. It opens silently as a burst of stale air flees the room beyond, like it were grateful for the freedom the movement granted.

A gasp escapes my lips at what we find on the other side of the once sealed door.

CHAPTER TWELVE

THEA

The musty air from inside Morwen's chamber assaults my senses and I scrunch my nose in disgust. If it were not for the layers of grime and some substance that could quite possibly be mold, it might be pleasant in here. Underneath the refuse is that comforting scent of old books. "Let's try to be quick in here," I say taking in a breath through my mouth.

Cole steps around me and coughs, placing a hand in front of his nose. "And we are supposed to find something of use in this place?"

If the rest of the castle represented how Morwen portrays herself to her vampires, this room would be how I imagine the chaos inside her mind. There are piles of books on every surface: the floor, a blanket-less bed, the windowsills whose curtains are torn and shredded, a rotting bookshelf, and what looks like a weathered davenport desk, though the precarious stacks of books cover every surface. Various, mismatched leather armors are strewn around the floor and books, some with a dull brown stain.

"It might prove to be as fruitless as the library." Mica carefully steps over a collapsed pile of books and…something slimy, with a particularly twisted expression of revulsion. "I didn't think the King could keep something so filthy and disastrous." He examines the curtain on the far wall and gingerly pulls it back as if it might bite him. Or contaminate him. But the window behind the shredded cloth is clouded with age and the light from the sun can hardly penetrate. He frowns at the glass and drops his hand, wiping it on his jeans.

Images of Morwen after she revealed herself to me as the King flash in my mind. Her body was flooded with pure rage, her mind an unstable, faltering dam. Her truth is far from the calm and collected persona she typically wore. "I can," I whisper. The two of them look at me, but don't say anything.

Morwen is dangerous because of the power she can wield, sure. But power doesn't always mean evil.

The greatest threat from her is her twisted sense of justice.

Cole sighs and runs a hand through his dark hair. His facial hair is a bit stubbier than it was before. "So, I guess we each pick an area and see what we can find?" When Mica and I nod in tired agreement, Cole turns to the back right corner of the room, his eyes roving over the particularly high stack of books against the wall. He winces, noting some that reach for the ceiling. Pointing to the absurdity of it all, he turns to us and opens his mouth, just to be interrupted by Mica.

"Nope. That's your corner, Moretti," Mica jests. "Read fast." A corner of his mouth lifts when Cole growls and turns back around. Mica pulls out a familiar, small gray book that was tucked under his arm. I didn't notice it at all until now.

I jerk my chin toward it. "Is that the journal I took from the library?" I had left it on the table in the hall. He must have snatched it before entering the room.

Mica runs his fingertips over the blank cover before peering over to me. "Yes. I was curious about it."

To my left is a mound of old clothes. I reach over it and grab the first book I see. "I can spare you the time. That journal only has names written inside." The tome in my hands, a lightweight book with brown bindings, is blank inside. At some point in time, it wasn't. Faded remnants of ink are the only thing left on its yellowed sheets.

"Names?" Mica asks quietly. His tone catches my attention, and I watch as he opens it and flips through the sand-colored pages. His index finger moves from the top of each page to the bottom before he turns to the next. I am about to ask if he is looking for something when his hand stops. His jaw clenches, eyes pinned to something on that particular page of the journal. Those emotions from earlier slip away from his calm control, one more profound than the other.

Shock and anguish. Grief.

Does he recognize one of the names in that journal? My beta ability hums, wanting to reach him and take away the pain in his heart. I grip the book in my hand and take the smallest step toward him. "Mica?"

He squeezes his moss-colored eyes shut and I could swear they were rimmed with a tear. With a shake of his head, he flips more pages before opening his eyes again. He doesn't look at me when he says, his voice teetering, "It's nothing." The emotions that leaked from him disappear again, closed off from my prying magic. His page turning, now quicker than it was before, stops abruptly again. And now he looks to me, his eyes a little sadder than they were before. "Did you read through them all?"

I lift a brow at him. "No. I only actually looked at the first couple of pages before flipping through the rest."

With a second glance at the journal, he takes a step to me, carefully missing the questionable substance on the floor. "The last two names." He hands me the journal, kept open with a finger.

I take it and rest it on the brown book. My eyes scan the names. And then the room spins when I read the last two.

Nicolai Moretti.

Thea Knight.

Sweat pricks on my forehead as I read our names over and over again. They are written in the same elegant handwriting as the rest. The only difference is that they do not have a line slashed through them.

"What is this?" I breathe, my voice shaky. I mostly am asking myself. Or the journal perhaps. As if it would answer.

"I think I found something," Cole says warily from his chaotic corner. His voice carves its way through the muddled thoughts in my mind. Chiseling away as if all the names and their implications were layers of ice. It takes me a moment to realize what he said.

I close the journal and find Mica still standing in front of me. He is studying me, his expression unreadable. I give the journal back to him. "I don't want this." I don't need to have it in my hand to remember that our names had been etched onto a page of an ancient looking journal.

The first time I saw that journal in the library, I was drawn to it. Was my name in there then? Or had it been added recently? I don't know if it was Morwen who wrote all the names, but I have a sinking feeling that it was.

The sound of books tumbling to the floor tears through the room. "Guys?" Cole says after the last one hits the floor.

I look over to him, grateful to stick the contents of the journal into the back burner of my mind. Except something behind Cole catches my attention, and somehow I feel like the journal is the better of the two options for something to be dealing with.

Another shimmering veil.

Except before, the one that sealed this room was opalescent and this one flickers like a raven's wing. Or the night sky. Around the edges, it is dark with specks of light that twinkle like stars over a quiet forest. For a brief moment, I want to paint it. The center is what I imagine a black hole to be. An endless pit of blackness.

"This…" Cole starts but trails off. He stretches his arm

out, blocking me from getting too close. When I give him an inquisitive look, he says again, "This feels wrong. In a way, it feels like the seal you broke. Like a witch's magic," he observes, his voice chilling.

Mica steps up behind us. "Why do I sense a 'but' coming," he says dryly.

Cole shakes his head. His brows furrow and his gray eyes harden as he watches the flickering darkness. "But, it also doesn't."

I release my beta ability and it slithers toward the barrier hesitantly. An unsettling coldness touches my magic and it retreats back into me, afraid of the strange power behind that touch. The sensation spreads over my body and I shiver. It reminds me of death. But as cold as it is, there is also a sense of invitation that my beta ability felt.

I twist my body toward the entrance to Morwen's chamber. To where I left Vitamors leaning against the wall. I call it to my outstretched hand.

Mica swiftly steps to the side as the sword whizzes to my waiting palm. "What are you doing?"

"I need to get in there."

Mica grabs my wrist before I can turn back to the barrier. His green eyes are alight with their own sort of fire. "Just because that worked on the other seal, doesn't mean it will for this one."

"Let go," I snarl. He doesn't budge, even when I feel my vampiric features emerge. The room brightens and I can feel the wrongness of the magic layered into the barrier. But I don't care. I need to find out the secrets it is keeping hidden. Mica's grip tightens, almost painfully so. His irises remain green. I muster the strength to yank free of him.

"Thea," Cole says softly. His voice breaks the hot anger rising in my chest. "I think Mica is right. Using the sword here doesn't feel right." He might not have my beta ability, but he sure knows how to calm my erratic emotions.

I stop fighting against Mica's hold and close my eyes. Despite the anger and fear that still swirls ferociously in my mind, I relax, letting the world around me dim. "Sarah could be dying right now. This barrier, or whatever it is keeping locked away, holds an answer." I can feel it.

Mica releases my arm and the point of Vitamors' blade sticks into the wood floor. Cole steps up to me and says, "We will find a way. A safer way."

The symbol on my collarbone tingles uncomfortably, as if it were still imbedded with Morwen's will. It is as though she were here, laughing at my hopelessness, urging me to give up.

Sarah has always been the one to risk herself for me. And I hate that I can't even think of a single time where I did the same for her. Always too afraid of the consequences.

But not now. I won't be held back, won't let her risk her life for me. I will not give up.

My hand tightens on the sword hilt as it hums in my hand. "We don't have time," I say quietly, but with conviction. And before either of them have a chance to stop me, I plunge Vitamors into the black, endless magic.

And I scream.

It isn't like before. Breaking the seal to Morwen's room felt like cutting through stone and storm.

This is like lightning. Pure and powerful energy sears into my body. Vitamors vibrates in my grasp like it were crying out as well. A suffocating chill sweeps over my body, my limbs numbing slowly, as a single word is whispered into my mind in a voice that seems to pull the life from my soul.

Trust.

I feel warmth on my shoulders. That touch tries to fight off the cold and pull me free. "Let go, Thea!" Cole. He is yelling, though his voice sounds far away. I urge myself to focus on his voice, his touch. "Thea, let go."

He wants me to let go of Vitamors. I let my grip loosen, but Vitamors trembles with my release. That power that is lightning and the coldness of death, latches onto my sword. The magic will consume Vitamors if I let go.

So I focus on Cole and pull with all my strength on the hilt of my sword. With every tug and twist, the chilling magic seems to double its own strength. The pain of whatever is in the barrier wraps itself tightly around me, but I ignore it. Still focusing on Cole, I call forth my beta ability. It emerges, this time with more fury, and forms a layer around my body and Vitamors. Like a piece of magical armor, it shoves the barrier's hold on me back.

Cole catches me as we fall onto the grimy floor of Morwen's room, somehow knocking over only a single book from a stack beside us. Vitamors calms in my hand, gratitude flooding from it and into my body.

"Thank you," I say to Cole. My heart is stammering in my chest. From the touch of that barrier's magic, the voice that spoke in my mind, and the word it uttered.

Trust.

Behind us, Mica grunts. Horror floods my body when I see him clutching his shoulder. Underneath a tear in his white shirt, there is a sickly black color spreading slowly. His skin is paling. "A shard of the barrier broke free when you pulled Vitamors from it. I didn't even have time to react." He winces and sways a bit.

I rush to my feet and guide him to the dust-covered bed. "I'll try and flush it out." I tuck Vitamors under my arm because it doesn't want to part from me, even if I were to only put it on the floor or on the bed beside Mica. That barrier spooked it. My hands warm as I place them on his shoulder.

An iciness fights back, and it is not the familiar trace of his magic. There is a sentience to this powerful, black-tainted magic. Like that of the barrier. I shove my beta ability at it, concentrating on a pure, cleansing energy. The black magic hisses, retreating only a little. Mica grunts, his fingers digging into the ragged quilt.

My energy manipulation slithers around the unnerving blotch of magic, trying to form a barrier of its own. As my fingers touch Mica's cool skin underneath his torn shirt, visions flash through my mind, so fleeting that I can't grasp them. Their ghost leaves an ache in my chest and my magic stumbles, allowing the intruding magic to advance into his body. A phantom voice whispers Mica's name in my ear, so similar to mine, yet different all the same. Mica stiffens and inhales sharply, his expression twisting in pain.

I shove away the lingering sensations and shift my hands so they are hovering just slightly above his bare skin. Focusing on my magic, I push forward again. The foreign magic slams against mine, eliciting another pained noise from Mica. It is trying to force me out of his wound, all the while I can feel it digging itself farther into his body. The magic…growls at me, rearing for another attack. I feel it slicing through my beta ability as I form a wall to devour it.

But then, nothing.

That dark, foreign magic rushed toward mine and then disappeared. I can't feel even a single tendril of its presence.

"Thanks," Mica says, his rigid body relaxing. I remove my hand from him and he rolls his shoulder, all signs of discomfort gone.

I blink, watching as the wound slowly closes, then I look at my hands, still tingling with my beta ability. "I…" I let the sentence trail off. Did I destroy the magic in his body? It sure didn't feel that way, but I felt nothing. Maybe when it rushed at me, it dissolved on contact? He seems to be in no more pain, so that should be a good thing, right?

Mica lifts a blond brow at me before examining his shirt, a frown forming on his lips. "This was one of my favorite shirts," he says.

"You have dozens of those shirts," Cole jests, a crinkly, tarnished parchment in his hand. "It's all I've ever seen you wear."

Mica narrows his green gaze at Cole before jerking his chin at the paper. "What is that?"

Cole glances at the paper's contents, his lips pressed into a thin line. He turns the paper over to reveal the scrawling letters. "Would either of you know who, or what, Vitamors is?"

My sword hums at its name. "Yes, why?" I ask, stepping over a small broken table so I can look at the parchment. The handwriting is hardly legible. Nothing at all like the elegant letters in that journal. It doesn't help that there are stains covering most of it.

Cole's eyes glisten with surprise. "This paper was stuffed in one of the books here." He points to a small stack on the desk.

"You were so worried about me getting stabbed by whatever that is," Mica gestures to the still intact barrier and I could have sworn it rippled as he mentioned it. The others must have noticed, too, because they both froze. Mica stops talking and we all just stare at it for a moment.

Cole clears his throat after a moment of stillness and steps between me and the now tranquil barrier. "Did you want me to hold your hand?"

Mica sticks his middle finger up at Cole.

I pluck the paper from Cole's hand and scan the words. "This..." my eyes widen. "This is a way out of the dimension."

CHAPTER THIRTEEN

THEA

The invisible wall that Sarah had placed to lock us in the castle shattered just as Morwen's magic did when I plunged Vitamors into it. But where Morwen's broke like glass, Sarah's magic crumbled like snowflakes dancing in a winter wind. Gentle and beautiful.

"So let me get this straight," Oba says between breaths as we make our way to the portal on the beach. The sun shines brightly overhead, like a beacon of hope. "You are going to leave some of your what here?"

"Essence," I inform him. He and Cole are on my left side while Alec is in front. The trees pass by in a blur of green and brown as we run to the portal.

Oba huffs. "What does that even mean?"

"It means," Mica, who is behind all of us, answers, "that we are surely running to our deaths."

Alec makes a noise that sounds like he agrees with Mica.

"We won't be," I growl. Vitamors warms in the makeshift scabbard strapped to my back. It, at least, agrees with me. Or it might be warming to the thought of fighting Morwen.

"I'll make sure the King isn't around before we run to help Sarah. And if he is, we will change our strategy." I tell them my plan again. And the part where I will go regardless of who joins me.

"The witches and wolves are our allies," Cole adds. "We need them." His gray eyes shoot to mine with a look that says, *You will never have to be alone.*

When we reach the beach, the air is quiet. The waves stretch onto the sands, but in tranquil movements. The stone archway stands alone, almost beckoning us forward. There is no sign of the battle that had just occurred here, the vampires we killed already having melted away into the earth.

"Here," I say, unsheathing Vitamors. It sings as I slash it through the air. We stop at the edge of the beach. That liminal space between sand and grass, the forest to our backs.

Cole removes that shriveled parchment from the pocket of his jeans. He steps in front of me, standing in the sand as my feet are planted in the grass. "Ready?"

"Yes," I say, placing the cold metal of my sword to my left palm.

He starts reading from the paper. Half of script is in English, the other in some strange language Cole is certain that he can read correctly. "Thresholds are places of in between. They hold potential, but also uncertainty. They are neither whole nor incomplete." He looks to me and signals the next part of the ritual.

I slide Vitamors against the skin of my hand. Blood pools in my palm, wetting Vitamors and dripping into the grass. When the point of the sword is coated in crimson, I stick it into the line between the two landscapes. Power ripples from the sword and in my blood, spreading through the ground.

Cole resumes reading from the paper, this time in that strange language. It sounds like a song, if that song were conjuring a demon. He said the spell mentioned the borrowing of the giver's soul and power for the favor of escaping. And he is certain that it is not for an indefinite amount of time. He places a hand on me as I collapse to a knee, still holding onto Vitamors.

I grunt, clenching my teeth as a wave of dizziness creeps over me. Cole's grip on my shoulder tightens and I focus on his touch. It keeps me from falling to the ground, despite already on my knees. The spell moves its web-like fingers down my body, collecting my magic as a debt. I feel it merge with the castle, with the magic-made earth below, and the air above. This dimension is holding my power, keeping it like a ransom. It seems more than happy to crush this borrowed magic—and me—should I not return in time.

I rise to my feet when the spell—or the dimension—stops pulling from me. I don't know when Cole stopped speaking in that language, but he was quiet before the dimension was finished extracting what it wanted. I can feel the absence of my magic. Like a hollow part of a tree. Without that piece, I feel unstable.

But it doesn't matter. So, with my comrades behind me and Vitamors once again strapped to my back, I push forward. My feet slide across the sand as we run toward that glistening, white stone portal.

And I could swear it was whispering, *chanting*, our demise.

CHAPTER FOURTEEN

THEA

The magic of the portal coats me like a spiderweb. It seems to touch every part of my body, inside and out. The sensation is strange but energizing at the same time. The piece of my magic left behind sits like a hole in my chest.

The moment my body is free of the portal's watery-like surface, I take in our surroundings. The air is acrid, a putrid weight hovering and pushing on my chest. I scrunch my nose, trying to ignore its strength. The trees here are bare, no greenery on their scraggly branches, reminiscent of a pond created by a beaver or an old wetland.

I summon my beta ability. Like we planned, I let it rove over this rotten landscape. When I don't sense Morwen, I call upon my vampiric speed and break into a run. I know I should wait to make sure everyone else gets through the portal, but I can't. Not with Sarah's life on the line. My vampire comrades will undoubtably hear my footsteps and be able to follow.

As I run, I take in as much of the landscape as I can, noting that my eyes see more now than when I first ran at this speed all those weeks ago.

The trees become more sparce, making way for tall, brown

grasses that sway in a light wind. My foot sinks into the soft ground, and I stumble to a stop as it seems to pull at my shoe. I hear the others quickly approaching from behind. Looking ahead, there is a vast wetland with patches of grasses and water. Far in the background, a thick line of trees covered in mosses jut out from the right, blocking the view of what lies beyond.

"What's wrong?" Cole asks, concern flitting through his eyes. He glances at our surroundings and I feel the air stirring around us. "Do you sense the King?"

Pulling my foot out of the muck, I say, "It's a marsh. It'll be too difficult to run through here." My body vibrates with the need to keep moving.

"It smells horrid," Oba observes, his nose pressed to the crook of his arm.

I am about to express that I agree when I see Mica's face. It has paled to a ghostly white, his eyes a dull green. "What is it?" My body tenses, what little magic still remains pulses to my hands to defend, my palms heating.

His throat bobs as he swallows. His hand moves shakily to tuck a lock of blond hair behind his ear. "I've been here before." From the expression on his face, his last visit must not have been pleasant. "The King—"

The smell hits me like a brick. And by the flash of red in his eyes, Mica likely smells it too. There's blood here. So much of it. Clashing parts of me fight to take control. The enticing aroma calls to the hungry vampire. It wants to follow the scent and feast on what may remain.

The part of me that knows what I am smelling is likely that of our allies recoils at the smell. It snarls and tugs to keep control. The ribbon scent of fear fights against that part of me as well.

Silence pounds in my ears as fire seeps into my hands. I close my fingers into a tight fist, extinguishing the flames as I ignore the waters and muddy ground and push forward. The sound of our footsteps slurping in the mud covers the eerie silence of the wetland.

Each step onward is strenuous. The mud is so thick in some places that we have to help each other free our swallowed feet. Cole keeps by my left, leading our small group through the marsh, Oba behind slightly on the right. Alec and Mica, the latter still colorless, remains a few paces behind us all. I can't help but wonder what nightmares fill Mica's head.

Foolish. It was so, utterly foolish for them to come face Morwen on their own. To lock us up while they raced to their deaths. Sarah's need to be the protector is one of her strengths, but also a serious fault. She wanted to protect us—protect *me*—from the danger of facing the King of the Brais. But Cole and I might be the only ones able to even stand against her.

Mica curses behind us and we all turn. The mud has swallowed his left foot all the way up to his knee. Alec and I move toward him to help, but he waves us off, his magic freezing the ground around his leg. It shatters when he pulls his limb free. He winces and rolls his shoulder as he flexes his left hand. His face is ashen as he looks up, gaze moving past me, and takes a step forward.

"Mica, can you freeze the mud?" Cole asks, his breathing labored. "We could get there faster if it weren't for this soft ground."

"Yeah," Mica whispers, his voice unsteady. He shakes his hands and I feel the temperature in the air plummet. The ground around him becomes hard with ice. It slowly spreads to where Alec and I are standing, the ice becoming thinner and thinner. It stops just beyond us before cracking and melting. Mica grinds his teeth together and releases his magic and a heavy breath. The air warms again. "I can't." He casts his gaze downward, his chest heaving. "There might be some magic in the marsh preventing me from using mine."

"I don't feel anything," Oba says, a light wind gliding between us.

I turn to Mica. "You don't have to keep going," I say, gripping his arm. His skin is cold, and I wonder if it is solely because of his magic or due to whatever fear lingers within him.

Mica twists to me, brows knitted together. Sweat beads on his forehead. "I'm here. I'm going to help." Though his words sound sure, I can feel a subtle shake under my grip on him. Pulling his arm free of my hold, he moves past me.

My eyes find Cole's. His lips are pressed into a thin line. I follow after Mica, the other two moving into step again. Oba has fallen to walk with Alec in the back of the group, Cole and me in the center and Mica leading.

We walk more in silence, still unable to move at a quicker speed. My nerves are ravaging me on the inside. While we take our time getting to wherever this murky path leads, Sarah and the others could be in danger. They could be dying and we have no way of knowing.

Shoving my fire magic down, I tug on my energy manipulation. Where there is a hole in my fire magic, my beta ability feels full. Like the dimension only took from one. Slowly, it spreads from my body with its invisible tendrils. No one notices it touching them. I almost sigh at Cole's warm, inviting energy. If we were not here, I would let myself get swallowed up in it.

My magic touches the energy that I remember as Alec's. Cold and closed off like it was that first day back in the castle. Though now I note a sliver of something else. I can't quite discern what it feels like. I resist the urge to look at him, or to probe his energy for more clues.

At the same time, I feel another's energy eddying beside Alec's. Oba. Where Alec's has a definitive, hard border, Oba's is open and seems to swirl like mist into the air. There is an eagerness to his energy that pours into my magic, sending it flying outward, ready to do what it needs to.

And it slams right into Mica. I see his muscles tense for a heartbeat, and I brace myself for him to yell at my invasion of privacy, but he pushes forward like it was nothing. The last time I felt his energy, it was reminiscent of Cole's. Now… My magic spreads across the surface of his. That warmth is there, but it is clouded. My energy rounds his, unable to move through the solidity of those jumbled, heavy emotions.

Driven by the same urgency that I feel, my magic lurches forward. I can feel, more than see, its path. It rounds the scraggly tree ahead and to the right, to where it is no longer visible to us. Thorny vines hang like a curtain from the tree's bare, pale branches. It is one in a line of trees, all dead and covered in uninviting vines, that create a wall blocking the rest of the marsh. To our left sits a large copse of barkless trees so thick and dense that nothing could pass through them, at least not in a hurry. The vegetation—as barren as it is—is leading us toward that rounded corner of vine-covered trees.

A sick feeling spins in my gut. And whether the others feel the same, they don't let on.

I almost trip on my own feet as my magic brushes against something familiar and a sob escapes my lips. I take the next couple steps slowly and wipe the stray tears from my eyes. My magic touches Sarah's energy—a coziness that feels like home, like sitting by the fireplace with her and Valeria, watching a winter storm blanket the world in fluffy white. Or staying up late and dyeing our hair the most bizarre colors on the shelves and laughing ourselves silly at the results. Like sneaking gingerbread cookies that Valeria made for Yule and eating enough to upset our stomachs.

Cole and Mica turn to me, their expressions searching. "Thea?" Cole asks, his brows up in worry.

But I don't stop. No, I push myself through the marsh,

ignoring the scrape of sticks and the pull of the thick mud. I don't care if I lose a shoe. Sarah is alive. My magic tells me so.

"Thea?" Cole calls again, his voice hurried and dripping in concern.

"I feel her," I say through a cry. My foot sinks just a bit too much into a pit of soft, watery earth. I yank once and it hardly budges. There is a chilly wind blowing from behind, stiffening the ground enough that I can pull my shoe free. The wind continues, propelling me faster to my friend. I feel so light in this place of emptiness and despair.

The sight when I turn the corner of scraggly trees, however, knocks the breath from my lungs. At the lifeless, blood-covered bodies laid out in a circle. The witches. They either went out together in one attack, or someone put them like this. Their battered bodies create a wall around—

"Sarah!" My friend is kneeling, her back against a post protruding from a patch of brown grass at the center of the circle of bodies, her wrists are tied over her bowed, motionless head. I run to her, only to be stopped by a wall, invisible like the one that trapped us in the castle. Another sob wracks my body as I punch that invisible wall. "Sarah!" I yell again. She doesn't move.

"What the hell?" Cole whispers as he steps beside me, his arm brushing against mine.

"Are they alive?" Oba asks quietly.

He can't possibly be asking about all the witches laid out in a circle. Whose eyes were left open, unseeing, toward the gloomy sky. But that is when I notice the other person tied to a post. Amelia is tied like Sarah hardly two feet away. They face each other, though neither seem to be awake. But where Sarah's bindings are rope, Amelia's are chains.

I scan them, noting how both are covered in blood. Sarah's cloak is missing and her clothes are lathered in crimson-stained mud. I can hear her heartbeat from here, so she isn't dead.

The blood I see on Amelia comes from a deep gash along her chest. My hands dig into the barrier. Her wound isn't bleeding anymore, but there is blood that dribbles out from her mouth and down her neck. I don't hear anything from her. No heartbeat or staggering breath.

"Sarah!" I punch the wall again, with enough strength that my knuckles sting. And then again and again and again. I'm faintly aware of Cole's hand on my back in silent comfort. But I ignore him and punch the wall two more times. My beta ability pours around my fist with the last strike, and it causes the barrier to shimmer like a faltering digital screen.

I unsheathe Vitamors and strike at the invisible wall. "Sarah!" I strike again. Vitamors doesn't even crack the wall. Why? Why doesn't it work here? Tears sting my eyes as I slash at the barrier again.

"It might be a while before she awakes." A silky voice purrs from behind us. And if the world wasn't quiet before, now it has gone deathly silent. It's like we all hold our breaths, turning to face Morwen standing at the edge of the marsh. She's picking at her nails as if they were the most interesting thing here.

Cole growls and pulls a wooden stake from his belt, his other hand engulfed in a violent wind. Oba wields a stake as well, his left hand glowing that sickly green. Mica and Alec stand frozen, their faces a picture of fear as they gape at the King.

Morwen looks up from her nails and frowns briefly at the shimmering barrier before surveying each of us. Hatred flashes across her features when her gaze lands on Mica and Alec, then to Oba. And when it moves to Cole and me, that hatred turns to a cruel grin. She takes one careful step into the muddy marsh, her foot moving smoothly across a dry spot, as she says, "And here shall your bodies rot, *Vincula*."

And then she strikes.

CHAPTER FIFTEEN

COLE

The King moves so fast it is hard to see. A blast of black, menacing flames hurtles right at Thea and me, cutting through the air at lethal speed. There isn't a moment to warn Thea, so I send my air magic at her, dropping my stake in the movement, as I jump out of the way. My shoulder hits the soft, muddy ground, but I get to my feet in the same breath.

Oba surges forward, striking while she gathers more flames in both of her hands. I try to cry out for him to be cautious, but he is already throwing a wooden dagger at her. As true as ever, his aim sends that weapon right at her heart.

Morwen's right hand moves, still wreathed in flames, as she plucks the dagger from the air, directing an annoyed look at Oba. But that wasn't his main move. That green glow around his hand has doubled in size within his palm, twisting to form a whip. A lash of poison, capable of bringing even a vampire down. While she catches the stake, his green whip lashes out at her.

But it isn't fast enough.

So I help it.

My air magic whirls in my palm. It gathers around us all

and races to the King. Oba's sickly green magic rides the wave of wind, moving at an incredible speed.

Her eyes widen just barely, and she moves at a speed akin to teleportation. One beat she is standing where she caught his stake, the next she is gone. Oba's magic cracks into a tree, dissolving it to the ground almost immediately. His magic evaporates just as fast.

Then, Oba gasps. I turn, horror building in my chest. The King appeared behind him. That dagger found its mark, not in the King's chest, but in Oba's.

"No!" I shriek, gathering a torrent of violent winds. It roars around us, a monster come alive. Born from the surge of dread coursing through my veins. I mold it into a thin tunnel and aim it right where the King stands behind Oba, who is now dropping to the ground.

The King faces the wind, her leg retreating a single step as she pushes against the magicked air. She angles her head down, bracing against my magic as it slices past. Out of the corner of my eye, I see Thea getting up. I don't dare take my attention off of the King to make sure that Thea is okay. Neither Mica nor Alec have made a move yet, and I curse at bringing them. They can't even fight against Morwen without harming themselves.

Flames ignite to my right, weaker than they usually would be. The King turns her head in a snarl toward that bright magic as her left hand fights against the wind and slowly rises, fingers curled. The stake imbedded into Oba shakes. She is using the same power that I have to summon that weapon. I push harder on my magic, trying to knock her down. She digs her heels into the ground.

Thea releases her fire. It isn't much at all, but it merges with my wind, nonetheless. Her magic feels like her. Determined, precise, and sure. It wraps around my own magic, the two swirling around each other in a joyous dance. I pull at the end of the wind torrent so that it circles around the King. The two magics become a tornado of flame and wind. Hungrily, they engulf the King of the Brais.

As the tornado rises into the sky, a moment of panic has me searching the ground for Oba. But then I see that Mica has finally found his courage and carried Oba safely away.

And that moment cost me.

I let that left side of the tornado falter. It was weak enough that the King darted through it, cloaked in her own black flames. Out of those deathly flames, a wooden stake thrown, cutting into my air current.

I flinch, but it wasn't aimed at me. The flames stop abruptly and horror threatens to bring me to my knees. The stake pierced Thea's upper chest, so achingly close to her heart. Thea drops to a knee and clutches the stake.

And in a heartbeat, the King vanishes again. I brace myself, expecting her to reappear next to me. But she doesn't.

My head snaps to beyond that charred piece of the marsh, to where the other three are. Mica and Alec stand over Oba, who is slowly getting back to his feet.

The King emerges from nothing, right in between Mica and Alec. Her muddy boot connects to Oba's jaw as she grabs Mica and Alec by their necks and hurtles them to the line of trees as if they were pieces of paper.

So fast. She moves *so* fast. I thought that I had sharpened my senses enough to be able to keep up. But that fight at the castle wasn't even close to how quick she really is.

If she wanted to, she could stake us all before we even had time to breathe. That thought is deeply nerve wracking.

Mica and Alec don't even hit the trees before the King moves toward me, her steps so sure and unfaltering. The marsh made our trek here a hassle, but the King has no issue. Her steps glide over the uneven ground with ease.

Something flashes to my right, but I don't have time to look. The King reaches me before I can even throw a wall of wind up as a shield. Her claw-like nails dig into my neck, gripping so hard that I feel muscle and tendon snapping. Cherry black hair whips in the air from her quick movements, swiping across her face when she stopped in front of me.

Her other hand grabs mine in a quick motion. White dots flash in my vision as she snaps the bones in my hand. First my right, then my left. My scream cuts through the thick air and her wild eyes flash ruby, a hunger that has nothing to do with blood fills her sharp features.

There is a cruel smile tugging at her crimson lips, but her voice is venom as she says, "You are born to die." Her free hand pulls back, fingers pressing together to form a dagger of sharp nails. "So die."

And in that agonizingly long second, as I watch her hand move with lethal precision toward my heart, visions swim through my mind. Images of lives lived. Memories that I cannot recall. They flash by with emotions and warm sunlight, with heartache and pain, laughter and home. And at the center of it all is her. Thea, there with me. But it is also not her all the same.

And all of a sudden, the words I uttered to Thea when I was dying in that castle dimension make sense. As impossible as they sounded then, they make sense now. I have always found Thea. Her soul has always called to mine, and I have answered.

Like I will do again.

Dark wisps filter into those visions of life. Death, coming to claim me. A thousand times, I see it take my life. In some images, it is a quick death. In others, I am screaming in pain.

The King. No, Morwen. It is her face that swirls with that mist of black death. Eyes like burning gold and a ruthless grin in the darkness.

A flash of light, and I collapse to the ground, clawing at my crushed throat with my broken hands. I shift to my vampire features, the magic that heals flowing a little faster as I gulp down air. When I am no longer feeling like I am breathing through a broken straw, I look up. What I see almost knocks the air from my lungs again.

Thea is forcing Morwen to take the defensive. With Vitamors. Thea swings it with invigorating accuracy. Her first strike must have been the one that made Morwen release me. A long, brutal gash that is already stitching itself back together runs from her shoulder to the middle of her side.

My nails dig into the mud, still taking in deep breaths. I can't help but watch Thea's glorious display of swordsmanship. She and I never trained with swords. Everything that she has learned was from the Brais. I wonder if Morwen is cursing herself for all that teaching now.

With how quickly Thea picked up hand-to-hand combat during our training sessions, her aptitude for this doesn't surprise me. Something in my mind knows that she has always had this ability.

One sure strike after another. Each one flows expertly into the next in a calm, fluid movement. Thea's feet slide gracefully across the uneven terrain as she raises the sword in the air, preparing for another strike, when Morwen throws a lash of black flames at her. The King stumbles but manages to dodge the fire by leaping to her left and rolling.

"I'm so grateful you brought my sword back to me," Morwen says as she prowls to Thea. A predator stalking its prey.

Thea stabs at the ground, the sword slicing through the soft mud. She uses it as a crutch as she stands. "Finders keepers," she says, somehow managing to keep her expression neutral. Even as Morwen snarls at her.

And despite the pain rippling through my throat, I stifle an amused cough.

The King's nostrils flare. "That is *mine*." The words are guttural as her irises blaze like a pit of molten lava. Her magic pours from her skin, black flames drip to the ground, steam hissing as it scalds the earth. Even with the almost twenty feet between us, I can feel the heat flowing from her. It weighs the air down, making it too heavy for my own conjured air to latch on to.

It feels as though we entered an oven. My fingers flex at my side as I create a barrier around myself, Thea, and the others. Around Amelia, Sarah, and her witches. A protective shield of air that won't blister our insides. It doesn't seem to bother Morwen, though, but I am not taking any chances.

Thea looks down at the sword as if she were listening to it. Then, her steady gaze returns to the wild vampire stalking toward her. "I think it likes me better."

Morwen ignites. Her magic bursts like a wall from her body and barrels toward Thea like a broken dam. Thea holds her ground, though I know she doesn't have enough magic to block this attack. So I send my own out to be her shield, a cyclone of wind encircling her body.

Straining against the King's heat, my magicked air pushes against the menacing flames. The black fire spreads and swells around my shield, trying to find the smallest crack. The moment our powers collide, a surge of crippling fear hits me. It uses my magic as a bridge to get into my mind. It manifests as images of Thea and everyone else being broken and torn to shreds. I almost collapse with a sob, the visions so lifelike. My shield falters, the black flames pushing harder against my air. Sweat beads on my forehead and runs down my back. My fingers tremble as I try to hold steady, ignoring the constant flashing of blood and screaming that fills my mind.

A voice croons in my head, more images of gore with it. *They're dying. Your allies are dying. Thea is screaming, don't you hear her?*

This isn't real. None of it is real.

Thea is fine. My wind magic is protecting her.

Her body is breaking. Don't you want to run to her side?

But what if she isn't? What if my protective barriers weren't enough to save them from the King's ancient and malicious magic? Thea could be burning right now. The screams hear…it could be hers.

That foreign fear pushes harder against my mind. It caresses my thoughts like wisps of smoke. *Do you really want to watch her die again? You could save her. You know you could. Just let go of your magic. Run to her, Tempest. Save her.*

She's dying. The King's magic was stronger than mine, and now it is shredding away at Thea.

Tears prick into my vision, and I am about to break my shield when a voice calls out from the clashing of magic. "Cole! Cole, I'm okay. Don't let her manipulate you."

Thea. Her voice is like the melody of an all-consuming song. One that raptures me into pure bliss where nothing matters but the notes of the instruments and how they swirl into my body.

It calms that induced fear and silences the screaming and the visions. I can feel that voice pounding against my mind, though I can no longer hear it. Like Thea's voice cast its own protective shield. I push harder on Morwen's magic. Her black flames bounce back, as if they became afraid of *me*. And then I swing my magicked air, engulfing them in a vortex of my own creation. With a deep breath, I squeeze my magic around Morwen's and deprive it of air.

The black flames suffocate and wither away, revealing the vampire behind. Morwen seethes, savage gaze searing me to the bone. Her daggerlike pointed fingers drop to her side with the last of those disappearing flames.

She snarls. "You have always ruined things." She curls her fingers into fists.

I open my mouth but am cut off by the sound of snapping wood. Thea pauses, the sword in her hands raised, and listens. Tree limbs snap and shatter behind Morwen, to where the trunks are thick and impenetrable. I shift into a sturdier, defensive position, half expecting an army to emerge from the dark forest. Instead, the breaking tree limbs just hover in the air, their sharp ends turning to point at both Thea and me. My eyes widen in horror as Morwen's snarl twists into a grin.

"Run, Cole," Thea whispers as she raises the sword in front of her body. As if that could stop the hundreds of lethal stakes aimed at us. "Take Sarah and run."

I tear my eyes from what surely will kill us both to stare at Thea. She doesn't turn to look at me. There isn't a tremble to her words, not even in her body. She stands firm against what faces us.

"No," I say. More and more branches snap from the trees and join the others that hover. They create a wall. A bodiless army, commanded by a soulless vampire who watches us like a predator who knows their prey will soon fall. One motion, and she could send those stakes flying toward us. "I will not leave you," I tell Thea.

Thea closes her eyes for a moment. "I'll find you again," she says. Orange flames seep out of her and move up the sword. It isn't enough. Her magic can't stop projectiles like that.

My voice cracks as I say her name. I could stand here and die with her. There is no way that both of us can make it out of this. Morwen would likely just throw more. And with half of her magic stored in that castle dimension, Thea probably isn't fast enough to dodge them. I could try to run and push her out of the way, but would it clear her of all the stakes?

One thing is for sure: if I don't run back to grab Sarah, she will surely get caught in the crossfire. And regardless of what happened, Thea would never forgive me if I failed to save her best friend. Even if that friend is the reason why one of us is going to die here.

"Cute, but I intend to rid myself of both of you. Right here." Morwen's cold voice filters through the snapping of wood. She lifts her hands, the stakes behind her vibrating with her magic coiled around them. Her piercing ruby eyes linger on Thea as she says, her voice so low I can hardly hear it, "In the next life then."

It is too late. Even with my speed, I can't get out of the way fast enough. Not if I want to save myself and Sarah. I force myself to move, to tear my gaze from the woman who is my heart. Who has been since the start of life itself. Stepping over the bodies of the witches, I run to Sarah. To shield her from the onslaught of Morwen's magic.

Thea and I will just have to find each other again. In our next lives.

Together.

I feel the weight of Morwen's magic slam into me as she undoubtably releases her tether to those lethal stakes.

And then a bone chilling wind.

CHAPTER SIXTEEN

THEA

I hear Cole turn toward Sarah. The tremble in my body takes over, no longer having to hold steady for him. Vitamors hums in my grip, as if it were trying to offer comfort. I hold the sword tighter, my flames inching toward the point. My beta ability cannot stop this attack, nor can the little bit of fire I have.

But at least Cole might be able to escape it. With Sarah.

Morwen's expression turns triumphant as those stakes she created whiz by her. She doesn't even blink as they pass, not a single one nearing her back. I feel her invisible magic slam into me first, almost knocking me off my wobbling feet.

The air in my lungs freeze. And so does everything in front of me. As if a blizzard carrying ice blows through the space, winds churn and snow whips around. It snuffs out the flames on both my arms and Vitamors.

When the chilling ice storm stops churning, I almost gasp. Morwen and her weapons are frozen in an enormous, house-sized chunk of ice, a look of surprise on her face. A handful of the stakes were frozen only five feet from where I stand.

I drop my stance, my heart pounding in my chest. The

sound of an agonizing cough pulls at my attention. I first look to where Cole was, only to find him standing in front of Sarah's unconscious body, his own like a shield in front of her. My legs threaten to give in at the sight. At his willingness to sacrifice himself for my friend. Because I asked him to save her.

Then that cough again, this time with the stale scent of blood. The acrid scent of a vampire's blood. I whip my gaze to the left and see Mica kneeling in the mud. A line of ice stretches across the ground from him to the iceberg that engulfed Morwen.

"Mica!" I run to him, ignoring the shakiness still clutching my limbs. Even the ground was affected by his magic. It isn't the soft mud that it was before, but a cold, uneven surface that is reminiscent of the earth in early autumn. I somehow avoid all the ankle-breaking dips in the marsh as I make my way to him, dropping to my knees beside him.

Blood drips from his mouth as he keeps coughing, each sounding more painful than the last. I search his body for a wooden stake that might have hit him, even though he seems far enough away.

"What happened? Are you hurt?" I ask frantically when I am unable to find any reason for his pain.

He doesn't speak, only lifts a shaking, bloody hand, and points to his neck. That's when it registers. The curse. That damned silence curse. On the surface of his body, there is no indication that the spell is gripping him. No sickly coloring or scent. If it weren't for his shaking and the blood dribbling from his lips, I wouldn't even know he was affected.

He fought against it, *against her,* again. Just like in the clearing of the castle dimension, he attacked the King. Despite the curse's lethal claws around his throat.

Behind us, Alec is stirring. I glance over my shoulder when I hear him grunt and survey Oba who is still prone on the ground. Cole is untying Sarah from the post with such gentleness. I curse under my breath at the state of us all.

Mica's ragged breathing mellows, and he stops coughing blood. He lifts his head and stares at what his magic has done. Everything is still encased in the ice, unmoving.

Cole's energy reaches me before I hear his heavy steps. He is carrying Sarah in his arms. My eyes flit over her body, examining to again make sure that she is still breathing.

"She'll be all right," Cole says as he stops beside me. "Her bleeding has stopped and her breathing and heartbeat sound normal."

I let out a breath. "Thank you."

Cole's gaze softens, though he looks me over for any injury. The stake Morwen threw at me wasn't poisoned, so my body healed naturally. Even if it was, Vitamors could heal me of that. Like it had done when I fought Commander Kael.

A thump on my chest, like someone took a hammer and tapped me with it. The dimension that holds my magic is telling me to hurry. I shrug it off and say, "We need to get out of here."

"We should finish the King. Here and now," Alec says, his voice hard.

"There isn't time," I say through gritted teeth. Because that thumping is getting harder to ignore. I look to Mica and ask, "Are you okay to stand?"

He gives a curt nod, a wince following, but motions to stand. I put my free hand on his arm in an attempt to help, when there is a deafening cracking sound that comes from the iceberg.

We all pause and look to where Morwen still stands, mid attack. Around her body there is a slight discoloration to the ice. It also seems to flow a little like a person's aura would.

Or like water.

"We need to go," I say alarmingly as I tug on Mica.

The ice cracks with each step we take backward. It echoes into the silence of the marsh. A chunk of the ice breaks from the side, followed by another on top. Shards of it land in front of us and Cole swears. Already the heat of her fury reaches us as the holes melt rapidly.

I glance to Alec who is attempting to fling Oba over his shoulder, his eyes wide with fear. His gaze meets mine and he mouths "portal".

The portal is far away, and on the other side of the ice. I survey the distance and the rate at which Mica's ice is melting. Dread fills my gut. There is absolutely no way we can make it around and out of the marsh before she is free of that ice.

"Can you freeze her again?" Cole asks as we make it to Alec and Oba. Another chunk explodes off of the iceberg, this time flying over the treetops. Wide cracks bend through the entirety of it.

Mica flexes his hands and small ice shards form at the tips. We all watch grimly as they appear much slower than they usually would. He collapses to a knee and I am beside him again, offering a hand. "No, I don't think I can," he answers solemnly.

"That's too bad," Morwen's voice says, colder than Mica's power. The ice explodes, roaring like thunder. Shards whiz past us, some scratch me in my arms and legs. "Out of every vampire's abilities, yours was always the one I felt would be a problem against me. It is why I made you mine. Why I *branded* you." Morwen moved silently from her frozen prison. Her magic, so similar to Cole's psychic abilities, pushes us back with phantom hands. All of us except for Mica. Him she holds, her nails drawing blood as she grips his neck so tightly. He wheezes, a gurgling noise coming from his lips as he unsuccessfully tries to pry her off. There is pure panic on his face as both his strength and his magic fail him.

I push myself to my feet and run at her, Vitamors held

firm in my grasp. But something solid stops me. It punches the air out of my lungs as my body slams into some invisible force.

I'm so tired of walls that I cannot see.

Stumbling backward, I notice the slight shimmer of a barrier. Exactly like the one that had encircled Sarah. "Morwen! Let him go," I plead. But she ignores me, her fingers seem to tighten harder.

A stake slides out from her other hand. No, no, no. I slam my fist against the barrier and again it shimmers like iridescent scales. I grip Vitamors and thrust it at the wall in an arc. This gets Morwen's attention. Her head moves toward my direction as I bring it down upon the barrier. And cut a hole right through the damned thing. It shatters and Morwen drops Mica, her fury now wholly settled on me and Vitamors. My energy manipulation catches the wrath that flows out of her like a waterfall, promising a sure and painful end. But I just take a defensive stance and pull all the training I have ever had to the forefront of my mind. All those self-defense sessions with my dad. The training with Cole and Sarah. Even the lessons with Morwen and Commander Kael.

There is an odd *twang* sound from behind Morwen as she charges at me, and I hardly have time to register before three stakes emerge from her body, bloody and sharp. One in each of her thighs and another in her left shoulder. She stumbles and glances down at them with a confused sort of surveying expression. Like she is trying to register what is happening. And then two more are fired and sent into her stomach.

She takes a half step forward to catch herself from collapsing. Though I notice people emerging from the thick line of trees behind her, I don't dare take my attention off of Morwen. I grip Vitamors tighter when her gaze lifts back to me, a promise of hatred blazing within.

She clutches her bleeding stomach and snarls at me as she says, "You bring an army. Then I shall, too." More wooden bolts are fired at her, but this time she dodges, her impossible speed on full display once again. The stakes whistle in the air as they fly by us, some sticking into the ground. "You think there was a war before? I will flatten everything." She lifts her chin, her upper lip pulled back. "And when I've destroyed everyone you love, you will beg me *again* for death."

I'm about to snarl right back at her that I have never and will never concede to her, but something stops me. A memory shoved deep in my mind grumbles its fear.

But as she moved before, Morwen seemingly vanishes from where she was. Though this time I notice the blur of her body as she speeds off in retreat. A part of me wants to chase her, but I know that would be foolish. In my hands, Vitamors quiets, the constant simmering hum lessening until it is still.

I want to let out a breath of relief but, instead, turn my attention to the dozen of people at the edge of the forest. Each of them are holding a crossbow, though it is no longer aimed at a target. I do note, however, that they aren't sheathing their weapons either.

"Isaiah," Cole calls out with a wary sigh. "Your timing was quite perfect."

I look to Cole with knitted brows, wondering how he knows one of their names. He just remains watching the crossbow holders.

The man Cole calls Isaiah drops his weapon to his side as he steps farther out from the compact tree line. The others with him relax a bit at his command, though don't entirely loosen their guard. He seems familiar, from the way he moves to the fierceness in his eyes. He is tall, probably the same height as Oba. He wears a black short-sleeved shirt with some sort of green tactical vest over it. Muscled arms are covered with tattoos. "You're welcome," he says. His voice has a bit of amusement in it, though I can't see any in his neutral expression.

When he takes another step out of the darkness of the

forest, I notice the plethora of wooden stakes and glass vials attached to the vest.

He shifts his brown eyes to me and studies me for a moment before asking, "Are you Thea Knight?"

I stiffen. "How do you know my name?"

A sad smile at that, and my heart lurches, already knowing the answer. "I knew your parents, Connor and Evelyn."

CHAPTER SEVENTEEN

THEA

The wind howls as it blows through the quiet marsh. It carries the scent of the dead with its symphony. Vitamors almost slips from my grasp, my fingers trembling as I look to Isaiah, still standing close to his group of vampire hunters. "How?" The question hardly comes out, and I realize the answer as I ask. I remember the things Cole and I found in the basement of my family's home. The panel in the wall that hid weapons so similar to Isaiah's. There were empty vials in there as well, and letters, one of which was addressed to my father from my grandfather. "They were vampire hunters."

Isaiah signals to the other hunters behind him by waving a hand in the air. Half of them put their weapons away. "Yes." He takes another few steps closer, and Cole growls in warning beside me. Isaiah stops his slow advancement and looks to Cole, his hands up in surrender and an amused smirk on his face. "Relax. Truce, remember?"

I furrow my brows, regaining some semblance of sense. "How do you two know each other?" He has never mentioned being allied with hunters. And back in my family's basement, when we stumbled upon that open panel, Cole looked stunned. It seemed to have more to do with vampire hunters than with my family in general.

Isaiah tilts his head. "I met him through your witch friend there," he says, jerking his chin toward Sarah, who is still in Cole's arms. "You were," he pauses. "Out of our reach then."

And that is when I remember. "You were following us. That day I was with Amaund. You pointed right at me."

He inclines his head. "I was following you, indeed. Your magic, anyhow."

I am about to ask him to elaborate when the pain in my chest spears to the rest of my body. I wince, clutching at the pounding headache.

"The spell. We need to get back to the dimension," Cole presses as he walks closer, readjusting Sarah in his arms.

Mica grumbles his tone raspy, "We've stayed too long."

I look back to Isaiah who is watching me curiously. With a hand still on my temple, I say, "Come to the castle with us and we can talk more."

The vampire hunter shakes his head apologetically. "We cannot." He clasps the circular charm around his neck and his body flickers like light. With a gesture to his comrades, he says, "The forest around this marsh is impenetrable for physical bodies. We used our magic to conjure these illusions." He pulls one of the crossbow bolts from the quiver on his belt and holds it on an open palm. "These are just concentrated bursts of our magic." A squeeze of his fingers and the bolt disintegrates into an iridescent dust. "The distance our magic needed to travel to get here was tiresome, but we pushed through. And now, we need to release the illusions." It is then that I notice the beads of sweat along his brow. Isaiah reaches into a pocket and I can feel my allies tense. Though it is not a weapon that the hunter reveals, but a crumpled-up note. "When you find a way out of that dimension indefinitely, come find me." He shows me the contents of the note, an address located on the outskirts of my hometown. It vanishes like the crossbow bolt. Before they disappear in the dark woods, he turns and says, "I'd like to call you an ally, Thea Knight." And then they all vanish into the haunting darkness of the forest.

"We need to go," Cole says urgently.

I nod at him through a pained gaze. The ache in my head increases with each pulse. Looking to Cole, I frown at Sarah in his arms, then turning to the lifeless wolf shifter still chained to the post. Sarah's coven is still splayed out around her. "I don't want to leave them," I whisper and make my way to Amelia.

"Thea," Mica warns. "We don't have time. We can't bring them all back." His words are harsh, though I can hear the sympathy in them. Cole snarls at him and Mica huffs in response, but he doesn't push further.

I fight the burning in my eyes. The heartache of leaving those who Sarah loves behind crushes me. But Amelia, I can't. Someone who filled my friend's heart with joy. I can't just leave her here. No one stops me as I step over the fallen witches and walk to the werewolf. Her arms are pale and bloodied, her clothes shredded. The chains are cold like her skin, and I flinch at the tendril of pain that slices into my headache when I touch it. "I'm sorry," I whisper to her.

The chains snap, and in the same breath, a strong and feral hand clutches around my throat. My head slams into the mud, my vision blurs, and the pulsing becomes excruciating. My lungs are deprived of air, and I struggle to break free of whatever is holding me. I must have dropped Vitamors in the attack, my empty hand grasping at a deadly-cold grip.

Someone yells and in a haze of movement, rips my attacker off of me. I gulp in air, my body shivering profusely. When the world stops swaying in my vision, I look up and see Alec. My mouth drops open at who he yanked off from me.

Amelia is snarling at Alec, her eyes the color of rubies.

With a pair of sharp fangs poking from her upper lip. He has her arms pinned, and it seems like he is struggling to do so.

I blink, trying to register what I'm seeing. Amelia is a…vampire?

Cole hurriedly makes his way over here with Sarah in his arms, his body tilted so that if she woke up, she couldn't see anything.

My head is pounding and nausea roils in my gut. We need to get back to the castle dimension soon. Shakily, I stand and use Cole's arm as a crutch.

"Can you handle bringing her back with us?" I ask Alec.

He grunts as she tries to yank free of him. "I can try," he responds gruffly, though his expression conveys a different answer.

I frown at him. "I can hold her if you can't."

He shakes his head before I even finish the sentence. "No, you can't." Amelia tries to loosen his grip again by lunging forward, her eyes more rabid than any hungry vampire I have seen before. But Alec doesn't let up. "I think," he grumbles, "her wolf side is fighting the vampire."

A wave of dizziness crashes over me and I stumble forward. Amelia lunges at me, her arm successfully pulling out of Alec's grip. He curses as Cole moves his body so fast, his shoulder catching me in the chest as he kneels. I want to curse at him for putting Sarah in the path of Amelia just to save me, but then the wolf shifter's gaze lands on her lover. Like a switch being flipped, Amelia stops her struggling. Her eyes soften, the color dimming just a little that I know she is gaining some semblance of control.

We all seem to blow a breath of relief at that.

And finally, we are getting the hell out of this marsh of misery. Alec leads the way, setting the pace, with Amelia who now seems to be more compliant, though his hold on her is still strong. Cole is carrying Sarah while I hold on to him for support. Behind us, Mica and Oba use each other as a crutch.

With each step to the portal, I feel the strain on my severed magic lessening. The ache in my head clears just enough that I no longer wince every time my foot gets caught in the mud and I have to yank it free. Everyone is too preoccupied with their misery that I don't have to snap at them for talking. I think someone's voice would bring me to my knees. It's the first time in my entire life that I am thankful to not hear any birdsong or trickle of a stream.

My thoughts roam to Isaiah. He has a connection to my parents, and I need to know all I can. It kills me that I can't learn anything until we find a way to untether me from the dimension. There are so many questions that I would ask him about my parents. Like why they decided to stop hunting vampires and if they had any magic of their own. I remember seeing Isaiah talk to Amaund that day while being brought to the Brais. He used some sort of spell that made it impossible to overhear his and Amaund's conversation.

If my parents possessed magic as vampire hunters, did they give that up when they quit? And what would that mean for me, if anything? I doubt that a vampire can use vampire hunter magic.

We reach the portal and Amelia starts thrashing in Alec's arms again. She shoves her boots into the ground, refusing to go any farther. Alec growls, but his voice is soothing when he speaks in her ear. "It leads to the castle. You've been there before." But Amelia continues to push against him and leans away from the inky portal.

"Wait," Cole calls to Alec.

Amelia calms when Alec stops trying to push her through. Cole and I make our way there slowly and the two of them watch us. Amelia's eyes, still ruby in color, never leave Sarah. I don't know if I want to shield my friend from her gaze or be grateful for her need to be protective. Emotions as a vampire can all feel like hunger, so I don't fully trust Amelia to be around Sarah while she is still unconscious.

Cole waits until we are beside Alec and Amelia before saying, "Let us go through first. Amelia will follow."

And she does. The prickle of the portal hardly finishes washing over the two of us when Amelia emerges through, Alec loosely holding her arms. Her eyes scan our surroundings quickly before they settle on Sarah again. Behind them, Mica passes through with Oba.

The sands below my feet seem to hum and pulse like a heartbeat. I can feel my magic that the dimension was holding surge toward us. It flows from each grain of silt, every leaf and blade of grass, even the droplets of rain that fall from the gray sky. The mass of it all returning at once has my tired body collapsing, my knees hitting the warmed sand.

My body feels like it is being shoved into an unwelcoming, blazing fire. With heaving breaths, I push through the searing pain and welcome my magic back. My nails dig into the sand, and I fight a cry that bubbles in my throat. I hold up a halting hand when I hear one of my comrades shuffle toward me. No one moves and we all remain silent for a few moments.

When the magic completely returns to me and the heat subsides, I release a shivering breath. The clouds darken above, answering my call for Amelia's safety. We will have to get her a sun totem soon. I turn to look at everyone behind me, to urge Cole and Alec to get in the castle so Sarah and Oba can rest, when their panicked expressions make me pause. They flinch at me, each of them taking a sharp, startled breath. Even Amelia reacts to whatever it is, her back pressing into Mica as she retreats a step.

Cole is the first to regain his composure. "Your eyes." His voice is quiet, thoughtful. "They just aren't expected."

"They look like the King's," Mica murmurs. Alec closes his mouth and nods somberly.

"I'm sorry," I rasp and rub my face with a hand. The image of Morwen's golden gaze flashes in my mind. I've seen my own look the same, just once. When I almost erupted in fury and to take out the garage that revealed so much pain. The vehicle that told me the story of how the Brais—no, how the King—inserted herself into my life, changing it for the worse.

Cole presses his arm to mine in comfort.

Well, not completely for the worse.

~

BACK IN THE CASTLE, Oba rests on the couches in the foyer and Mica and Alec offered to help Amelia with her transition, utilizing the bags in the cellars. She didn't hesitate when she decided to follow through with becoming a vampire, having made the decision while still watching Sarah. Cole and I watch as they depart down the corridor, aiming for the small cellar far away from the room still coated in those innocents' bodies and blood.

The wolf-turned-vampire relaxed immensely as we entered and the door closed behind. She even let out an audible sigh when Cole gently placed Sarah down on the couch opposite of Oba. There are hundreds of rooms in this castle, but waking in a foreign chamber would likely freak the two of them out, so we opted for the known foyer.

Cole and I stand watch over the two of them in silence for a while. I'd like to be around when Sarah wakes up, but I also desperately want to get out of these clothes. My blood has dried over the caked-on mud, making it uncomfortable to remain dressed in.

Hunger roils in my gut, but I ignore it. Later, I promise it.

"I would offer clothes for you, but I have none," I say to Cole with a regretful shrug. "Though, I'm sure there is a room here that has something that will fit." I catch myself admiring him again, the muscles under his shirt and his broad shoulders, heat creeping up my neck.

I don't miss the smug grin on his lips before he says, "I'm

sure I can find something." His fingers brush against my shoulder, drawing my attention back to his face. He twirls a lock of my hair, picking a small clump of mud from the end before brushing his hand down the length of my arm. His touch is pure electricity.

We say each other's names at the same time, then share a mutual smile.

Being here, in front of him, makes my heart race. I want nothing more than to touch him. I think I convinced myself in that dream sanctuary that it was just that, a dream. While there, unable to feel his skin against mine, almost made my brain convince itself that it was all just a dream. We haven't talked about it, not that we had a chance to. But now, being able to do all of that and physically feel him? It is terrifying, in a good way. And I know he would reciprocate it but making that first step is like leaping off a cliff.

No risk, no reward.

I look at Sarah, asleep on the couch. "Let's find something," I manage to choke out as I walk down the hall and away from the foyer. Cole's replying chuckle sends pleasant shivers down my spine.

"What are you thinking about?" he asks, having caught up to my pace without me even noticing. There is amusement in his question and I know he is smirking. Still, I don't look at him. If our eyes locked, I don't think the strongest force in the world could have stopped me from wrapping myself around him. The thought of it is consuming, out-competing even the pangs of hunger. Just hearing his voice stirs something in me. The thought of me kissing him while Sarah is down the hall, even unconscious, is weird to me.

Out of the corner of my eye, I see that beautiful, half grin that he always gives. The one that flutters my stomach. "Nothing," I breathe.

"Liar."

We turn a corner, entering a wide corridor that seems to

have fewer flickering candles than others. A beam of sunlight stretches through a slender window at the end of the hallway. "Thea." The roughness in Cole's voice forces me to stop walking and actually look at him. The edge of sunlight soaks into the color of his irises, a star among morning mist.

His smokey eyes consume all that there is to me and I think I might have stopped breathing. Peering into his gaze feels like a homecoming that my heart has been grieving and missing for years. Cole slowly brings a hand to my face as if he were afraid I might disappear if he moved too quickly. When his hand touches my cheek, a tendril of electricity flutters to my heart and travels lower.

My lips part at his touch and his gaze drops to them, perhaps remembering the promise he made when we met in that dream sanctuary. When his eyes move back to mine, my knees threaten to give out. It is like thousands of moments like this, losing myself in his perfection, come crashing into my mind. I wonder, as his breathing hitches, if the same is happening to him.

Finally remembering to move the rest of my body, I lift a hand and place it on his side. "Kiss me," I breathe. My heart stammers in my chest as those electric tendrils dance between us, pulling like we were both magnets searching for the other.

And he obliges. His free hand moves to the other side of my cheek as his lips find mine. Gentle to start, our kiss is like the soft first touch after finding something long since lost. In this moment, our lips together is all I know. All I need.

I tighten my hand on his side, clutching at his shirt. I hardly register the wall pressing against my back. Our kisses become greedier, like if we let go, we might lose each other again. But I won't ever let that happen. Not again. I part my lips, inviting his tongue to meet mine. He indulges as one hand moves to the nape of my neck, his fingers curling in my hair. With a gentle tug, he tips my head back and presses his body against mine. I let out a groan at his warmth, getting annoyed at the barrier of clothes between us. I slip my hand under his shirt and press my palm against the smoothness of his skin. His approving noise vibrates into my mouth, and I lightly scrape my nails against his side.

His hand caresses my cheek before moving down my neck, eliciting a shiver down my spine, and I arch into him. Something I can only describe as an eruption of sparks spiraling between us. Like our souls are colliding with each other in a euphoric reunion. Thousands of lifetimes and moments merge into this one.

Someone pointedly coughs and the sound of footsteps stomping down the adjacent staircase register into my mind. Alec rounds the stairwell banister as Cole and I break apart, our heavy breathing preventing us from hiding what we were doing. That and our rhythmic heartbeats seem to echo into the spacious length of the hall. And our faces are flushed.

"These are from Mica," Alec says as he hands Cole a pile of neatly folded clothes. "He's still with the shifter and I went to fetch us something clean to wear. He told me to give you his pair."

Cole extends his hand and accepts the outfit. "Thank you."

Alec bobs his head before twisting and making his way back to the foyer. "I'll watch over the two of them while you two…clean up," he calls out, his voice too loud for what he is implying with that teasing tone. I stare at his back as he walks away, a brow raised. For someone who seemed so standoffish when I first met him, he really has opened up.

Cole follows me as we make our way to the fourth floor to where my room is. I tell him to wait out in the hall while I grab a change of clothes. Having him come in would not help the butterflies in my stomach. A few doors down from my room is a bathing chamber with stone baths and a few showers. Luckily, the showers offer privacy because I would not be able to handle it if they didn't. I would just have to make Cole wait.

Even with the seven-foot stone wall that separates our two showers, knowing that Cole is right beside me is torture. Out of all the ones he could have chosen, he picked the one adjacent to mine.

I, at least, have enough sense of control that I manage to remain in my own shower. Letting the warm water cleanse away all the dried blood and mud on my body and in my hair mostly distracts me from the thoughts that run through my mind.

My lips still tingle from our kissing and that primal part of me wants more of it. More of him. I was a breath away from finding a secluded room before Alec interrupted us. My skin craves more of Cole's enticing touch. Electricity courses through my body the more I think of him.

"What are you thinking about now?" Cole asks, his rough voice seems to swim through the wall and water, snaking around my skin.

I place my face into the stream of warm water before answering. "Nothing," I say again, focusing on the feel of the stone floor against my toes.

Cole's responding chuckle sends a shiver down my spine despite the water's warmth. "Liar."

CHAPTER EIGHTEEN

AMELIA

"I've heard that wolf packs kill their members who become tainted by another species. Tell me, alpha, would your pack do that to you?" The vampire bitch King tightens the silver shackles around my wrists. The metal bites my skin, cold like the mud under my knees.

My pack. Who I told to stay at Sarah's house. Where they sat in a circle, offering me their power through a pack ritual so I could take on the vampire with the coven. A werewolf pack's last resort option when facing a powerful foe. And it wasn't enough.

The vampire walks around the post I am tied to and squats before me. Her long black hair is like the night sky without a moon. I snarl at her, noting the unmarred skin where all the gashes once were. All the damage Sarah did is already being undone with her supernatural healing. I lunge at her with teeth barred, but the chains are stronger than my exhausted and aching body. She smiles, her two sharp teeth gleaming.

"I'm going to rip your throat out," I say, voice guttural. No, my wolf said that. Its primal fury is unbearable. If my body wasn't on the brink of collapsing, my wolf would take control and shift. But after the fighting, all my magical stores are depleted. And my pack...they gave me everything. I don't know what state they are in after what I pulled from them. *Are they even conscious? Can they sense the terror and hate I feel right now?*

A muscle ticks in the vampire's jaw. "You've already tried, pup."

I growl at her, lunging again. Still, the chains hold. "Where is Sarah?" I didn't see what happened to her. Not after Alain attacked me, her spell rendering me unconscious.

That wicked smile again. "I'm glad you asked." The King looks beyond me.

Alain walks into my view, carrying an unconscious Sarah. Opposite of me, there is another wooden post sticking out of the muck. I lunge again, this time with more force as my wolf lets out a harsh growl. But the King stands and places her foot on my chest, pinning my back to the post.

The Kings clicks her tongue at me, her piercing gaze overflowing with feral delight. "Not yet, pup. We aren't done yet."

I can't move. The chains are strong and so is the vampire. "Please," I rasp. My wolf recoils at the pleading. "Don't kill her."

The vampire crouches, blocking my view of Alain wrapping Sarah's wrists in rope. She unsheathes a dagger that was hidden behind her back and twirls it effortlessly. "Oh, I am not the one who will kill her."

The tiniest flower of hope blooms in my chest, but then her words register. "What—"

She plunges the dagger into my chest and I cry out from the sharp pain. "Do you know how vampires are created, little pup?"

Even over the pain, the nickname stirs something in me. A deeply rooted terror. But the thoughts vanish when the King drags the dagger across my chest and my blood pours from the wound, the fresh scent of iron filling the air.

She leans closer and I shrink from her presence and the dagger. "When your blood runs dry and your body gives out, I'll give you a dash of my own blood. Should you survive the transition, you'll wake up famished." She rips the dagger from my body, and I bite back a scream as tears sting my eyes. "And because I am generous, I have left you your first meal." She stands, revealing Sarah behind her, helplessly confined to the post.

"I-I won't" I say, the words only a whisper. My head is spinning. If it weren't for the chains keeping my arms upright, I would collapse to the mud. My body is too tired to hold itself up, my magic too depleted for any sort of healing.

The Brais vampire looms over me like the thunderstorm before the hurricane. "And that is the fun, isn't it? Will your love triumph, or will the hunger?" She returns to eye level with me, positioning herself so I can see both her and Sarah, as she examines my wound. "For me, the hunger came as a result of the love that left me in pieces." Her gaze drifts downward, to her hands. When she speaks again, it doesn't seem to be to anyone but herself. "Sometimes I convince myself that when I kill, it is to find that love again. That the next time will be different." Her ice blue eyes are devoid of emotion when she brings them back to me. "But it never is. The universe tells me so over and over again."

Even with hardly any strength left, I look to her, a snarl on my lips. "Tells you what?" I wanted to say something snarky, to laugh in her face about the misery that is her life. But the sliver of curiosity slipped out before I could reel it in.

"Love is a weakness." She grips my hair, pulling my head back. "Love is just a weapon that the gods can use against us. Without them, perhaps it would be different. But, here we are, little pup." I struggle against her hold, my vision becoming gray around the edges. Sarah's body is blurred in the background. Morwen leans closer to me, blood trickling out of a small wound on her wrist. "And here is my last offering to you in this little game. Should you survive this transition and love indeed triumphs over hunger, do not fight me. I will not be so generous next time." Her lips brush against my ear, her voice a cold promise. "I am Morwen Trethaway, and I am the King of the Brais."

A searing, agonizing pain explodes along my neck and into my head. It is like someone poured lava down my throat. Tears sting my eyes as those dull colors around the outskirts of my vision leap over me like a panther.

~

With a startled gasp, I awake. I run a hand over my abdomen, where the King's blade had sliced into me. Not even a scar remains. He killed me. Turned me into a vampire. And almost killed Sarah. I look to my love, asleep on my lap as we sit on the couch within the foyer of this castle.

My wolf is rabid. Absolutely feral at everything that has happened. At the horrible loss we suffered from fighting the King. At the betrayal from Sarah's coven member. I can still feel the nightmarish pain from Alain's magic stabbing into my mind. My wolf snarls at the thought of seeing that witch again, already conjuring plans of ripping out her throat.

But most of all, my wolf is ready to destroy the world for what it has done to Sarah. For all the agony in her life. The memory alone of her body being torn to shreds because of that spell upon her neck threatens to unravel the hold I have on the wolf. That now grips its claws around my neck.

Strangely, becoming a vampire has not angered my wolf as much as I thought it would. Initially, the two parts of me warred with each other. But the moment my eyes landed on Sarah, they calmed. The wolf and the vampire side of me want to protect her. And with the transition comes more power that will help destroy the Brais and the corrupt world they seek to establish.

"Amelia?" Thea's kind voice snaps me out of the madness. I look up at her and note her soft, cautious gaze. I haven't said a word since waking up in that disgusting marsh. My voice doesn't work, not while I wait anxiously for Sarah to awake. I twist my fingers in her soft black hair for both comfort and to hide the shake in them. Thea takes one small step forward, her hand gently landing on the back of the couch. I fight the growl in my chest at someone getting too close to Sarah while she is prone like this.

"Can I get you anything?" Thea asks in a tone that makes me wonder if she asked that already. Her hazel eyes flick down to Sarah briefly before returning to me and my wolf rumbles in defense.

I shake my head, still not able to form any words. My fingers move gently through Sarah's hair, combing out bits of dried mud and leaves tangled within. Occasionally, I stop to stare at her chest to make sure that it still rises and falls with her breath. And every time I do, I notice the sound of her heartbeat. My mouth waters at the symphony of it, stifled so quickly by the wolf inside. For as long as I have lived, my wolf has protected me. And now, it is keeping Sarah safe by taming the vampire side.

I wonder what my parents would think about me now if they knew what I have become. Their youngest child, half wolf, half bloodsucker. If they have heard of my exploits across the country, they haven't reached out. Not that I ever expected them to. All of their energy always went into the eldest of the Bordon siblings.

My wolf notices a moment before I do. Sarah's head tilts, her throat bobbing. The wound on her bottom lip cracks a little as she opens her mouth. "Amelia?" Her voice is weak and hardly audible.

I want to cry with how happy I am. "I'm here," I whisper back, stroking her soft hair with my palms. Tears streak down the side of her cheek and that is all it takes for my own to fall.

Slowly, she rises into a sitting position, a wince flashing across her features. Her lips tremble as she scans my face, more tears falling. "I thought I lost you."

I place a hand on her cheek and brush a tear away with my thumb. "You will never lose me, petal." At the nickname, she lets out a relief-filled sob and pulls me in for an embrace. I close my eyes and soak in her soft touch, the delicate scent of lavender that seems to push against all the dirt and stench of the marsh that still clings to her. She buries her face into the crook of my shoulder, her tears dripping irregularly on my shirt. A crack of hatred spikes at her pain.

The wolf wants revenge. Now. Knowing that Sarah is safe, it wants to leap from this couch and run to wherever the King is now. To tear into his neck and watch as those cold, ruby-colored eyes fade into nothing. There is a subtle sharpness along my collarbone, where I know that terrible curse lingers. At that, my wolf snarls louder in that space of limbo within my mind.

But that new, foreign part of me that is still adjusting to life, seeks to wait. It is just as ravenously angry like my wolf, but it knows patience. Some ancient knowing of waiting and planning in the shadows.

My wolf calms ever so slightly.

Someone swallows from a place that seems so far away. The sound bounces in my senses, louder than what it should have been. I glance up and see Thea and Cole standing at the back of the couch across from us. Behind them is Mica, leaning aloofly against the cold fireplace mantel.

I gently place a hand on the back of Sarah's head and breathe in her scent. Quietly, I say, "There is someone else who is happy to see you awake, love."

Sarah sniffles, pauses, then pulls away quickly like she just remembered where she is. Her honeyed eyes scan the room before landing on those of her friend's. "Thea," her voice breaks again. She motions to push off the couch, but her limbs are weak and she stumbles. I catch her before she falls on her hands and knees, Thea doing the same. She moved so quickly that I didn't notice.

I used to hate how fast vampires could move, would choose to move. Their speed can surpass even a werewolf, and not a single bloodsucker is unaware of that. Of how frightening it can be to lose sight of something dangerous, only to have it reappear in front of them.

It surprises me now that my wolf seems content with Thea's display of her undead prowess.

Both of us help Sarah back on to the couch. Thea sits on

the square coffee table, her hands interlaced with Sarah's. Her hazel eyes show no sign of their ability to change into an unnatural red. A lock of brown hair falls from behind her ear, but she ignores it.

"I needed to…" Sarah starts. Her faltering voice cuts off as her eyes bounce between Thea's, her tongue searching for the right words. "I'm sorry."

"Sarah," Thea whispers.

Sarah tightens her fingers around Thea's. "No. What I did…" She swallows hard. "What I did was wrong. I felt that I needed to handle this on my own for what the King did to my mother. And now…" She closes her eyes, letting a few tears drop to her bare arms. "And now most my coven is gone."

The young witches, the ones whose mothers were part of Valeria's coven, who vowed their allegiance to Sarah, to be the new Minuit coven. The young witches who Sarah has known most of her life. Their bodies are still in the horrible marsh, used as tools for the King's barrier spell. My heart is a stone of grief and rage. Those witches may have known what they were getting into—may have made that conscious decision to follow their coven leader, like I did, but Sarah will carry that guilt for the rest of her life.

"You are my sister." Her brows turn with sorrow, but she keeps her voice steady as she continues. "I'm so glad we found you. Your mom would have haunted me if I let anything happen to you." She chuckles sadly at that. "I love you so much."

Sarah's lips twitch ever so slightly with a smile, but it is gone quickly. I am grateful for Thea. And happy that she is still here for Sarah. Still alive, despite all that the King has thrown at her.

The King's name dances on my tongue, unable to be formed into words with the curse lingering in the shadows. His last words in my ear, his *declaration*, will haunt me for the rest of my life.

"Nothing that has happened has been of our fault. The King started this war. Those we care for, they all went into this with love and protection in their hearts. The King will fall for all the lives taken," Thea adds, her tone carrying the promise. "*We* will make sure of that. You and I, together. And when everything is done, we will hold a vigil for every life lost."

Sarah wipes at her cheek. "No more acting out of fear," she vows.

Thea smiles faintly. "I recently remembered a piece of advice I was given once. That you and I are a force to be reckoned with. Together."

"My mother," Sarah murmurs, the spark of something better in her eyes. An emotion other than the heavy ones that have been plaguing her for the last few months. It is refreshing to see on her.

Thea smiles. "I knew you were listening that day." A fire ignites in Thea's own eyes as she nudges Sarah's shoulder. "Those who stand against us and threaten the well-being of others? They won't see their goals come to fruition so long as we are alive."

Sarah clasps her hands on Thea's, a renewed strength in her frail body. "You are my sister as well and I will fight with you, Thea. I will follow you." She shakes her head slightly, her lips trembling. "No more solo acts."

I refrain from speaking my opinion that we could have won that last fight. If it weren't for Alain who betrayed the coven. Betrayed Sarah. I look at the charred, empty fireplace, shoving down the growing anger. The pointed gaze of a vampire's attention pokes at my mind. I look up and see Mica watching me with a knowing expression. He may try to hide it, but there is deep pain in his heart. I recognize it because it echoes in my own. And at the center of it all: the King.

CHAPTER NINETEEN

THEA

"I feel like I've never been this tired before," I say to no one in particular as I toss the empty bag of blood into the bin. Our stash of blood bags is down to only seven, so Cole, Mica, and I shared this one. The musty quiet of the storage room is comforting somehow. It certainly helps that it is as far away from the dungeon as possible. The little spider from the corner is no longer there and a part of me is sad about that.

"Maybe you should get some rest," Cole suggests. "A lot happened today."

That's an understatement.

"Cole is right," Mica chimes. Our voices bounce off the stone walls in this small, chilly room. The large, white refrigerator sized coolers line the walls of this storage room. Mica leans against the single cooler that has blood in it, the others long since empty. The three candles in iron chandelier above hold a steady light in this draft less room. "We all should be recovering."

I chew on my cheek. Rest does sound wonderful right about now. And the thought of sleeping beside Cole… I shake my head and clear my throat. "There's still the sealed-off door in the King's room to investigate."

"Tomorrow," they both say in unison.

~

"This isn't exactly taking it easy," Cole jests half an hour later as he and I walk along the dimension's northernmost forested trail. He steps over a smooth, large rock. "I thought you were tired."

Ducking under a low-hanging pine branch, I shrug. "I am." Overhead, a waning moon shines brightly, its silvery light filtering through the trees. It offers more than enough light for a couple of vampires to see. "I was told that there is a pond somewhere along this path. I wanted to see it underneath the moonlight."

Cole nods in understanding, then he grins gloriously at me. The silver light sparkles in his eyes, making them look even more like swirling mists.

I almost stumble on a root. Heat blooms along my neck and I quickly focus back on the path in front of us, dodging obstructions that seem to want to see me fall on my face. His following low chuckle sends a wave of something through my body that has my toes curling. The image of us tangled together on a bed of moss pushes into my mind, and I blow out a breath. Clearing my throat, I say, "What?" My tone is more demanding than I intended it to be, which only causes him to laugh again. "Is my being flustered funny to you, Cole?"

I can hear the amusement on his lips. "I think it is rather adorable. Is this a date, Thea?" Not even a breath between the two sentences.

My heart jumps from my chest as I whirl around. Cole is standing so close. All the words evaporate from my tongue and my mind blanks. I don't even know if I am going to joke about this or deny my intentions. Actually, I don't even remember my intentions. All I can think about is how close he is and the crispness of his woodsy scent. He smells more of the forests I love than this magically crafted one that we currently reside in. The one we are standing in so close together that our breaths mingle. His irises dance in the light of the moon. A light breeze slithers through the trees, rustling the leaves and our hair.

I swallow and he watches the movement. My knees almost give out at the attention. "Are you doing that?" I whisper, needing to fill the silence between our heartbeats. "The wind?" Even as the question leaves my lips, I know that it isn't he who controls it. I can feel the magic of the dimension singing with my emotions, that mark on my collarbone warm.

His attention is wholly on me now. "I'm not," he says, his voice quiet but rough. One of his hands comes to brush my hair from my face, the touch so rapturing that it is all I know. "I can't stop thinking about our kiss." His gaze drops to my mouth before his thumb runs gently along my lower lip. "The memory of it. It is there, nestled beneath every thought I have."

"For me, too." My voice is carried away, silenced by the magnet between our bodies. A shiver runs down my spine at his touch. So gentle, yet so consuming. It is then that I remember my body. My hands clutch his shirt, pulling him so that he closes the distance. "Remind me again," I breathe onto his lips.

When our lips crash, I lose myself entirely. I feel my soul tether to his in a relieving sigh. The forest around us disappears, one plant at a time, until it is just us in a blissful eternity. Cole brings his other hand up so that he is clasping both sides of my face. I splay my hands on his chest and move them up, slow enough that I can feel each defined muscle under his shirt. My fingers reach the bare skin above his neckline just as his tongue greets mine. A glorious heat rolls down my body, craving more of him.

I wrap my fingers around the back of his neck, tucking them under his shirt so that my fingertips graze his skin. Something reminiscent of an approving purr vibrates from his throat. His own hands move down my body at a painstakingly slow pace. His touch is soft but firm, enough so that the cotton shirt I wear may as well be nothing at all. Each deliberate touch of his fingers leaves a trail of fire along my skin. When they caress the tender spot below my breasts, I almost melt. My nails dig into his skin when his thumb strokes again, his hands then moving down to grasp my thighs.

Our lips are still together when he lifts me off the ground.

And my hair snags on a branch, the tree's limb bumping my head then scraping down my back as he lifts me. I grunt at its point that digs into my skin.

Cole immediately places me on the ground, a regretful sound escaping his lips. "Thea, I'm so sorry."

I can't help but laugh then, the feel of his kiss still lingering on my mouth. My body is still humming. "It's okay." At the concern still etched on his face, I place a hand on his cheek. "Cole, it's all right."

He smooths my hair back down and kisses the top of my head. Studying my face, his eyes are glassy as he exhales a long breath. After a moment, he says, "You unravel me."

Those tender words sink into my memories. Like a gentle claw trying to pry something free, they slip through a dense fog. A barrier of some sort, cast around hidden places in my mind. I furrow my brows, noting a similar expression on Cole's face.

"I feel like you said that to me before," I admit, still searching my memories. Though I can't grasp it, I know it is more than a déjà vu moment. It feels like the memories of another life colliding with my current one.

The sound of Cole's phone ringing startles us both. He

looks to me before pulling it free from the pocket of his jeans. "It's Mica," he says after a few blinks, his voice distant.

As much as I don't want to move away, I say, "Answer it. It could be about Sarah."

He does, pressing the speaker button. "What's up?"

"I think I found a way through that seal in the King's room. And by the sound of it, what lays within will help us defeat the King." Mica sounds as if he drank a dozen cups of caffeine.

"I thought you were going to get some sleep?" I jest.

Mica laughs. "I could say the same to the both of you, Kindria."

"What did you find, Mica?" Cole says as he shifts on his feet.

There is the sound of a book closing, a hefty one by the deep thud and echo it makes through the speaker. "I think you will want to come to me for this information. I'm in the library." He lets out a long sigh. "Things are bigger than even I thought they were."

Cole and I exchange a concerned look. In my time here at the castle, training under Morwen, Mica always seemed to know the goings-on within the walls. He knew every vampire who lived under the tiled roof, and when groups were sent out to fight or gather information. The fact that even he was surprised by a piece of information worries me. And Cole, who has known Mica longer, him being worried is even more unnerving.

"We'll be right there."

"The King did what?" I ask, having to snap my mouth shut. Cole and I are standing opposite Mica at one of the long tables in the center of the library. There are numerous books strewn about, some opened and some closed with whatever object Mica could find to keep his place.

"He made a deal with the god of death," Mica says gravely. "Well, *a* god of death, apparently. I'm guessing it is how the King became who he is now."

"A witch turned vampire," Cole offered. Mica doesn't so much as nod in confirmation, but we all know the story.

"We are assuming here that gods are real," I say, running a hand through my long hair. My fingers catch on a few knots.

Mica's lips turn down. "I'm inclined to believe that they are. After all, vampires exist."

"And so do witches and werewolves," Cole adds, reminding me of a conversation we had once in the kitchen of my apartment. It seems like eons ago. When he was telling me about this supernatural world that lives in and out of the shadows, all unseen from mortal eyes, nonetheless.

I cross my arms. "You told me once that there are also fae and dragons."

Cole shrugs and shoves his hands into the pockets of his jeans. "I've only read about them. Never have I actually met one." His jaw clenches. "That I am aware of, anyhow. I think Oba had dealings once with the fae. He won't talk about it though."

"Somehow I feel like we would know if we met a *dragon*." I emphasize the last word, my eyes rounding.

"Actually, no."

Cole and I snap our heads to Mica. "Do tell," I say, almost wishing that he would just admit to joking.

Mica runs a hand through his pale hair before wrapping it in a bun at the nape of his neck. "Like werewolves, dragons are a type of shifter. They look just like you and I when they are in their human form."

"That's comforting," Cole says warily. "You've met one?"

Those green eyes focus on a spot somewhere behind Cole and me as if he were reminiscing in his mind in those memories. "Yes, but that is a tale for another time." He sighs heavily. "The short story is that centuries ago, the King was allied with a vampire who despised the dragon shifters and sought to wage a war on them."

"Why?" I ask even though the room spins a little. If the dragons despise Morwen, perhaps we could use that against her, seek an allyship of our own. But how does one find a dragon shifter?

"I'm not privy to all the details, but the vampire the King allied with was the one calling the shots. The King was just a commander in those battles."

Cole places a hand on the back of the chair in front of him. "How did it end?"

"With the death of the King's vampire ally and with the rest of them retreating," Mica answers smugly. "Kind of wish I was there to see. Although I probably would have been on the front lines and killed."

I glance to the back wall of the library, where all I can see are the cobwebs hanging from the ceiling. The layers of bookshelves hide that tormenting statue. Hopefully Morwen doesn't have some unknown spell on it that allows her to hear what we are saying. "The dragons are that strong?" Mentally noting to not make an enemy out of them, should I ever recognize one. "Do you think we could seek their help in fighting the King?"

"No," Mica says before I even finish the sentence. "The vampires and dragons have a sort of peace right now. They would never ally with our kind." He frowns, his voice quieting. "Even if it is to rid the world of a vampire they don't like."

There is a moment of silence between us all. Even the air in the library seems to still at the thoughts that churn within our minds. Having allies as strong as these dragon shifters could mean a sure victory against Morwen. But if what Mica says is true, seeking them out could likely have severe consequences.

"At least we don't have to worry about," I pause, pulling the name that sits on the tip of my tongue back in. I don't know how Mica and Sarah can move through life constantly worrying about what they are saying and if it will trigger the silence curse. "The King won't be calling on that other vampire for aid."

"Thankfully," Cole agrees. "So what did this piece of the King's past have to do with getting into his chambers?"

Mica reaches to the closed book on the table in front of him, opens it, and removes the smaller book that was likely holding his place. "This castle didn't start off in this dimension. It was originally built to honor the god that the King made a pact with. When the dimension was created, it was then brought here at its center." He points to a paragraph on the open page. "This page mentions the sealed-off room." He looks at the book, his brows furrowing.

"What is it?" I ask, leaning forward to inspect the pages. The writing appears to be handwritten, witch scribbles and notes in the margin. It looks like a large journal.

"It is unclear whether the King had the seal put in place or if the fact of bringing the castle into this dimension, essentially hiding it from humans, angered the god it was meant to acknowledge." He flips the page, his palm moving across the surface of the old paper. "I think it might be the latter."

A light chill runs across my skin. Whether the other two felt it as well, they don't let on. "Are you saying that this castle was built as a place to worship this death god? And by moving it into this dimension, the King pissed off the god?"

Mica nods. "Essentially, yes. And I think that is how we get access. Play on the hatred the god has with the King."

Cole and I exchange a look. The idea of getting ourselves mixed up with a god of death is a lot to process. The fact that this thought even runs through my mind is bizarre.

"I feel like that could go wrong in so many ways. Do we

even need to get into that room?" I ponder, running a finger over the smooth cover of a tome.

The doors to the library open and we all turn to see Oba shuffling inside. He takes in the room in its entirety, his gaze holding briefly on the sword-shaped sundial in the center before making his way toward us. "I knew I would find you lot here." He still dons his fully-stocked bandolier, though his leather armor has been replaced by a gray shirt and black pants. "Resting is not something that any of you can ever do, eh?"

Cole chuckles. "You usually do enough snoozing for the rest of us, Oba."

Oba smirks, his hand moving to the hilt of a dagger. "Don't make me use one of these on you, Moretti."

"You couldn't even hit a building if you tried."

"I recall his aim earlier being particularly on point," Mica chimes in with equal amusement.

Cole grunts, the smile waning from his expression. "I'm surprised you noticed at all, Mica, considering how much you hesitated at the marsh."

"Yeah," he responds, voice trailing. "I'm sorry." Mica's attention is on me when the apology comes out. He rubs his shoulder as he says, "I underestimated the King's grip on my fear."

I put a gentle hand on Cole's arm, noting how tense he is and offer a light, comforting squeeze. At the head of the table, Oba remains quiet. Before saying anything, I take a moment to actually look at my three comrades here. Exhaustion plagues each of their features, as I'm sure it does mine. They all stand silently as if waiting for my judgement.

Eventually, I take a deep breath and say, "The King has been in my life for almost the entirety of it, wielding my fate from the shadows like an instrument for his own benefit. There is an inherent fear that comes with knowing that. In knowing that the path I am on is because of him, that everything major in my life has occurred because he has placed me at the right crossroads. I'm at the point where every action I take now comes with the thought of 'is this what the King wants me to do?'" I squeeze Cole's arm again, but it is Mica who I look at. "You have been living in the King's shadow for so long. You do not have to apologize for your fears. None of us can possibly know what torments you have experienced and lived through. Yes, you froze back there. You were facing what I imagine as the demons of your past that relentlessly haunt you. And yet, you fought against that fear when we needed you to. Regardless of your plans for moving forward, I will still gladly call you my comrade, Mica." Silver rims his eyes, and I get that tug in my mind again, pulled by his emerald irises. "Whether you choose to fight with us or not, know that I will do everything in my power to free you of your demons."

Mica swallows and breaks our eye contact, glancing down at the table where he mindlessly taps the surface with a knuckle. His voice is throaty as he says, "I once told you that you couldn't trust yourself in this castle." He lifts his gaze, those emerald irises so piercing. "Every decision you have made here has been of your own volition. The King," Mica's hand balls into a tight fist, "he might have steered you, but every decision you made here had him changing plans. You kept him unbalanced. *That* I know.

"I will fight with you," he continues, meeting all of our eyes this time. "Whatever I can do with this curse on my neck, I will. I owe it to you all, but I also owe it to the person who I lost so long ago." To me, he says finally, "I will help rid the *world* of this King that haunts it."

Cole takes a half step forward and drops his arms to his side. "For a moment, back when we were fighting, I thought that you were turning on us. When you didn't fight back, didn't defend us, I was ready to let my magic destroy you." The tension in the room eases just a little at his words, and I find myself feeling content with these three vampires, a steady and pleasant bond forming between us all. Cole clears his throat. "I'm sorry. For doubting you and dismissing what you have gone through in the past."

Mica manages a small half smile. "Thank you, though, I imagine my past actions never really helped."

Cole mimics the expression. "True." The smile fades. "But still, I am sorry. Since you two are doing it, I might as well verbally pledge myself to defeating the King with you as well."

I lean into Cole, soaking in the warmth of his energy as it seeps into my own.

The three of us look to Oba now. His brown eyes widen and he steps away from the table. "Oye," he says. "I'm in, but I'm still piecing together the fact that—"

"Do not finish that sentence," Mica warns. He pulls on the collar of his shirt, revealing that dooming mark there. The black ink is circular in shape with small lines extending outward, disappearing into his skin. It reminds me of what I sometimes loosely sketch on paper when creating an art land-scape with the sun in the background. "It is best to keep those thoughts in your head."

Oba glances to the mark on Mica's neck and winces. He rubs his own throat, likely imagining how things could have gone if he kept speaking. "Thanks, mate."

"Is that really all it would take to trigger the curse?" Cole asks.

"To be honest, I'm not entirely sure. But it's just best to avoid the risk in my opinion."

Another beat of silence falls between us all. I don't know what is racing through their minds. In my own head, I can't help but notice the thoughts that always seem to rise to the surface, just to disintegrate the moment I give them attention. Before becoming a vampire, none of this has ever happened to me. All my thoughts and memories were my own.

I shove my hands into the pockets of my sweater, my mind shifting to the battle earlier. To Isaiah and how he knows my parents. To the address he offered as a place to talk about them. If I ever free myself of being the anchor.

Vampires. Witches. Hunters. Werewolves.

Each species caught in the grasp of a single, bloodthirsty vampire. And for what? Morwen wants revenge on the humans and witches who had wronged her in the past. This seems like so much more than that, though.

"How can we win against someone who has the ability to just force opponents into submission?" I ask into the open library as I stare at one of the opened books on the table. It looks like one that hasn't been used in a while. Dust is layered heavily along the top edge, the papers lightly discolored. A fresh pile of dust is gathered beside the book, likely from when Mica placed it on the table. Out of the corner of my eye, toward the back of the library, I notice a flickering candle extinguishing. Smoke streams into the air like a snake.

It isn't until the next two candles burn out that the others take notice. The hair on the back of my neck stands as goose-flesh races down my arms. I'm unnervingly reminded of the last time this happened while I was in this room. Somehow, it is strangely more nerve-wracking when there is no glass rattling thunder above.

"What is happening?" Oba asks. He grips one of his daggers and yanks it free of the bandolier.

None of us respond, stunned into silence as more and more candles extinguish so that only a single one remains lit. A small, tapered candle that sits in a sconce burns steady above a pedestal where a single, heavy tome rests. If I could look at the layout of the library from above, I would likely be able to determine that this book is directly across from the painting of the sword I found a while ago.

"I think something is telling us to look at that book," Cole observes warily.

Oba sheathes his dagger, though doesn't remove his grip from its hilt. "I hate ghosts."

Mica moves around the table toward Cole and me. The book is about twenty paces from where we stand. "I don't think this is the work of a ghost, Oba."

"If you are about to tell me that a god of death is pointing you toward that book… I'm just going to leave now." We all turn and stare at him, eyes narrowed. Oba shrugs. "I overheard you talking before I came in here. You lot are looking at me like you were planning to keep the information about a damned god a secret."

Cole shakes his head. "We would have told you."

Oba just hums in a disagreeing tone.

"Right. So who wants to be the one to grab the book?" Mica asks.

When no one responds immediately, I let out a sigh and take a step forward. I'm not too eager to grab some object from this place that might plunge me back into a vision. But I don't want that to happen to the others, either. Before I can say anything, Cole grips my arm and pulls me back. "I'll get it."

He moves before I can protest. I think I hold my breath as he walks over to it. He glances down each aisle before proceeding to grab the book. There is no flash of light or thunder. Cole doesn't crumple onto the ground as his mind is pulled to some far-off memory. He just holds the book, tucked against his chest, as he walks over to us.

I let out a relieving breath. Beside me, Mica moves some of the other books and slides a candelabra to the center of the table.

"Do you mind, Kindria?"

I grumble at the name but decide to light the candles anyway. In the dark of the library, I hold up a hand in front of Mica's face. Only when the conjured flame ignites on the tip of my sole finger does the green-eyed vampire look at me flipping him off. Surprise followed by amusement flashes across Mica's face as Cole places the tome down on the now cleared spot on the table. The book is black, seeming to devour the light of the candle flames. There is no title on the cloth cover.

"Yes, very helpful," Oba jests. Even with the possibility of ghosts or gods, he maintains his childish jabs.

I snort a laugh. "Just because there is no title doesn't mean the information inside isn't going to be helpful. Sometimes old books only have the title on the spine." I grab the book to turn it over, but a searing pain travels from the book into my arms and to the rest of my body. And then I am plunged into darkness.

CHAPTER TWENTY

THEA

An endless darkness swallows me. It is ever present, stretching far in every direction. I turn and see the scraggly skeleton of a pine tree, spectral in this dim lighting. The apex of the tree points to a full moon that brightens the surroundings in a ghostly light. Below me is a shallow body of black water, wraithlike mists rising low before disappearing into the night.

It is that nightmare. The one I had so many times, though I haven't had to endure in months. They stopped shortly after being taken to the castle dimension by Amaund.

"Cole!" I yell, panic forming a lump in my throat. "Co—"

A sharp throb lances from my head down to my right arm. I fold into myself, crouching from the pain, sending ripples through the water with the movement. It subsides rather quickly, though now seems to be concentrating as a slicing pain in my palm. Shakily, I hold out my hand. There is a gash in my palm, as if a blade carved into my skin. Blood pours out and drips into the murky water.

And then visions speed into my mind, so fast that I can hardly register them.

Someone chanting. A blood offering. A sealed, arched door bordered in runes. The full moon.

A darkness, so greedy and hungry that it might devour all.

And it does. The darkness swirls like a living entity, swallowing the moon and the tree beneath. It slithers over the surface of the water, dispersing the mists. I hardly have enough time to try and get away before it reaches me. The wisps spiral around my legs like a snake readying to take down its prey. It sears my skin, the touch so cold that it feels like it is burning.

I want to scream in agony, but nothing comes out. I can only stand there and let the darkness consume me.

And so it does.

"THEA! THEA, PLEASE." Cole's frantic voice trickles into my ravaged mind. A dull throb lingers in the center of my head. My eyelids flutter, the light from a few candles too bright. "Thea?" Cole's warm hand on my cheek pulls me all the way back into my body.

"I'm here," I whisper, my throat burning. Cole leans forward, resting his forehead on mine. His body blocks out the bright lights, soothing my eyesight. Somewhere behind him, I hear Oba curse quietly.

"What happened?" Mica asks. He must be kneeling right behind my head. His voice is so close.

Cole lifts his head and hisses at Mica. "Let her recover first."

I bring a hand to my aching head. My eyes adjust to the room just as Cole straightens. His gray eyes are cloaked in concern, fear rippling from his body in waves of black energy. "I'm okay," I say. "Help me stand, please."

It isn't until Cole moves that I notice my head was placed

on his lap. He slides an arm under my back and gently helps me rise to a sitting position. "Take it slow," he says.

"I'm okay," I repeat, taking a deep breath. The pain has significantly subsided, mostly just leaving me with the eerie reminder of it all.

When I finally get to my feet, I note the book still sitting on the table. I clench my jaw, wary of it. It seems the library is alight with the candles that line the walls again. I'm grateful for that, though I wonder if they lit by themselves or if one of the others found a match.

"The moment you touched the book you were overcome with some strange magic," Mica says.

Oba clicks his tongue. "I'd call it the death god's magic."

"Your eyes went black," Mica continues, ignoring the wind user at the end of the table.

"I pulled it out of your hands," Cole finishes, his expression distant. "And then you collapsed."

I swallow, forcing the memory of that nightmarish place out of my mind. "How long was I out?"

"Not long. Maybe a few minutes."

The doors to the library slam open. Amelia barges in with Sarah huffing behind her. Alec brings in the rear, his eyes wide, arm sizzling with flame. They look equally concerned but also ready for a fight, their eyes assessing the room for any threat. "What happened?"

Sarah's attention lands on me and she pushes in front of Amelia. "Is everything okay? We heard screaming."

"I'm okay," I repeat again, for the third time. "We're okay."

They should know. Everyone here, as a part of our alliance, should know everything. All that I have discovered while living and training with Morwen. The visions, the influences she had on my past. Everything. "We should sit. I need to tell you all something."

And so, at the table in the library, I tell them all I know.

THE SUN ROSE by the time we all left the library. After telling them everything, Cole opened the black book. Every page was covered in a language that none of us knew. The characters looked similar to languages in Asia. Mica and Alec said they weren't. Frustrated at another roadblock, we called it a night.

Now, I lie on the bed in my room, my head resting on my hands, staring at the ceiling. Cole offered to meet me here after grabbing a glass of blood for us. He didn't say much after everything that I told the group. But I didn't, either.

This bed has never been comfortable, but with exhaustion plaguing me, it doesn't really matter. I close my eyes, falling into the quiet of the room.

A knock at the door wakes me up, though I couldn't have been asleep for too long. I'm still in the same position as when I closed my eyes. "Cole, you can just come in," I say as I sit up and rub the sleepiness away.

The knock comes again. A forceful pounding.

I freeze, my palm still pressed into my face. Outside, the moon is shining. Was I asleep for an entire day? Why didn't anyone wake me?

The person on the other side of the door pounds on it again.

"Who's there?" Slowly, I rise from the bed, the hair on the back of my neck standing.

Knock. Knock. Knock. Again and again. The sound clobbers around in my skull.

My heart thumps loudly in my chest as I reach for the doorknob. In my left hand, I call upon my flames.

They don't come. I feel no magic humming in my veins, just an emptiness where it should be.

I'm about to step away from the door when I hear a voice, the sound a tsunami of relief. "Thea?" Cole calls from the other side.

I yank the door open, already forgetting about the lack of magic. And then terror floods my body. It is not Cole's warm, gray eyes that greet me. It's the horrifying, amused gaze of Morwen.

CHAPTER TWENTY-ONE

THEA

"Hello, Thea." Morwen is calm as she always was, like she is visiting a friend. Like what she used to be. To me. But that was a one-sided friendship.

No. It wasn't a friendship at all. She manipulated me into thinking it was.

But in my mind, it still feels like she was. And the betrayal of that false friendship still hurts. How many times has she stood in this doorway, offering her help in this desolate place? A place she created. This castle dimension is just an extension of who she truly is.

A monster. Murderer.

Ruby red lips curve into a smile, one of her dark brows rising. "Aren't you going to let me in your room?"

"How?" I manage to say. It is the only word that my brain can come up with.

"Easily. You just open the door more and step aside." She sweeps her pale, deceivingly delicate looking hand.

I shake my head, finally remembering myself. "No." Again, I try to call on my magic, but nothing answers. I grasp at my back, to where Vitamors should be.

Morwen clicks her tongue. "Attacking me won't work here,

I'm afraid." She takes a step closer, the sound of her heel on the stone floor pulling more fear out of me.

The grip I have on the doorknob tightens. Cole never came to bed. I stretch my hearing and notice that I cannot sense anyone else in the castle. "What did you do to the others?" My voice is a growl. A warning.

It doesn't faze her in the slightest. She laughs, the soft sound of it not fitting what I now know of her. "Sometimes I am amazed at how you are still alive, Thea." Her gaze flicks to my hand. "You are so naïve. Or perhaps just senseless."

I need to leave. Letting her bait me into a fight would end very poorly on my account. There is no way that I can win against her alone, especially without any magic. Summoning all my strength and speed, I slam the door.

It stops just before closing. And then Morwen is pushing on it, hard enough that I am forced to let go, or I'd lose my balance and fall. I manage to move to my closet. To where Vitamors might be.

But it isn't there either. Nor are my clothes and shoes. The closet is empty. Confused, I glance to the bed. Helios is not there. He isn't curled up at the end. And then I look to the windowsill. Where there shouldn't be a lavender plant, since I threw the reminder of Morwen in the trash. But it is there, soaking in silvery moonlight.

"This is a dream world," I murmur. Like the sanctuary that Cole conjured in order for us to still be together when I was trapped with the vampire who now stands before me.

Morwen hums. "Maybe you are a little smarter than I give you credit for."

I whip my head to her, a smile already forming again on her lips. The rage inside me boils, but I manage to let it simmer down. "How? I thought…" I let the sentence trail off.

"You thought your dearest Cole and that wicked witch of the Minuit coven were the only ones who could do this?" Her smile is predatory now. Like she knows she caught me.

Trapped in a cage of a room. In a world I have no idea how to escape.

"I knew he visited you the very first night. I was sad you didn't come and tell me about it." She playfully pouts.

"Why didn't you say anything, then?" I survey the space between her and the door. If I can manage to get past her, perhaps I can find a way out of this dream. There has to be a finite barrier somewhere. I just need to find it, and perhaps push my way through it.

She shrugs. "I had a façade to protect. And it was actually mostly Cole, you know. He just used the witch as a tether more or less."

"Why not just come to the castle? Why go through all this?" Not that I want her to come here.

She picks at something on the sleeve of her cherry-red blouse. "For giving up my tie as the anchor, and then leaving the dimension, I can no longer step foot in that place." My brows rise at that reveal, and Morwen chuckles. "I hope you aren't thinking about hiding in the dimension." Her eyes darken with a predatory gleam. "There are other ways to flush you and your allies out." She glances to a spot behind me.

And I move. My palm strikes her hard in the chest. I don't wait to see if it causes her to be knocked prone or not. I don't have the luxury of time. Morwen is fast and I need every second I can spare to get away from her.

Moving as quickly and as silently as possible, I run toward the side stairs to the left of my room. But the moment I turn the corner, Morwen is there, leaning against the banister. She is still looking at her nails, as if she teleported from the place she stood in my room. When she lifts her chin at me, she smirks. "You've certainly gotten faster than when you last ran away from me. Which is impressive, considering it wasn't that long ago."

I rip the closest painting off the wall and throw it at her, doubling back the moment it leaves my fingers. If not those stairs, then the central ones. And if not those...then I'll jump out a window.

But I hardly make it ten steps before her slender fingers wrap around my throat and my head slams against the wall. Stars dance in my vision, pain lancing through me.

Dream world or not, I can feel pain here.

"I only came here to talk," she hisses, her nails digging into my neck. Her face is inches away from mine, her fangs a delicate, lethal point a breath away from ripping into me. When she lets go, I drop to the cold, stone floor, gasping for breath.

I glare up at her, trying to regain control of myself. She leans against the wall, waiting until my breathing returns to normal. When it does, I stand and say, "Speak."

There is an amused glitter in her azure eyes. "I've come to offer you a deal."

With a narrowed gaze, I watch her for any signs of trickery. I don't find any tells, but I know firsthand her proficiency with the skill of deceiving others. At least here, she can't use her ability to manipulate my emotions. "I'm listening, though I highly doubt that I will agree to whatever you have to say."

She crosses her arms, her expression still amused. "You've dragged a whole lot of people into this mess. Most of them, if not all, will die by the end of it. You and your... *lover* included." The smile on her lips is coated in poison now, a sneer replacing the previous calmness.

"I'm waiting for you to get past these delusions of yours and get to the point." I cross my own arms now, mustering the confidence I need. This visit from Morwen, the deal she is implying, makes me think that she is concerned with losing this war.

She pushes off from the wall. "These are not delusions, Thea. I won't lose. I *know* that you and your allies will." She takes two steps toward me, her heels echoing in the hall. "I'm just trying to minimalize the casualties."

Despite her closing the distance, I don't move. "Why?" I ask. "You've never cared before."

"On the contrary. Believe it or not, Thea, but I don't like the idea of other vampires dying in this fight of ours."

"Because you will lose your playthings?" I take a step to her this time. "I know Cole and I are the only ones immune to your curse."

A muscle in her cheek moves. "You've been busy."

I cock my head at her non-answer. "Why did you create that curse? Why force others to fight with you?"

Morwen doesn't answer, she just watches me with cool disinterest. For the briefest moment, her irises change to ruby.

"I thought it was just because you are a sadist. A monster who enjoys ruining others." Her face reveals nothing. "Is it because you are alone?" Still, nothing. "Or is it for protection?"

Her lip curls. "Enough. Give yourself to me, and I will allow your allies to live through this war."

I can't help the tug of a smile. "What are you afraid of, Morwen?"

She drops her hands to her sides. "I am afraid of *nothing*," she spits the last word. "You, on the other hand, should be. Every time you thought you were close to ridding yourself of me, you lost. And this time, if you don't agree to this deal, I will arrive with an army and destroy everything. I will make sure your death is slow and painful. You and your lover."

At my silence, that malicious smile returns.

"I'm sure you know by now." She chuckles, a laugh that is like claws scraping on a metal surface, and then leans in. "You, Cole, and I have been playing this dance of death for centuries."

The only thing I can trust about her is her ability to manipulate. So I hold my chin high and try not to let anything she says burrow into my thoughts. And somewhere deep in my mind, a spark lights. It shines with the memories long forgotten.

"All your defective past lives still live in your soul." Her hand grips my chin, forcing me to look in her eyes. "They've been clawing at your mind, trying to get you to remember." She surveys my face, likely taking in the mix of horror and disbelief. "I've killed you so many times. I've *won* so many times."

I remember. Memories flash in my mind. Memories of me dying. Of Cole dying. Over and over and over again. Sometimes in agony, sometimes so quick that we felt nothing.

"And every glorious time that I kill you two, I get stronger." Her breath is hot on my cheek.

More memories flood my thoughts. Painful ones, of screaming and fire and blood. It is like those pieces of my soul are warning me. That death by Morwen's hand is inevitable.

But she already killed me once in this lifetime.

It won't happen again.

"Let go of me," I snipe at her. The back of my right hand smacks the inside of her wrist and she releases me. I move away from her, fury growing in my chest. "Why didn't you just kill me that day? When my parents died?"

Her face darkens, stripped clear of any amusement that still lingered. "The more you suffer in each lifetime, the easier it is to kill you in the next."

"Don't lie to me. The more I suffer the stronger I become," I fume.

"Hmm." The sound is sharp, unrepentant.

"Why? After all these years, why do you still hate us?" The castle seems to sway, a light hum sings outside. There is a thunder-like roar from somewhere outside. The castle shakes and pieces of the ceiling hit the floor behind Morwen. Neither of us flinch at it.

"This dream world is crumbling. I've held it open for too

long. Do you agree to this deal, or shall I visit again with an army?"

If I agree to this, I can spare Cole from risking his life. He will be furious, that I know. If I don't agree, so many of those I care for might die. And if either Cole or I die by her hand in an all-out war, the whole thing is likely forfeit. Everyone else can be affected by her silence curse, forced into submission for her.

Forced to protect her. Against something that is powerful enough to frighten even her. If we can figure that out, perhaps the tide of this war will dip greatly in our favor.

This is my fight. And I won't lose a second time.

"I agree."

Her smile is feline. "Lovely." Morwen waves a hand and a document appears in her palm.

"What is that?" The uneasiness increases. It was one thing to verbally agree to this deal, but if this is what I think it is…

She shrugs. "I learned long ago from my mentor to always prepare a contract." From her coat pocket, she pulls out a small knife. "To be signed in our blood, of course." She extends the knife to me.

Morwen is utterly enjoying this.

The floor beneath our feet vibrates rather aggressively. I move to her and take the knife before looking at the parchment. Thankfully, the contract is short. In no way would I sign this without reading it wholly.

Just a handful of lines. The first states our names and the formation of this binding agreement. The second prevents either of us from discussing this meeting and its outcome with anyone. A knot forms in my chest at this line, but I continue to read. The third stipulation provides the coordinates to where we shall meet under the next new moon.

I tap the paper. "How am I supposed to meet you if I can't leave your castle dimension?"

An unbothered, borderline bored, smile curves on her lips. "You've done it once, I'm sure you can again."

I grind my teeth but return to the contract. Four: neither of us can attack the other before the new moon. "Why the new moon? Why not just get on with it now?"

Her gaze drops to her hands as she examines her nails. "Not that you understand, but I need the new moon for what I have planned. And I need you alive until then."

Grinding my teeth, I look back to the paper. The final line states that I must come to the ritual site with only Mica.

I shake my head. "Not Mica. You will only get me for this. No one else."

She clicks her tongue. "Mica knows those coordinates to the ritual site. You will need him to show you the way."

A *ritual*.

The thought of being a sacrifice at a ritual site is enough for me to want to turn around and let this dream world collapse on our heads. I told Sarah that we would do this together. I've been saying that defeating Morwen is not something that any of us can do alone.

Yet here I am, holding a contract that I am going to sign. A contract that spells out my inevitable death. I glance at the four lines, committing them to memory. In two weeks, upon the night of the full moon, I will meet her. I glance at the paper again. Maybe there is a loophole that I am not seeing yet. I prick my finger with this knife and press my blood to the paper, right next to a dried smudge of Morwen's blood.

The knife and paper disappear and I feel myself crumbling.

There is a burning sensation on my right wrist. I look down and see a golden line forming, encircling my wrist like a tattooed bracelet. "It is done," Morwen says, taking a step away from me. She holds up her own marked wrist, a twin to mine. "A reminder of our time here. It will only be visible under the light of a fire. If you break this contract, you will die. As will I if I break it." She turns her back to me.

Though the walls and ceiling are breaking apart, I call out to her as she departs. "Just tell me." She turns around, her expression triumphant. "Why do you do this?"

"To you specifically?" Her fangs protrude from her upper lip as she smiles. She pauses for a moment, her eyes shimmering wildly. "Because when we were mortal, we were lovers. I've destroyed every version of you, looking to find the one who would love me again." She lets out a rough laugh. "It has taken me too long to realize the lesson I should have learned back then." Ruby irises gleam in the dust of the collapsing building. Her face twists in a primal rage. "To love is to be weak. To be hopeful is the same. And with this final death of yours, I will be free of more than one torment."

I am too stunned to move as Morwen disappears from view, the castle collapsing on top of me.

CHAPTER TWENTY-TWO

THEA

I wake, my eyes opening calmly despite my racing heart. My head still rests in my palms. The early morning sun shines through the slender window, still in the same position it was in when I closed my eyes. Helios is curled up at my feet.

Morwen and I were *lovers*. I scrub at my face, my palms digging into my eyes as I try and comprehend what she told me. I can't even imagine a life when I would love someone like her. Then again, it has been centuries. Her hardships have changed her for the worst, it seems. She has been given hundreds of years to better herself, but the only thing she has been concerned with was the past and how to bring it back.

Putting an end to her life almost feels like a mercy now. A way to honor who we were in our first lives.

But that just got a lot harder with what just transpired. I would think the entirety of that dream was exactly that, a dream, if it weren't for the mark still etched around my wrist, glowing faintly in the fire writhing on my fingertips. I snuff out my magic and the golden band disappears. A tear escapes as I close my eyes and roll to face the wall. Did I just secure my death? Had she manipulated me again?

The reflection of a light on the wall catches my attention. I look down and see Vitamors nestled beside me.

At least I can bring the sword. The contract never said I had to go unarmed, or that I couldn't challenge her to a fight.

When I challenged Commander Kael to a fight to the death, I almost lost my life. If it weren't for Morwen arriving when she did, I wouldn't be here. And Morwen would still be locked in this dimension. Did Morwen know I was going to challenge Kael to a *Necaut Necare*? Maybe she did and used that as a way to rightfully kill Kael.

I've never actually seen Morwen wield a sword before. Not in a real fight. When we were training, she only instructed while I held a wooden sword. I watched her take Kael's head off. And I saw—and felt—her stab Vitamors through my chest.

If I challenge her to a fight, her speed alone could be the reason I die, no matter if we use magic or swords.

I sigh and roll to my back again, my hands resting on my stomach. My left thumb brushes over the mark of our contract. Two weeks until the new moon. Two weeks to figure this all out. Alone.

The bedroom door opens and I flinch, my palm heating with my magic. Cole enters and I offer a smile, trying to mask the fear. To further hide my emotions, I wrap myself in a calm aura of my beta ability. Just like Morwen always had done.

"Hey," he says gently. Helios lifts his head at Cole's voice and lets out a small purr before putting his head back down.

I pull my sleeve down, hiding the mark. "Hey."

Cole hands me a glass filled halfway with blood. It really has only been a few minutes here. Being with Morwen again felt like many excruciating hours. "Thank you," I say.

He gives a curt nod before sitting at the end of the bed, leaving a few feet between us. His chest rises with a deep breath, his black shirt stretching across the muscles there. He takes a drink from the glass, then combs a hand through his dark hair before resting his gaze downward. We sit in silence, replenishing our bodies with the blood. It doesn't have that same, intoxicating taste as it once had. Maybe it is just the situation we are in.

I look out the window, my gaze scanning over the tops of the trees in the forest below. There is a ring of dirt on the windowsill where the lavender plant once sat.

"Are you all right?" Cole asks gently, his eyes on the tight grip I have on the glass.

I clear my throat and put the almost-emptied glass on the nightstand. "Define all right."

He bobs his head in agreement. "A lot has happened." He rubs his hand along the prickly hair on his jaw.

That's an understatement. I wonder how he would react to the entirety of this war being rooted to the fact that Morwen has been obsessed with resurrecting the past.

I rub my hand on my sleeve, pulling them down even more. "I'm sorry I didn't tell you about everything earlier. That you had to learn when everyone else did."

Cole takes a deep breath as he shifts and grabs my hand. "When you were filling us in, I did find myself a bit frustrated that I was *just* finding out."

"Cole," I start, my voice betraying the guilt.

"Hold on," he says, giving my hand a squeeze. "I was just confused why you didn't mention anything during our trysts, or even while we were together here. And I'll admit, I did suggest you returning to your room while I grabbed us a meal because I needed a moment." To this, I squeeze his hand. "And the whole walk to the cellars, even with Oba babbling on and on, I found myself thinking how ridiculous it was to be upset with you."

"It's not, though." I wish I could tell him what just happened. How I'm bound to die again.

He shakes his head. "It is. And then, Oba said something, just to himself maybe, but it really knocked me out of the stupor. He said, 'It is crazy how strong she ought to be for dealing with all that.'" Cole turned to fully face me, then. "Thea, I understand why there might be things you don't tell me. And I trust that anything important, you will when the time is right. I am here, right by your side. And I intend to be for as long as you will have me."

Another damned tear falls down my cheek. He moves closer so that our knees touch and wipes the tear away. There is a lump forming in my throat. Of all the things I want to tell him but can't. For this man, that I would die for. *Will* die for, if things work out as they have for centuries. "Cole," I breathe. His attention is wholly on me, and it threatens more tears to escape. I cup his face in my hands, memorizing the feel of the curve of his sharp jawline and the small scar hidden beneath his facial hair. "I love you. I always have."

For centuries, I have loved him, and I can feel that now. That love that has blossomed for so long.

He smiles sullenly, a fire burning in his smokey eyes. "I love you, too, Thea. I think, from the moment I saw you handle that guy in the bar, I have loved you." He pulls my face to his, our lips meeting in an electrified kiss.

The world melts away with each second. Cedarwood envelopes me, grounding me to this moment. The scent of him. Of home. I don't even register myself moving to his lap, my thighs wrapping around his waist. One hand is in his hair, the other resting against his neck. Our kisses become deeper, his tongue moving into my mouth. I moan at the sensation, so much more intoxicating than before, as impossible as that sounds.

He moves his hand down on my back, a pleasant shiver coursing through me. At the hem of my shirt, he tucks his fingers underneath, pressing his palm against the skin of my back. His other hand grips underneath my thigh.

I decide that I need more. More of this, more of him. He groans when I simultaneously grind against him and tug at his hair. The hand on my back moves to the clasp of my bra, gently roaming underneath the strap. His fingers dig into my thigh as he pulls away. The look in his eyes yanks the breath from my lungs. They are lidded with desire.

"Thea," he says quietly, his voice heady. "I'm one touch away from tearing your clothes off and taking you on this horribly uncomfortable bed."

I smile onto his lips, my fingers trailing across his jawline. "I very much want you to do that."

That is all the confirmation he needs as he pulls my shirt off. I do the same to his, our gazes never leaving the other's. I move off him, my fingers grazing his bare skin, eliciting a knee-quaking noise from his chest. We remove the rest of our clothes, the desire thick in the air.

At some point of our de-clothing, Helios jumps off the end of the bed and into his nook within the closet.

Cole lifts me gently and places me down on the bed before resting on top. Our bodies fit together like two parts of a casting, reunited to create a beautiful piece of art. We kiss, melding our lips together gloriously. It's hard to tell where I end and he begins. He kisses me more, his arms shaking just enough for me to detect as he holds himself half up. I kiss him hungrily, never wanting this moment to end as I wrap my legs around him and pull him into me.

In this lifetime, one of hundreds, we mend our souls together underneath the light of the morning sun. No curse or evil vampire can keep us apart from each other. And I hope, in our next life, we will be able to meet again.

We lie together, after our intimate entwining. Cole's heartbeat is a song, his breathing steady as he sleeps. I listen to him, nestled in his arms on this horribly uncomfortable bed, and brush away the stray tears that fall into his hair.

When we were mortal, we were lovers. Morwen's words clang around in my head. They spark a small piece of my mind that knows them to be truth. A piece that remembers a time when we were each other's world. And it is that part of me that fights the hardest for Morwen to be put to rest. So that she may find true peace for once.

Morwen will not win again. She made me like this, orchestrated how my life played out. But she will learn that in doing so, she has made me her downfall. Because this time, she will be the one who is destroyed.

CHAPTER TWENTY-THREE

THEA

As hard as I try, the rain clouds do not break over the castle. The dimension grips the sadness that lingers in my heart, casting a never-ending storm cloud overhead. Sarah and Amelia informed us that it has been raining since early this morning, making many of my allies here change their original plans of training outdoors. Since becoming the anchor, I can feel the connection I have to the nature of this place. There is nothing interfering or different about the connection that I can perceive. But for some reason, I just can't seem to stop the torrential rain like I could before.

"I guess just keep an umbrella handy," I say, igniting the fireplace with my left hand, my right hand tucked safely in the pocket of a sweater. I move to the couch and sit next to Cole, then jerk my chin at Mica who sits on the couch across from us. "Or you can keep him with you. He's basically a humanoid umbrella."

Oba chuckles, but Mica finds no humor in my joke. "Don't you think its suspicious that your control of the weather here is waning? We don't know enough about the magic that binds you here. The King could still have some control."

"Oye, are you implying that the King is coming here?" Oba straightens, his posture alert and ready.

"He isn't stampeding the dimension," I say firmly, immediately wishing I hadn't said anything.

"He could be," Mica adds. "Don't get too comfortable here, it isn't exactly a safe place."

I shoot him a glare. "I know that. We do have our defenses though." Amelia's werewolves stand guard at the portal inside the dimension. "And I can tell when someone moves through the portal." The single portal, since I destroyed the second one while pursuing Morwen.

Cole leans forward slightly, his shoulder brushing against mine. "Okay. We all are all a little on edge, but let's not argue with each other. True, the King could try coming here and fighting us, but we aren't completely vulnerable."

Sarah steps in. "Cole is right. Amelia and I do have some news though." I study my best friend, noticing how at ease she appears, despite everything. She wears a comfortable, loose yellow shirt and black pants and her brown hair is tied back in a low bun. She looks better, like she did before everything happened.

"Good or bad news?" Cole asks, his hand resting on my leg.

We slept for almost twenty-four hours. And when we awoke, it took only a look at each other to return to being entangled again. Even here, in front of everyone, his touch ignites my core. I have to fight with myself to not kick everyone out so we can have more time alone.

Sarah frowns. "It depends how you look at it, I guess."

Oba lets out a long, loud breath. "Great."

"We were combing through my grimoire and trying to figure out what your vision meant, Thea." She steps away from the fireplace. The crackle of the fire echoes between her words. "Most of the time, when someone has a true vision, the information they receive isn't meant to be taken literally. So, we started looking into it with that in mind.

"It didn't make sense, and the more we looked into it, the clearer it became that the images were actually meant to be taken at face value." She walks to the front of the room, so that we can all see the paper she pulls from her pocket. "First, the sealed door. You told us about the door in the King's chamber. I think that is what you saw."

I shake my head. "Sure, but the one in the vision looked a little different."

She looks at the drawing on the paper, the one I sketched for her in the library. "It is similar in shape, but the difference is the markings. Sometimes seals can alter the profile of something, hide some markings or a keyhole. There is always a way around that because laws of nature demand a balance. Nothing can be finite."

I resist the urge to rub at the invisible mark of the contract. Instead, I tug on the sleeve of my cozy sweater. The fireplace is far enough away that I don't think its light will illuminate the mark, but I can't be too sure. The last thing I need right now is to lie to everyone about what the mark means. All morning I've been debating what I would say if needed, to no avail.

She taps the moon on the paper. "And I think that is where the moon comes into play. Well, part of it. Full moons are powerful for spells like nullifiers. I think that under that particular phase, we might see what the door truly looks like. And it will be easier to see the seal on the door in general. Maybe it'll even reveal the spell for the ritual."

Ritual. The word conjures an image of me strapped to an altar, bleeding, while Morwen stands over me with a knife in her crimson-stained hands.

"Wait," Oba interrupts. "Different moon phases work for different spells?"

"Yes," Sarah answers.

"Interesting."

I battle with myself, debating whether I should say anything. The direness of the situation, and my curiosity, wins. "So, if full moons are for nullifying, what are new moons for?"

Sarah dips her head. "Full moons are good for other things too, like manifesting or summoning. But new moons can be used for spells regarding beginnings, clarity, banishment, and other things."

"A little off topic," Alec notes calmly. He sits in the chaise at the end of the couches.

I shrug, resting into Cole's side. "Witch things make me curious."

Sarah smiles briefly at that, her face resuming all seriousness once she returns to the paper. "The other two things from your vision makes me think that all these combined," she taps each item on the list, "is to remove the seal. You need a witch to chant a spell under the full moon. Someone will need to offer their blood as a binding agent to that spell. And the door is, well, the door."

Mica stands from the couch and straightens his green shirt. "Well, you are the expert. We wait for the moon to get inside, then. And hopefully when we do, there'll be some mysterious, all-powerful weapon to destroy the King with."

Wouldn't that be nice.

"Let me guess, the next full moon isn't for another month?" Oba asks, his hand gripping the leather strap of his bandolier. I've learned, in my short time of knowing him, that Oba is always prepared for a fight. Not a bad trait to have during a time of war, I suppose.

Sarah folds the paper gingerly and tucks it back into her pocket. "Tonight, actually."

Oba blinks at her, trying to determine if she speaks the truth, no doubt. With all the chaos lately, the luck of being in the right time is strange. "That's oddly lucky for us."

"Maybe there is a death god somewhere, looking out for us," Cole jests to his friend.

Oba puts a palm up. "Nope." He shakes his head dramatically. "I'm just going to go with the fact that we've run out of bad luck, so now we've got nothing but good luck."

Cole lifts a brow, a wicked smile curving on his beautiful face. "So ghosts and gods, Oba? That's what scares you? What else? Goblins?"

"You're pushing it, Moretti," Oba warns. He lets go of his bandolier and points at Cole. "Keep talking and we'll finally get a crack at the long overdue brawl rematch."

The genuine laugh that comes out of Cole skitters along my body as he stands, his hand running along my arm. "Ghouls?"

Oba's brown eyes widen. "You know very well that those damn things are terrifying." He unclasps his bandolier and hands it mindlessly to Alec, who is getting the right sense to remove himself from their soon to be area of disaster.

"Are you just afraid of things that start with the letter 'G'?" Cole steps forward, his hands forming fists. He ducks the moment Oba swings a punch at him and brings his own fist upward to Oba's side. The latter twists just in time to avoid a direct hit, but Cole pushes him back, knocking him off balance. They exchange a fury of blows and blocks, two equal brawlers not giving up against the other.

We all watch the two of them go at it, needing the momentary distraction. I keep the smile on my face, my energy manipulation holding a joyful, yellow aura. But the depth of my thoughts is nothing like what appears on the outside.

If I was right about Morwen using the silence curse to keep a layer of protection, then that likely means that there is something that frightens her. Likely something strong enough to end her, something powerful. And if what Mica implied was correct, that means Morwen pissed off a death god at some point in her miserable existence.

A damned *god*. Could that be what she wants protection from? I need to figure out how to play that fear against her. Tonight is the full moon, which means I have approximately fifteen days until the new moon. Two weeks to figure out how to best her without involving the others. At least, until the day of, when I'll need Mica to take me to the coordinates.

I survey the pale-haired vampire. He stands beside Sarah and Amelia, watching the two brutes brawl it out. He wears an expression of enjoyment, but like me, it is a mask. I can see it in the downward crinkle between his brows. I wonder what thoughts race through his mind as he forces this outward appearance to the rest of us.

Mica glances at me, and I curse myself for looking too long at him. I turn back to Cole and Oba, who are still sharing punches and blocks. Neither of them look worn out, but rather exhilarated. Their eyes are wild with this friendly battle of fists.

Someone clears their throat beside me. "I'm going to take a walk. Care to join me, Kindria?"

I look one last time at Cole, who glances at me. The distraction cost him a punch to the jaw. I wince at the impact, but Cole is already swinging back in retaliation.

"Sure," I decide, following him out the two main doors of the castle. The rain is still heavy, the pathway almost flooded. We stand on the outside of the doors where the overhang protects us from the weather. "If you call me Kindria again, I'm going to shoot fire at you."

Mica chuckles. "Habits." He steps out of the cover of the castle and I expect him to be instantly soaked from the rain. Instead, the water hits an invisible wall just above his head then runs down to the ground beside him. He remains completely dry.

"So you *are* an umbrella," I say through a laugh.

His expression lightens. "Do you want cover, or not?"

I step closer to him. It is one thing to see his water shield, but to be under it, watching the rain stop just above my head…it is pure magic. "That's incredible," I say.

We start walking as Mica says, "If you tell anyone that I… am an umbrella, I'll deny it even with my dying breath."

Come to the ritual site with only Mica.

Mica's jest erases what little contentment was left in me at the moment. What if it isn't just my life that Morwen wants to take at that ritual, but Mica's as well? She might have chosen that place just because he would be the only one who knows of it, and I would be forced to bring him. More than once he has fought through the silence curse to fight her. That has to infuriate her.

"Everything all right?" Mica asks after a few moments of silent walking. We took a right off the main path, leading to the eastern side of the dimension. If we keep going straight on this path, we will eventually reach the disintegrating garage. I don't think I can handle seeing the vehicle with the Brais' crest right now. There, I would remember how Morwen once held me, calming me after almost losing myself entirely to my anger and grief.

We reach a smaller path that branches from the one we walk on now. Before I can even turn, Mica does first. "Everything is peachy," I say.

"That's a lie," he says. "Just like that false aura you've been projecting."

I almost stop walking, ready to interrogate him. But I stick to ignorance. "I have no idea what you mean."

Mica grabs my arm, forcing me to look at him. His nostrils flare, green eyes somehow more piercing. "Come on, Thea. You might have fooled everyone else back there, but I've lived with the King long enough to know when someone's emotions are forced."

My mouth opens, but I close it. Mica silently watches me

struggle with my thoughts. There is nothing that I can tell him, not without worrying that what I reveal might break the contract. This is my own silence curse, one that I signed willingly. And if it breaks, and I die before the new moon, Morwen will no doubt march on my friends. All of their deaths would be because I couldn't burden myself with this weight.

"I'm just…afraid," I say finally. "Afraid for what the future is going to bring." I fiddle with my fingers. "I'm trying not to add to anyone else's fears." A truth, but not the one he is looking for. And I think he knows that.

Mica searches my face as if he could pull the entire truth from me. I hold my breath with his silence, only releasing it when he runs a hand through his hair. "I get it." We continue down the slender path, walking so that our shoulders are almost touching as to avoid the rain-wet shrubbery along the sides. "You're not alone, you know. Every single one of us in that castle has your back." He pauses then hums.

I snort as I step over a puddle. "I appreciate all of you being here." I nudge his shoulder. "Even when you get on my nerves."

"Me? Impossible."

We walk in a pleasant silence for a while, only stopping and turning around once we reach a part of the path completely inundated from the rain and runoff. I contemplate asking him about the coordinates and get a feel for where the ritual will take place. The only reason I don't is because I'm not sure if that would break the contract. Morwen is allowing me to tell him so that he can bring me, so surely it doesn't matter when I do, right?

"Why do you think the King hasn't attacked yet?" Mica asks, right as I was getting enough nerve to talk about Morwen's location. "You seemed pretty adamant back there that we are safe."

I run through all the answers in my head, searching for

one that doesn't hint to the fact that I have her contracted word for it. "It's just a gut feeling. We showed her—*him*, I'm sorry." I wince at using Morwen's feminine pronouns again.

He waves me off. "Don't worry. It's honestly refreshing to hear someone talk about the King without the mark influencing their words." Halfway through the sentence, he winces. "You're betting on our safety based on a gut feeling?" The question isn't impolite, just curious.

I nod. "We showed the King how many allies we have. She doesn't know that the hunters haven't officially joined us. When they arrived, she retreated. I think right now she is regrouping and figuring out a new tactic. So, I think we are okay for a bit."

He cups his chin in contemplation. "That does seem likely. The King is arrogant most of the time, but I think when it comes to…this, he will play more on the safe side." Mica glances at me. "I wouldn't put it past the King to try and reach out to you discreetly somehow."

Now. I can tell him now.

Again, I open my mouth to tell him, but then close it. I can't risk it, not yet. I'll have to wait until the day of the new moon. I just hope that he won't be too suspicious.

Keeping my gaze steady, I say, "I'll let you know if she does."

Disappointment flashes across his face. He knows I'm keeping something, but he won't push. The rest of the walk to the castle is in silence, a little less comfortable than before.

Something in my chest twists at his expression, and at the gap he puts between the two of us.

CHAPTER TWENTY-FOUR

THEA

It turns out, waiting for the day to pass so we can unseal a mysterious door takes a lot out of you. Cole and I are lounging on a bench outside, fighting boredom as we watch the sun set beyond the tree line. The evening's air is cool, thanks to the rain that finally stopped about an hour ago. Now, the clouds part, revealing a darkening sky to the front of the castle.

"I feel bad for Helios." The poor, adventurous cat has been locked in my room since he arrived. It isn't the first time he has lived in a small space, but at least when we were traveling together in the airstream trailer, he got to explore the outdoors on our hikes. Some nights he wakes us up meowing at the door. But when I open it for him, he glances down each side of the hallway and darts back into the bedroom.

"Well, while you were out this morning on a stroll with Mica, I was looking at other rooms. Larger ones with bigger beds." He lingers enough on Mica's name that I half hear the rest of what he says.

"Were you jealous, Nicolai Moretti?" I grin wickedly at him and poke at his chest.

He catches my hand before it reaches him. "No," he says,

his voice deep. His gray eyes flash red, though not from anger, and my heart jumps at the sight. He brings my hand to his lips and kisses the back of it, then turns it over and places another on the inside of my wrist.

Lightning courses between us, traveling from his lips to my chest, and then lower when he pulls my other hand and does the same. All of my senses focus on his mouth touching my skin, on the tantalizing caress of his other hand making lazy circles in my hair. I let out a breathy noise when he closes in and kisses the sensitive spot under my ear, sending pleasant shivers down my body. Slowly, he leaves a trail of kisses over my jawline. My entire body reacts to his touch and I am utterly at his mercy.

His kissing reaches my lips and I turn into him, eager for more. Except he pulls himself away. It takes a moment for me to come back to myself, my body still tingling. And when I do, I glare at him.

"Are you being a tease?"

The corner of his lips turn up. "No," he says again, in the same tone as before.

"Liar." I put my hand on his chest to push him away but feel the erratic beat of his heart. Instead, I wrap his shirt in my fist and tug him closer. This time, he kisses me. The sweetness of his mouth is something I crave now, never able to get enough. "Liar," I repeat when we break away.

He chuckles and stands, offering me a hand. "We should probably head inside; it is almost time to get started."

I pout but accept his hand regardless, ignoring the growing nerves for what we are about to do.

He pulls me into an embrace. All thoughts of what is to come are erased from my mind as his breath caresses my ear. "And Thea? Next time you call me Nicolai, I'm going to kiss you in *other* places until you are writhing and begging."

I still stare at the spot far into the distance, my breathing erratic, when his tug on my hand has me moving toward the castle.

Cole holds the door open for me. We enter the castle and I offer my hand for him, not realizing which one until it is too late.

"What is that?" he asks, snatching my wrist before I can pull it away. Under the glow of the candlelit sconces, the golden band gleams. He runs his thumb over the mark. My heart sinks, annoyed at my stupidity for not remembering about the firelight.

I yank my arm away from him, a flash of hurt crossing his perfect features. "It's nothing," I say, my heart breaking at the lie.

Cole's arm drops slowly to his side and I want to shrink away from his pained expression. "When did you get it?" He takes a step closer but stops when I retreat, shoving my sleeve far beyond the mark.

There is nothing that I can say to him. My mind falters on anything that could salvage this conversation. "It's nothing," I repeat.

Frustration mixes into his saddened energy. "That's a lie, Thea."

I struggle to keep my voice from rising. From letting all the anger spill out at him. At the one person who least deserves that. "I've got it under control."

He steps away, the space crushing me. That, I deserve. Was this Morwen's plan? To wedge distrust between the two of us? Making it so I couldn't talk to my allies about this deal. After all that talk from me about us doing this together. Did she know about that before making me stay quiet? I dig my nails into my palms, letting the pain consume me.

"Are you two coming?" Alec says in a quiet voice. There's no doubt in my mind that he overheard everything.

Cole pushes past me and I reach for him, stopping just

before my sleeve reveals the mark again. I follow behind the two of them, regret numbing my body.

By the time we arrive to the northern wing, the others are already there. Oba stands to the back of the group while Sarah and Mica talk closer to the door. Amelia leans against the stone wall, her arms crossed and a protective gaze never leaving her lover.

The hallway is darker than most within the castle. There aren't any sconces along the walls, the only light coming from the candelabras on the side table and the spooky glow of the shimmering veil. Someone cleared a path from the door to Morwen's room to the barrier, books and clothes tossed in more piles along its sides.

I'm grateful for the lack of candles. Still, I tug on my sleeve. Cole watches me, his brows furrowed, but doesn't say anything.

Oba snorts when we round the corner. "Look at that, the stars of the show. You two took your time getting here. What were you even doing?"

"Nothing," Cole says coldly.

Oba's playful expression wanes as he glances to me. "Your witch friend says that you two are the keys for opening this door."

I clear my throat and shake off the shame. "How?" The answer comes to me the moment I ask the question. Because it has been rattling around in my mind since the meeting with Morwen.

Sarah frowns, closing a worn-out book in her hands. "A hunch." Her fingers run along the cover of that old tome, a sadness looming in her eyes. "This was my mother's grimoire." My heart wrenches at those words, filled with so much emotion, each echoing in my own soul. Anger. Grief. The need for revenge. "There is a lot of information inside.

I've been pouring over it all for the last couple of days. I can't tell you any specifics of what I found." She winces, a hand moving to her neck, and I understand. The reason Cole and I are important for this must trigger the curse around her throat.

"I'm sorry," she adds sorrily.

"I think you know why, don't you, Thea?" Mica asks.

I feel Cole's gaze on me and resist meeting it. "I don't." The lie rolls easily off my tongue. The risk of this conversation breaking the contract is too great. I won't risk their deaths. I will lie to their faces about this if it means protecting them from her. Even if the words are like daggers to my heart the moment they leave my lips.

I look away from Mica's hard stare to see Sarah examining the seal. It's raven black wings sway in some invisible wind.

Sarah opens the grimoire to a page near the middle, her finger scanning the contents. After a few moments of silence, she glances up to the ceiling. Her soft features are scrunched in concentration. We all remain still, silently watching the witch prepare.

I can still feel Mica's scrutinizing stare. He knows. Somehow, he knows. Could he have somehow noticed the mark on my wrist? Instinctively, I wrench down on the sleeve, keeping it in place between my fingers and palm. Maybe Morwen visited him as well and taunted the contract. Or maybe he has known all along about what Morwen has planned.

A disturbing thought crosses my mind then. Could Mica still be allied with Morwen? Just thinking that makes me nauseous. After everything that he told me, everything that he has done, surely, he wouldn't still be fighting for her. The one who murdered his lover and forced him into her service? He fought Morwen in the clearing when she was trying to escape the dimension. But he hesitated at the marsh.

But he came through in the end. He wouldn't have fought her twice now if he was still allies with her, right?

Come to the ritual site with only Mica.

An image of Mica and me walking through a portal to meet Morwen flashes across my mind. The site causes something unpleasant to stir in my gut.

I am about to halt the entire thing when Sarah says, "It's time." As if she conjured it, a sliver of moonlight stretches from the single, slender window on the ceiling, shining right at the door.

Everyone stirs at her words. Cole steps forward, as does Amelia. Oba and Alec remain in the back, though their arms have dropped to their sides in anticipation of something. Mica pushes off the wall, his attention finally moving from me to the shimmering seal.

"Wait," I say, fighting the urge to step away from it all. Everyone seems to tense at my tone, the urgency in it.

Sarah frowns. "We can't. If we don't do this now, we will have to wait another month. The war won't wait that long."

Morwen won't wait that long.

I swallow, feeling every set of eyes on me, Mica's included. But where it was scrutiny just moments ago, it is now of curiosity. *Worry*, even.

"What's wrong?" Cole asks, concern flitting across the hurt still lingering on his face. His gray eyes glisten in the moonlight.

I don't know whether breaking this seal is the right move or not, but there is the slight chance that doing so could help us fight Morwen. Help *them* fight against her, I suppose. I let out a long breath as I say, "It's nothing." And then I wince at my response as Cole's lips press into a thin line.

Cole turns to Sarah and asks, "What do we need to do?"

She pulls out a small dagger from a pouch strapped to her side. It is ordinary in shape and decoration, made of gleaming silver. She must have raided the castle somewhere because she didn't have that on her before. With a quick movement, she flips the dagger, the handle side facing Cole and I. "You both need to spill your blood. Enough to pool in your palms. Let the blood drip to the floor inside the seal. And try not to let the wounds heal until we're done." She steps away when Cole grabs the weapon, refocusing on the grimoire. "While you do that, I will be casting an opening spell. This spell, it was placed here by the King. Only by the two of you could it be broken."

That leaves me with some questions, but because we are on the moon's schedule, I refrain.

If Morwen had ever come to me about this, I would be immediately suspicious of it all. Even with her façade of loving research. Because of my own curiosity, she might have gotten me to go along with it, but opening the door would lead to so many questions. About her, and the Brais, and whatever is hidden inside.

With a nod from Sarah, Cole presses the point of the dagger into his palm and drags it a few inches. I can't help but stiffen at the scent of his blood as it hits my nose the moment it rushes from the wound. Iron and woodsmoke. My magic hums under my skin, ready to fight whatever is hurting Cole. I shove those thoughts down as I take the dagger from him.

The weapon is sharp. It pierces my skin the moment I put the point to my left palm. Gritting my teeth, I press down harder and drag the silvered weapon along my skin. My blood pools into my palm, the sting of the wound a resonating numbness.

Amelia steps up to us and takes the dagger away before returning to the shadows behind.

Beside us, Sarah is chanting, a jumble of sounds similar to Latin, but with a melodic tone. Something reminiscent of what trees might whisper to each other under the soil, or when wind sings through a meadow clearing. Quiet at first, she gradually chants louder, her voice echoing down the corridors. It is a haunting but lovely sound.

At the same time, Cole and I push our bleeding hands

through the darkest part of the flickering veil. With a sensation similar to walking into the portals, our hands pass right through. The sound of our blood dripping to the floor beats to Sarah's chanting, a melancholy symphony.

I can feel the wound attempting to stitch itself back together, so I clench my hand into a fist, my nails digging in to keep the flow of blood. I grit my teeth harder, trying to distract from the pain in my hand.

Moonlight filters through the window, even brighter than before. It must be almost at its zenith now, shining high and bright in the sky. The veil reacts to the intensity of the moon, rippling and swaying vigorously. I want to step away but instead remain firm. Sarah's repeating chant hastens, her words moving at the speed of the swirling veil.

Something invisible grasps at my bleeding palm. Startled, I loosen my fist as I take in a sharp breath. My blood is being *syphoned* from my hand. The droplets hover above me then disappear. My hand turns cold, though the feeling ends abruptly where the veil drapes across my wrist. If Cole is experiencing the same sensations, he doesn't let on. His face is neutral, though he is staring at his own hand.

The air in the room hums, the veil thinning in front of us. Behind it, the door changes shape, revealing symbols carved along its arching border. Sarah was right, the door here is what I saw in that vision. The magic sealing the door acted like a curtain, hiding the shape and all the runes carved around it. Someone behind us gasps as the veil disintegrates, falling to the floor like snow.

Clouds move over the moon, just as the few candles in the corridor extinguish on a phantom wind.

Oba curses and I hear him unsheathe a dagger.

Instinctively, my right hand ignites with my magic, chasing away the frigid shadows that crept over us the moment the light left. The mark glows dimly on my wrist under the light of my flames. Before I can snuff them out, something pulls them from me, like claws scraping at my flesh. The runes around the door glow as they engulf my magic, consuming it hungrily. I can do nothing but stand frozen, letting it take and take and take.

"What's happening?" someone asks frantically, though I can't distinguish the voice over the roaring in my head. My hand feels as though it is being sliced into ribbons. Nausea roils in my gut and my head spins.

The door stops taking my magic, plunging us into darkness yet again. My body trembles at the ghost of the pain. Cole grabs on to me, though I can feel the tremors wracking his body as well. Whatever just happened to me was also happening to him.

A stale coldness sweeps through the corridor. It doesn't come from any flow of air like an open window or Cole's wind. The temperature just drops.

"Mica, please tell me that this is your magic?" Oba asks with trepidation.

"It isn't," the pale-haired vampire responds.

In a brief, blinding light, the runes blaze and a chilling dread filters through me. Cole and I simultaneously step away from the door shielding our eyes. And in the fire of the symbols, the silhouette of a shadowy figure stands before us.

An icy, omniscient voice echoes through the silence. A voice of death. "Good evening, Thea and Cole."

CHAPTER TWENTY-FIVE

THEA

The masculine voice is like frost on my bones. My body wants to retreat, but my legs are frozen in place, consumed by the innate fear this person brings. This god of death. There is no body, just a silhouette reminiscent of a living shadow. His energy slips around my senses, distant but unmistakably powerful. Like the summer hurricane whose winds and rains can be felt hundreds of miles away.

"Who are you?" Cole snarls, though his voice doesn't carry its usual resolve.

Though there is no face, no lips or eyes to peer into, I can tell that this being is smiling. "I am known by many names. But the last person who lived here called me Merikh."

The name slices through my mind like a sword cutting a body. Sharp and unforgiving, destined to elicit terror from its enemies. I whirl around to where Mica was standing, as he is likely the only one who knows who Merikh truly is. Or rather, *what* he truly is.

Only Mica isn't there. Nor are the others. It is just Cole and me, standing here with the god of death. The corridor around us is hazy, like a thick fog has settled in without our knowing.

Merikh snorts. "You will not find them here. It is just us three."

I snap my head back to the shadowy figure, my teeth baring. I will not lose anyone again. I don't care who I have to go through to ensure that. "What did you do to them?"

The death god smiles again. "Curious, that you fear for them, when it is the two of you who stand in the realm of a death god."

Cole's fury slams into me. He manages a step forward, blocking Merikh's path to me should he try anything. It is in this terrifying moment that I wonder how the speed of a god compares to that of a vampire. Would we even register him moving? Or would he cut us down in the span of a heartbeat. I grip Cole's arm.

A sound reminiscent of a chuckle vibrates from Merikh's shadow, sending a shiver skittering down my spine. "No need for any of that. Everyone, including the two of you, are safe. I have to desire to harm you."

"Then what do you want?" I ask, flames crackling on my arm. Not in a hostile display, just one of caution. I swallow at the unnerving observation of Merikh's shadow devouring the light of my magic.

Merikh's figure moves a step closer. Too close for comfort, though neither Cole nor I retreat. "It is more of what *you* want, my dear fire wielder, and how that can help me in turn."

Even with just the silhouette and the glow of his energy, I can tell that he is speaking the truth. There is no deceiving intent in his tone, no spark of malevolence. I'm silent for long enough that Cole's hand squeezes mine. Though he doesn't take his gaze off of Merikh, he says in a low voice, "We can't trust him, Thea. The god is his ally and a *death* god."

I step out from behind Cole. "I think we can." There is a flicker of anticipation that crosses Merikh's calm, icy energy.

Cole is quiet for a moment, but then says, "At least hear what he wants before you decide to trust him."

The death god hums. "You two seek to be free of the King you know as Morwen." He says her name easily, lingering on each syllable as if testing how they taste on his tongue. "In order to do that, you need to be free of this dimension. I can help with that."

"You are not cursed?" I ask, realizing that this is the first time I have heard someone other than Morwen or myself say her name out loud.

Merikh clicks his tongue. "I am a god, Thea." He says that as if it were an answer. "I will help you destroy that which tethers you here," he continues, not allowing any more questions regarding the curse.

"In exchange for what," Cole inquires warily.

There is a slight movement by Merikh's head, suggesting that he is shrugging. He almost reminds me a little of Morwen, and that makes me uneasy. "Morwen sealed me into this barrier." His shadowy arm gestures to the space around us. "For centuries, she has syphoned my power, used it as a catalyst for many powerful spells. The silence curse is one such spell." He pauses, letting that information sink in. I've always wondered how that curse could be so powerful. I wonder if that is why Merikh is immune to it, or if it is simply the fact that he is a god. "By breaking the seal, you have freed me—"

"Free Thea from this dimension, and we are even then."

That chilling smile again, like crystals of ice creeping along my skin. "On the contrary, you two will need more than just your magic and comrades to defeat the King of the vampires. You have tasted her power. Even with all that you have, it will not be enough. You will be slaughtered."

The sight of Cole, of the others, bleeding on some unnamed field, rips at my heart. If acquiring this god's magic means that they don't have to risk their lives, shouldn't it be an easy choice?

"And you can help with that, I'm assuming?" I say flatly.

"I will free you of your ties to this dimension for freeing me of this seal." Merikh moves in slow steps so that he is standing right in front of me. There is an earthy scent to him, like petrichor, that hides his darker parts. The layers of death. They waft through the calming scents of soil and leaves. "To defeat Morwen, I will make you my champion and give you some of my magic," he purrs, letting a sliver of his darkness touch my fire. There is so much power, even in that little piece.

My own magic hums to his. It wants so badly to take his offer, to use his power to annihilate the vampire who has devastatingly meddled in my life for too long. To watch her suffer for each life that she has been responsible for taking. And not just in this lifetime of mine, but all of them.

A wind spears between the god and me as Cole growls. "Just tell us what you get out of this. Stop toying with her emotions."

Amused, Merikh straightens and takes a step back, his magic retreating with him. My fire pouts, sputtering at the emptiness. "Very well. There is more to my desire to bargain with you than just seeing Morwen defeated."

"Naturally," Cole says under his breath.

Merikh doesn't react, he just continues speaking. "After so many centuries of using my power, Morwen developed a *taste* for the power of the gods." He chuckles at his word choice. "She discovered a ritual that would allow her to take my place as a god of death."

A ritual…could he mean the one that I voluntarily signed myself to be a part of? Or is there some other ritual she is planning?

Cole curses. "And what would happen if she succeeded?"

"Many more would die. The two of you included. The consequences of a god dying is great," Merikh says coldly. "Should Morwen succeed, the ritual will kill me. As the creator of vampires, I imagine that every single one would die as a result of my death." The shadow of his head tilts as if in contemplation. "Well, Morwen would not, considering she would then be a commander of death." He adds that last sentence as if he didn't drop a bomb on Cole and me.

"You… created vampires?" I ask, my voice unsteady.

"Yes," Merikh says pointedly, as if stumped that out of all the information he has given us, that is the piece we are stuck on. "But that is a story for another time, I'm afraid. Our time here together is coming to an end. Morwen has siphoned a great amount of my power, and I cannot keep this channel between us open much longer."

Cole runs a hand through his hair. "Say we stop Morwen from performing this ritual, what is to stop anyone else from doing it?"

The god of death shakes his head. "The ritual can only be done by someone tethered to me. There are only three beings who exist that fit that requirement." He pauses for a breath. "Morwen and the two of you."

I stop my jaw from smacking the floor. We are bound to a death god? A wisp of memory floats to the forefront of my mind. My soul knew this. It was why just being in Merikh's presence was so terrifying. Because he is responsible—and likely Morwen with whatever way she became a vampire—for the death of my first life. The moment that tethered me to not just him, but Morwen as well.

Merikh smiles as if he can see what thoughts plague my mind.

Cole says, in a low voice, "Brave of you to tell us a way that would kill you."

Merikh cocks his head. "Is it? I already told you, if I die then so do all the vampires who exist."

"You said you *think* that would happen," Cole corrects.

"If I had thought that either of you would have the gall to sacrifice the other in a ritual to take my place, we would be having a *very* different conversation here." The words are heavy, a warning.

Silence ripples between us and I fight the urge to look at that band on my wrist. Morwen is planning to sacrifice me in order to become a death god. I ball my hands into fists. "We are not like that."

Merikh inclines his shadowy head. "Hence my desire to share that information with you. It would be in your best interest to make sure that the ritual never happens. As it would be in mine." Power ripples from the death god, suffocating and unending. Even with the power that Morwen siphoned from him, he still has so much. "Do we have a bargain, then? I will help unchain you from this dimension as gratitude for freeing me of my prison. And I will loan you some of my power so that you may destroy Morwen."

Cole shakes his head. "No."

"I'll do it," I say, my heart thumping from the unknown of it all. There is a layer of adrenaline with making this deal, taking the power of a god.

Cole takes a step forward, half of his body blocking Merikh. "Thea, you freed him, you don't owe him anything else. We could be trading one tyrant for another."

Merikh doesn't respond, no indication of how he feels about Cole's belief. I look away from the death god and glance to him. Cole's eyes are so pure, so full of determination, glossed with worry and distrust. I place my hand on his cheek. "You just said it yourself. He is free. We unleashed him back into this world, why not use him to destroy one tyrant?" My thumb caresses against the roughness of his skin. I lower my voice as I say, "We will cross the other bridge should we get to that point."

Cole's jaw flexes underneath my palm before he presses his own hand over mine. His fingers lace mine as he pulls them away from his face. I can sense the distaste he has for this plan of action, but there is also a river of understanding flowing through his emotions. He knows that we cannot defeat Morwen as we are. Because we have tried. For centuries, we have tried. He returns to my side, his shoulder pressed to mine as he looks to the death god who watches us with a sort of curiosity. It reminds me of a spider watching an insect as it approaches its web.

"First, tell us how to get out of this dimension, *then* we will accept your bargain and save your life." Cole says the last half of the sentence slower, as if to remind Merikh the power that we have in this as well. Because as the god had said, it wouldn't be in our best interest to let this ritual be cast. But should we die, we would likely be reincarnated, where he will not be.

Merikh's shadow flickers and the pressure of his magic lightens slightly. "My hold onto this world is slipping. There isn't much time." His icy voice sounds more like a trickling stream.

I shrug, the smooth movement a mask against the nervousness. "Then talk fast."

Merikh is quiet for a breath then says, "Very well."

My heart stammers in my chest, the thought of reaching the crest of our hurtle getting closer. Being untethered to this dimension is another step closer to finishing this war. And another step to being able to fulfill the contract with Morwen.

"All dimensions need an anchor. Without them, they would crumble and cease to exist, along with anything and anyone inside. Before Morwen herself became the anchor, it was an object, crafted with the magic that formed the dimension. A piece of art created as if with otherworldly craftsmanship."

"There are rooms filled with art in this castle," Cole says flatly. "Can you be more specific?"

The silhouette of the death god turns to me. "I think she knows."

An image of the library and what awaits in the back

corner, flashes through my mind. "The statue," I whisper, hoping to be wrong.

"The statue of the first vampire," Merikh muses. "I offered Morwen the spell that could transfer the anchor from her back to that object. But it turned out that the spell necessary could only be done by a witch of her old coven's bloodline…" He lets the sentence trail off, goading Cole and me to finish.

Cole crosses his arms, his brows furrowed in uncertainty. "What bloodline?"

Merikh's smile widens, his shadow humming. There is a reason why Sarah's family is afflicted with the silence spell. Cursed with it from birth she told me. There's a reason why her mother was connected to the Brais, why they wanted her dead. And why Sarah felt so determined to finish this fight with Morwen, even if it meant forfeiting her own life. It wasn't just because of what the vampire-witch had done to me, or to her mother. It is for all that has occurred in the past. For the strife and battling between Morwen and the Minuit Coven.

Because Morwen is…

"The Minuit Coven," I whisper, bile rising in my throat. "Morwen was a part of Sarah's coven." It was Morwen who told me that she had created this dimension. But Mica was always under the impression that the Minuit Coven were responsible. I guess we were both right.

"Yes," Merikh confirms in a satisfactory tone. "Morwen made you the anchor because she wanted to get out of here to find an object that would help her with the ritual, keeping you here until she did. She would have waited however long it would have taken, centuries even, but…" Disdain sluices through his darkness. "Time is not in your favor anymore, is it, Thea?"

I glare daggers at him, trying to find words to deny his. The magical ring on my wrist itches as flames appear along my fingers.

"She'll have plenty with us by her side," Cole says.

Merikh says quietly, his shadow looking to the both of us, "Do not willingly sacrifice yourselves."

"I won't let it get that far," I cut in, extinguishing my flames. I look to Merikh, and say, "The answer is yes. Give me your magic so I can defeat her."

Merikh, pleased, straightens and lifts his arm. "Let me see your hand." A sphere of darkness forms above his palm, hovering and unmoving. It almost appears darker than that of his silhouette. "This will be enough for *one* powerful blast of magic. I will warn you," he says as I hold my left hand out for him. "Wielding the power of death, even a borrowed power, may have consequences. They may end up in your favor, or they might not."

"Do it," I hiss.

The death god's approving smile is audible as he says, "Very well." His magic rises from his palm and glides over to mine. In a light that is somehow both as dark as an endless trench of ocean and bright like the guiding north star, it sears itself into my skin and I grit my teeth. When the glow recedes, there is a mark left on my palm, only inches above the burn that represents my induction to the Brais. That day seems so long ago now. Cole and I peer at my shaking hand, at the forth mark to stain my skin after stepping foot into this dimension.

A cross with two half-moons on its horizontal axis, one curved upward, the other down.

"The sigil of death," Merikh croons.

CHAPTER TWENTY-SIX

THEA

The darkness of my room and the sound of Helios purring lulls me into a calmness. The moon's glow pressing upon the slender window reminds me of a time when everything made sense. My mother would be coming in to check if I was asleep, only to laugh that I was pretending, the book clutched in my hand a giveaway of my attempt to deceive. Sometimes she would lie on my bed and read a chapter with me, not even knowing what was happening in the book.

With a heavy sigh, I roll on my back, the bed creaking. Helios gives a short meow of disapproval at my movement, promptly stretching and relocating to his burrow in the closet. His purring continues with the crunching of his food.

I chuckle at the cat's antics as the door opens and Cole slides in. His expression conveys just how exhausted he is. "When this is all over, I desperately want to take a long, maybe never-ending, vacation."

I sit up in the bed, watching him slowly take off his shoes like his body were made of lead. "It went that well, huh?"

After the meeting with Merikh ended, we were sent back

to our bodies, where the others were hovering. The death god was right, we were in his realm while we were talking to him. Our bodies were left on the stone floor of the castle's corridor, leaving the others to believe that we died from that spell. We had no pulse, no breath drawing into our bodies. If we were human, I wonder if we would have never left that death realm with Merikh. After reassuring them over and over again that we were all right, they finally stopped asking. While we were unconscious, they noticed the golden band around my wrist and promptly asked about it. Mica knew what it was, what it meant.

Cole blows out a breath and makes his way to the bed. He lies down and I nestle in next to him, resting my head in the crook of his neck. "Sarah is quite upset about it all. So is Mica." Cole runs his fingers down my arm as he talks. "The others didn't say much after you left, though they agreed that they don't think you should go."

My fingers trace idle circles on his shirt. "I'll defeat her."

"I don't doubt you," he says quietly then pulls me in for a kiss.

A single kiss, turning into greedier ones that result into clothes being torn off and tossed to the floor. I wrap myself wholly around him, my heart and soul. Because when it is Cole and I, everything makes sense.

FORTUNATELY, there is no moon phase requirement for transferring the anchor to something else. Unfortunately, I have to face that statue of Morwen again in order to be free of this place. The library seems colder than it has ever been, darker even, despite the late afternoon sun shining above. Oba is standing beside one of the tables, scrutinizing the sundial like an artist when Cole and I enter.

The tall vampire has his typical weapons on him, all snug in the bandolier across his chest, but opted for a cotton shirt and black pants instead of his leather armor. It makes me wonder if he ever truly relaxes. Though I suppose that during a war, you can't.

"The witch and the wolf are in the back," Oba says in greeting. His usual joyful demeanor has been replaced with an indifferent one.

Cole takes the lead, a half smirk on his lips as he says, "Too afraid to join them, Oba? It's probably a good thing that you didn't, because those ghosts that you are frightened of might find you back there." He jerks his chin to the back, darker aisles of the library. The shadows there seem to slither as if alive.

Oba shoots him a glare but some of his amusement returns. "When this is over, Moretti, you and I are finally going to have a true duel. And when I win, maybe you will stop acting so tough all the time."

"So what are you two calling that fight you had in the foyer?" The grin that Cole gives me over his shoulder eases the cobwebs of nerves along my spine.

Oba remains in the center of the room as the two of us continue toward the back. He calls out to us, his voice reaching all corners of the library, "An unfinished warmup!"

Our laughter chases the rest of the worries away. When we reach Sarah and Amelia, I feel ready to get this over with. Amelia stands, arms crossed, a few feet away from Sarah, who is kneeling before the statue. Sarah's eyes are closed, hands clasped together on her lap. A cerulean blue aura surrounds her, and I can feel its tranquility from where Cole and I wait patiently at the corner of the aisle.

I look to Amelia, wondering how she is doing since her change. Since her death, really. Her blue eyes are sharp and clear, watchful as she stands like a guardian over Sarah. I've noticed that she hasn't said much since being turned, not that I knew her well enough before to compare. She also has a more preternatural air about her, about the way she can stand so perfectly still. She is the only vampire, aside from myself, I have ever witnessed go through the changes. We still haven't discovered what magic she has. Sarah was prompt about creating a sun totem for her, which turned out to be a necklace of a pine needles in resin, that she gave Amelia six months ago.

"Thea," Sarah says in a low, calm voice.

I step forward. "Yes?"

She opens her eyes and parts her hands. Between them is that talisman I saw her wield so long ago, the one with the leaf in the center. A birch tree leaf. "Are you ready?"

I look to the statue, to where the head once was, now only jagged edges. I'm glad the head is gone, or it would be Morwen's eyes always staring back. I imagine Morwen destroying parts of the statue in a fit of rage when she found out that she couldn't transfer the mark of the anchor to it again.

The memory of that vision of Morwen's past haunts me almost every time I close my eyes to sleep. And being here, at the statue again, likely about to place my hands on it, brings back the pain. The flames that encircled me, *her*.

I muster all the strength left in me as I walk a few more steps closer to Sarah. The statue seems to take all that away, though, leaving my nerves trembling. But a reassuring hand on my back warms the chill and my tensions calm. I let Cole's strength pour into me. "Yes," I say.

Sarah stands and offers me the talisman. "Here, when you put your hand on that symbol," she gestures to the chipped circle carved into the chest, "keep the talisman between you and the stone."

"Okay." The golden coin she hands me is hot, charged

with Sarah's witch magic. It seems to hum ever so lightly against my skin like the tiniest of lightning bolts.

Sarah sidesteps so that she is behind me. "When you are ready."

With a deep breath, I press my palm to the statue, trying my best to keep the talisman as a buffer. My body stiffens, expecting the ripples of agony from the vision to take over. But nothing happens. Sarah's talisman almost shifts underneath my palm. It fits perfectly in the circle on the statue's chest, like it was made for that slot.

Sarah puts her hands on my back and her magic rushes into me. It is equal parts fire and ice against my skin. It pours into my body like a floodgate opening, and races to my arms, meeting the coin and statue. I almost gasp at the sensation.

As the anchor, I felt all parts of the dimension as if they were an extension of my body. The spaces that people occupied were like tickles in my mind if I concentrated enough. I can't imagine what that felt like when the castle was full of all those Brais. Now, with Sarah chanting quietly behind me in that melodic language, and the coin vibrating beneath my palm, I feel everything magnify.

Amelia's wolves stand guard in front of the portal on the beach. One of them digs their foot into the sand. The other, in wolf form, is drumming their tail on the beach, sending vibrations into my body.

There are four fires blazing in different hearths within the castle, all of which warm empty rooms.

And in a small room sits a furry cat with his golden eyes set on the forest outside. Helios, as if he can feel my presence, purrs into the quiet of the bedroom.

Then, the mark along my collarbone burns. I grunt against the sting of it, grinding my teeth as I feel it move. Sarah's chanting becomes louder, enticing the mark to keep traveling. It heeds her command, making its way down my arm. It feels like someone is dragging a blade across my skin, tearing me open as it goes.

The bones in my hand feel as though they shatter when it reaches them. The mark cuts through with ease like a drop of water on snow. I think I let out a grunt, unable to grit through the searing pain. Sarah presses her palms harder into my back, urging the mark to keep moving.

And it does. It passes through my hands, the talisman pulling and pushing it into the statue. The second it leaves my body, the agony ceases. My jaw hurts from clamping down so hard.

Sarah's fingers curl around my shoulders, and she lightly pulls me back and away from the statue. I keep the talisman firmly in my grip, noticing that its humming has stopped. Sarah stops her chanting and we both stare at the glowing stone in front of us. Where the empty circle was etched onto the chest piece, now sits a symbol identical to the one that had been along my collarbone.

"Did it work?" Cole asks, stepping to my side. He narrows his gaze as he studies the statue.

"Thea?" Sarah says, though her tone suggests that she knows the answer.

I close my eyes, reaching beyond myself, trying to sense the rest of the dimension. But I can't. My attention only reaches those in this library. Amelia, who is still unmoving, Cole, and Sarah behind me. And Oba in the center of the room.

"I-I can't feel anything," I say with a growing smile. "I'm not the anchor anymore." I turn to Sarah, returning the golden coin to her. "Thank you."

She returns the smile. "Of course." The smile wanes. "Had I known that it would be this simple…I just wish we could have avoided other things." She glances down to my hand. To where Merikh's mark is.

I rub my palms on my pants, almost making myself laugh at the thought of the mark just being erased away. "Me too.

But it is what it is. Merikh's power will help defeat the King."
And if I ever see the death god again, which I have a feeling I
will, I'll have to thank him for getting us this far.

Sarah lets out an exasperated but amused breath of air.
"I'm glad that your optimism has never left you."

I beam at her, relishing in the familiarity of her words.
"My *immortal* optimism." Something reminiscent of hope
blooms in my chest.

CHAPTER TWENTY-SEVEN

THEA

"So remind me why Mica and Alec went ahead of us?" When I was scanning the dimension during the spell, it didn't register to me that I never sensed the two vampires. Understandably so, but I can't help feeling a little bit guilty for not wondering their whereabouts, even after. It wasn't until Oba mentioned them that I realized they were gone.

"Well, since you can't be present during their conversation, they went ahead to meet Isaiah and the other hunters and inform them about all that has occurred," Sarah answers as we step up to the portal. "They left as we were performing the transferring spell."

I touch the archway of the portal, content with feeling nothing from it. "Shouldn't they have been back already?" We severed my connection yesterday afternoon. No one else seems to be worried, but I can't help the unsettling feeling that has built in my gut. Not to mention that Mica has been uncharacteristically quiet toward me since unsealing the door.

Sarah tugs on the lapels of her maroon jacket, sliding the silver zipper up toward her chest. Though the weather here is calm and on the warmer side, once we pass through the portal, it will be the middle of autumn where it is usually a bit cold in Vermont. I decided to wear a sweater, though the cold won't bother me. Nor will it bother the other vampires in our group.

"Mica said they would likely stay there until we arrived, unless Isaiah kicked them out," she says.

The stone archway of the portal is cool to the touch. My finger catches on a chipped, rough piece. Behind the portal sits the seemingly endless ocean. But I know that it only looks that way. The edge of the dimension is not too far out. "I guess that is a good sign since they haven't come back."

Sarah nods her agreement. "I know Isaiah. He won't turn his back on us if we don't turn ours on his." I want to ask her more about how she knows a vampire hunter so well, but she turns to Amelia with soft eyes, a silent conversation passing between the two.

The rest of Amelia's pack are staying behind, albeit begrudgingly. Oba is also staying behind, which was surprising considering how much he enjoys fighting. Not that we are expecting to fight on this trip to see the hunters. Having another person to guard the dimension is comforting. He is rather fond of Helios, though, and despite me telling him that he can visit the cat in my room, he hardly does. I wouldn't be surprised if he spent some time while we were away giving some attention to the orange furball.

Cole had suggested Amelia stay with them, but the wolf alpha disagreed with that by way of snarling. She won't be leaving Sarah's side for a long while.

"Ready?" Cole asks as he steps beside me and hands over a small knife.

I take the weapon, noting how light it is compared to the dagger we had just used. "To get out of this place? Absolutely." Well, we won't be completely free of this dimension, at least not until Morwen is defeated. With only one entrance and exit, it is a tactical place to have a base. Though without my connection to the dimension, it is less safe than before considering I can no longer tell when someone is using the portal.

From my forefinger to the base of my palm, I slice. My blood pools in my hand and I let it drop onto the coarse sands between the two pillars of the portal's arch.

I take in a deep breath, recalling the place that Sarah instructed me to. Since I've never been to the hunter's dwelling, I could only get us so far. Not to mention all the defensive wards along their property that make it impossible for portals to open there.

"*Sol Invictus redit cum duobus.*"

There is enough of a pause between my reciting of the phrase and the ripple appearing that I worry I pronounced something incorrectly. It starts from the center, spinning counterclockwise in inky waves, until the entire portal is a sheer black curtain. By the time the portal is complete, my hand has stitched itself back together.

Cole insisted on being the first to step through. I hold his hand as he disappears, stifling my breath for any signal of enemies. Just the lightest squeeze of his fingers on mine and I will pull him back.

But there is nothing, so I step through next.

The park is just as I remember it, though quieter with the fall of the sun. Standing here, with Cole, feels like that day so long ago, when I learned that my new, undead life was more than just being a vampire.

The kidney-shaped pond is motionless, tranquil as the night approaches. A light breeze sweeps into the park, rustling leaves and creaking the metal swings. It would be eerie if I were human and unable to sense that we are the only ones here. And even though the forest beyond is dark, my eyes see perfectly fine into it.

Behind us, Sarah and Amelia step through. Sarah's hands seem to glow, an aftereffect of her warding the portal in hopes of protecting the others left behind. Should something happen to us here, she might have to break that spell in order to use her power to its fullest.

"All right, where to now?" I ask, scanning the park again, as if there'll be a sign that says, "Vampire Hunter Establishment this way".

Sarah pushes past Cole and me, Amelia on her heels. "This way." She leads us to the stone bridge that crosses the pond, toward a path that disappears into the State Forest.

The wind quiets down, plunging us into the silence of nature. Over the time I spent in the dimension, I missed hearing birdsong and the symphony of insects. But it isn't until right now that I realized just how much I missed it all. A few late evening birds are chirping into the darkening sky, and all around us are singing crickets. I close my eyes, stopping at the base of the bridge, and take it all in. Their songs fill my body, rejuvenating it with such joy and celebration. With a deep breath, I smell the crispness of autumn and let it wrap around me. I can't help but smile widely at the welcoming energy the forest gives. Like that first day I felt it, a pulsing wave of aliveness. Of life.

Cole's hand slips around mine. I feel the curious gaze of Sarah and Amelia, but it is Cole who my eyes lock on to. Smoke swirls in those endless irises, pulling me in. The smile that he gives makes me wish we were alone somewhere.

Cole leans into my ear when we start walking again, making our way across the bridge. "That day we were here, I wanted to hold your hand like this, too." He squeezes my hand in emphasis.

And despite all that we have done together, I feel a heat blooming on my cheeks. "Me too," I confess.

"I know," he says, his grin becoming wild.

We step off the bridge, colored leaves crunching under our feet. "You're a liar," I say through a chuckle. Sarah and

Amelia walk side by side ten feet in front of us, their own arms constantly brushing against each other.

"You couldn't stop staring at my hands. I thought you would bore a hole through them." Amusement glistens on his words.

"I'm surprised you noticed, considering how concerned you were with our surroundings and wanted nothing to do with me." I push my shoulder playfully into his as we enter the forest. There are less birds singing in this area, the darkness already having settled. Even the crickets have mostly ceased their songs, only those closer to the park entrance can be heard.

It is just occurring to me now how the time of day differs here than it did in the Brais dimension. We left when the sun was just past midday, but here, in the real world, it has already gone away for the day.

"That's true," he replies. "But I noticed you. I will always notice you." He brings my hand to his mouth and kisses the back of it, eliciting an army of butterflies in my stomach.

"As touching as your conversation is," Amelia calls out, startling me, "We shouldn't be making too much noise."

Not a second passes after her last sentence when a bone-chilling howl cuts through the air to the north, right in the direction we walk. Amelia's face blanches and she immediately moves into a defensive position.

"Please tell me that—"

"Not my pack," Amelia cuts Cole's plea off, her voice doused in cold rage. "This is my pack's territory. Someone else is encroaching on it." She snarls, a sound that most certainly would not come from a human, or even a vampire.

"Does M—the King work with werewolves?" I ask, really hoping for a no on this one.

"Not that I know of," Sarah answers instead, her tone grave. "But after you all defeated her, who knows what allies she has pulled from the darkness."

Great.

There are two more howls, one to the east and the other to the west. My entire body goes rigid, the hair on my neck standing straight up.

"They have us surrounded," Amelia murmurs. There is fear in her voice, though I don't think it is for herself. Or Cole and me for that matter.

We put our backs to each other just as we catch the first glimpse of a pure white wolf, as large as Amelia's. It darts between trees, a good distance away, in a toying sort of motion. Back and forth, back and forth.

Our wolf ally curses as a black and white wolf, larger than even Amelia's, darts toward us then jukes into the darkness of the forest, somehow vanishing. "It can't be," she says in a trembling voice.

"What?" Cole asks.

Another howl slices through the air. My magic responds, a flame igniting along my arms and hands. A pair of glowing, golden eyes catch in the light of my magic and my heart stammers. The wolf is far enough away that I can't hurl a fireball at it without torching the forest.

"That wolf. M-My father's beta," Amelia says. Her stumbling of words only makes me even more nervous. "Or he was, once. He was banished from the entire western coast territory. He's strong. And so is the pack he created."

A barrier of wind circles us, the trees swaying violently. "I doubt that they are here for anything other than blood, then. The fact that they are here doesn't feel like a coincidence."

"I agree," Sarah says. "We should assume that they are working with the King. Which means that they likely are here to take Thea, and maybe Cole, and are planning to kill Amelia and me."

I step away from my friends as my fire grows hotter. It creeps up to my shoulders and down my back like a cape. "They will not," is all I can say. With a hand of flame, I unsheathe Vitamors. The weapon is humming in my grasp, eager to defend or for bloodshed, I am not sure.

"How many wolves in his pack?" I can hear the churning in Cole's mind as he tries to think of a strategy for survival.

"I don't know. He was alone when he was banished."

A smaller, tan wolf jumps from a shadowy alcove between two trees but gets pushed back by Cole's wind. It retreats into the thick darkness, teeth bared. I reach out for it with my beta ability, a light wisp of magic to sneak through any enemy detection. The small wolf hasn't gone far. Then, I send out my energy manipulation even farther and in a thin wave. It touches the minds of those who are taunting us.

One, two, three… six, seven…ten, eleven, twelve. Thirteen wolves, their energies wild and raging.

And just as I am about to reel my magic back in, it touches the jagged mind of something else, cloaked wholly by that impenetrable darkness.

Cole's grunt pulls my attention back. His magic wanes, the barrier dissolving. I'm about to whirl on him to ask what happened when there is a shift in the air. Like the magic that vibrates around us is being consumed. That large, black and white wolf emerges from the trees, and transforms. A big wolf for a burly human. His square face is hardened with a variety of emotions, though there is a pleased curve to his lips as his eyes scan Amelia. His dark hair is tied into a tight bun at the back of his head. On his hip sits a gun in a leather holster.

A gun. And here I am with a sword.

Amelia's fear soaks into the air as the man steps closer. "Hello, little pup," he says in a deep voice. The light of my flames illuminates a scar that runs down the side of his face, disappearing beneath his shirt. "So far from home, you are."

A bit of Amelia's fear recedes as she snaps at him. "This is *my* territory, Fenrisulfir. Leave, or die."

The man, Fenrisulfir, raises his arms. "I see no other pack. Just you and these scums." He jerks his chin at the three of us.

Cole growls in warning, the sticks on the ground beside him trembling as he latches onto them with his beta ability.

The giant werewolf ignores Cole. "You could join me, little pup." His eyes survey her again, a predatory glaze to them. "My wolf needs a mate. You could have so much power with me."

Sarah bristles on my left flank, her power intensifying as it seems to fuse with the air around us. The earth vibrates under my feet, and I get the sense that I should take a step away.

Amelia's voice is guttural as she snarls, "I would rather be shredded apart." And before I can see it happen, she throws her arm forward, hand clenched in a fist, as a chunk of the ground hurtles to Fenrisulfir's smug face.

With quick reflexes, the massive man jumps out of the way, his eyes round as he rolls. It was too much to hope for it hitting him. "You'll get what you wish for, little pup," he sneers as the air shifts again. And instead of a crouching man, a large wolf stands, deadly teeth pulled back in a growl.

I half expect the wolves to charge at us but am surprised —and confused—when they step back instead. Their gazes shift to the right, eyeing five humanoid figures emerging from the darkness.

Vampires. Brais most likely. As if the wolves weren't going to be enough of a problem.

"Leave Fenrisulfir to me," Amelia says, shifting into her own sheer black wolf. And the two alphas lunge at each other, claws and teeth scraping and snapping.

I let Vitamors bathe in my fire. "Can you two focus on the other wolves? I've got the Brais." Cole and Sarah nod in acknowledgement, though I know the former wants to object. But even he knows that I can take them all. That the real threat here are the wolves and their massive alpha.

And so, I charge at the vampires, flaming sword in one hand and my other a fistful of flames.

CHAPTER TWENTY-EIGHT

AMELIA

The only day of my life that was better than when Fenrisulfir was banished from my father's pack was the day I met Sarah. For the longest time, I would only see this man's face when I closed my eyes at night. I built my way from a lone wolf to the alpha of the Northeast territory. Even then, with all the land and power that I had, I was still haunted by memories of my past.

Then I met Sarah. All it took was for our eyes to meet that day and I felt my sad, broken soul stir with hope.

And here, in this moment, I will fight for her. For myself. For any other person that this man has tormented.

That ambition, that *need* to win, drives me forward. My claws dig deep into the ground as I lunge at Fenrisulfir, my jaw aiming for his snout, his throat, anything that will hurt. He turns, forcing me to a skidding halt. The muscles in his legs twitch and I push myself back, readying for a retaliating bite.

The ground links to my will to evade. I feel myself pour into the earth as it reshapes itself and forms anew into mounds and valleys. With uneven footing, Fenrisulfir changes tactics. With speed only a powerful wolf can acquire, he jukes to the left. I hardly dodge his snapping maw that would have severely cut into my abdomen.

His speed is just like I remember my father's to be. Faster even than the vampires.

But so am I. My wolf greedily takes the swiftness of the vampire side of me, both wanting to destroy this man. The ground beneath my feet pushes back, urging me to move faster, to match his speed.

When he lunges, I pull back, retaliating immediately with a swipe of my claws. He dodges, though I can tell that my increasing speed is surprising him. In a fluid motion, he jumps at me again. There is a flash of light originating from somewhere to my right then a wall of flames hurtling toward Fenrisulfir.

He doesn't even seem panicked by the deadly fire as he gets out of its way. The heat of it stings my eyes, but I fight against it, not wanting to open myself for a blind attack. There are other vampires here, and surely, at least one of them can control the fire element, but I know that this burst was from Thea. She might not have been aiming for Fenrisulfir, but her miss still benefits.

In his leap to evade the flames, the giant wolf landed on the remolded ground. He lets out a noise that is half whine, half growl as his body rolls to catch the momentum of the jump, ankles twisting. Without a second thought, I charge at him, my mouth watering with the thought how his blood will taste as I end him. The ground flattens, my paws gliding seamlessly with each quickened step.

He is right there, lying helplessly on his side and recovering from the fall. One of his legs is bent at an irregular angle. Broken bones don't stop werewolves, especially if a vendetta is involved.

He is right there, the man who tormented me as a child. Made me despise myself.

I aim for the soft flesh of his stomach, my teeth sharper

than ever before. Colors brighten around me, the sound of his beating heart the only thing I hear.

And then something white hot erupts in my leg. My face hits the ground hard, and I can't help the cry that escapes my throat. I skid to a stop, pain lancing down my entire body. A wooden stake juts out of my leg, my blood staining the grass beneath.

A vampire is walking toward me, pulling out another stake from a belt across his waist.

A searing pain shoots up my leg. Vines. Thorny and angry vines wrap around my injured leg, pinning me in place.

Fenrisulfir gets to his feet, and lunges.

CHAPTER TWENTY-NINE

THEA

Even after all the strikes, Vitamors still swings cleanly. The vampires are adept enough to evade my attacks with the blade, though one has fallen to my fire. Out of the five vampires who arrived with the wolves, four can manipulate flames. The other is an earth wielder, like Amelia apparently is. If Sarah was just as surprised as I was about her lover's magical attribute when she threw that chuck of earth at Fenrisulfir, she didn't let on.

The first vampire has succumbed to my fiery attack and is already ashes in the wind. Now, three vampires stalk toward me, their eyes gleaming red. There was a forth vampire, but he has somehow vanished from my view and senses. With these three preparing for a joint attack, I don't have time to think about him.

I wasn't sure if they were working with Morwen or not, but since all of their attempts against me have been nonlethal so far, I am beginning to think they are her allies. One of the stakes cut me across the arm and it left no indication that it is coated in poison. The wound has already healed, but I can feel the stiffness of my dried blood.

I lift Vitamors as the three of them stalk closer, coating it in more of my fire. Finishing them off quickly would be ideal. Even though Amelia claimed to be okay, I want to be available to help her if needed. My attack on one of the vampires just barely missed the alpha wolf. I hope she took advantage of his retreat away from it.

"Let's go. I don't have all night," I say to the three Brais. One of them laughs viciously as their own fire forms in their palm.

His, however, is much weaker than mine. A pitiful flame compared to my inferno. The other two vampires form their own flames. In what is likely an attempt to move too fast for me, they dart out from behind their comrade. Even if their movement is a blur to my eyes, my beta ability can sense their energies. The three of them encircle me now, the heat from their flames pressing against me.

So I let mine burn hotter. I tug the magic from deep within myself, allowing it to engulf my entire body. Their energies mingle, moving together as if they were of one mind. The combined magic barrels toward me, and I release my own. Aware of where my allies are, I unleash my power just enough to swallow the three Brais standing around me.

My magic devours theirs.

One of them tries to jump out of the way, only to be caught in the back. My flames drag him back into the inferno and his screams mingle with that of his two comrades.

CHAPTER THIRTY

COLE

Sarah and I fight with our backs together, keeping the wolves in front of us and not letting them pass. I've fought so many vampires over the decades that I thought I could take on anything. But these past few months have shown me that won't always be the case. Werewolves and gods. Between those two, hopefully the former will be the only thing I have to face off against.

Even though the wolves don't have the magic that the vampires do, they are still tough opponents. Their agility alone is a threat, but combining that with their lethal claws and teeth...

Somewhere behind me, I feel the intensity of Thea's magic. The swirling heat douses me. A few of the wolves shift their gazes at the display, making the poor choice to take their eyes off me. I steal the air from a gray wolf to my left and hurl a stick with my beta ability to another on my right. The stick plants itself in the neck of that tan wolf. There is a gurgling noise as it tries to use its paws to swipe at the piece of wood. Blood spurts down its fur as it collapses.

The other wolf's death comes quieter. As it panics from the lack of oxygen, it shifts back into a human shape. Now, a slender, dark-haired woman is hunched over, clawing at the earth to breathe.

Out of the corner of my eye I see another wolf charging at me, its canine fangs bared. I throw up a hand, a blast of air booming from my palm. But it hardly affects the wolf, larger than the other two. The wolf, another gray one, positions itself like a torpedo, slicing through the gusts of wind that I throw at it.

With Sarah still at my back, I have no choice but to stand my ground. I pull my magic from the female werewolf who is still somehow alive and focus all my energy on my beta ability. With a breath in, my magic tethers itself to the various rocks and sticks littering the ground. And as I exhale, those projectiles are launched upward. The charging wolf, the female werewolf getting to her feet, and one other wolf in the back, are skewered with my makeshift weapons. They drop to the ground, writhing, then become still.

I double over, gasping for breath. Using both my air magic and my beta ability at the same time takes a heavy toll on my body. My hands are tingling with the ghostly impression of those dying wolves. An aftereffect of using my psychic abilities. I flex my hand with the familiar, though harrowing sensation.

I lift my pounding head when a low growl reverberates through the charged air. Another wolf comes to fight, then. It prowls closer to me, glancing at its slain packmates. Gooseflesh forms along my arms at the snarl that follows its morbid discovery. It is a sound of both agony and rabid fury. A pang of sympathy fills in my chest, but I shove it away quickly. I can't be distracted.

Where the other wolves rushed, this new one takes its time. I can see the wheels turning in its head, trying to decide the best course of action. It is likely looking for any opening or weak spot to launch an attack at.

My heart rate quickens with both exhaustion and adrenaline. I need to let my magic regenerate, so I opt for something that won't take too much of it. The wolf leans back on its haunches as I create weapons of compact air, tugging on stores of magic within my mind. Two wind scythes form in both of my hands just as the wolf launches at my unprotected side.

The scythes move, invisible to the wolf. They arc high over my head, the blade coming down, poised to strike the canine in its forehead. I put all my strength into this attack, for that will be what it takes. This wolf is large, its movement and aptitude to strategize an indication of battle experience.

Everything happens so fast.

The pinprick of another's energy barreling toward my unprotected backside.

The giant wolf getting impossibly faster.

I try and shift my right hand so the scythe swings to the back, but my movements are sure.

Something latches onto my leg, forcing me to my knee. The air magic holding the scythes dissipates, rendering me weaponless. Pain lances through my leg.

And then all I see is that large wolf's jaws as they open, aimed right for my throat.

CHAPTER THIRTY-ONE

SARAH

I will never forget the nights spent soothing a shivering wolf shifter. Or the horrid stories she told me as bile came out of her mouth. Amelia was a soul lost to the shadows of this world. And when I first saw her, I knew immediately that I needed to help her. To remind her body and mind that she is safe.

She is power.

And I will defend her with my life.

The ground quakes under the pressure of my magic, bending to my will. It cracks in jagged, endless depths as it races to the four massive werewolves charging at me. Shoulder to shoulder, they run forward in an unbreakable line.

But they don't know who they are fighting.

The medallion in my hand warms as I call upon the lost power of my ancestors. Of the Minuit Coven. The trees shiver to the spirits who heed my call. A ghostly wind races through the forest in their awakening.

These wolves follow a monster of an alpha. They followed him, despite all the death and destruction he brings. They are all no better than the Brais and their King.

And for that, they will all perish.

I let out a bellow of rage as a light explodes from my palms. Pure, white energy races toward them like a cavalry of peace. Of nature's divine vow for balance.

Nature is kind and loving.

But it can also take and destroy. For the purpose of equilibrium, it devastates those who cast shadows.

Like the protector and nurturer Mother Gaia, who sprouted the trees and forged the rivers with her pure, earthly power. I feel it in my blood. Her raw magic flows from the pockets of the slumbering earth, through the roots and rocks and sticks. It touches my feet and floods into my body, creating the light of the Mother that burns from my palms.

It disintegrates the four wolves in my path.

Sweat beads from my forehead, my body trembling from the rush of ancient magic. I look upon the field where the werewolves were. There is nothing. No bones or fur or teeth. No clothes or hair had they thought transforming might help. There are imprints of where their claws dug into the ground with each step forward, though they stop with no indication of their maker turning.

They vanished, as if they never were.

I can't help the slight smile that tugs at my lips, at the power I can wield. A part of me wants to march to the King right now. To keep Thea and Amelia and all the others from risking their lives.

But I made a promise to Thea. That we would do this together.

The medallion turns cold in my hand and I open my palm to say my gratitude. My heart stops at what I see. At the sliver of a crack that runs from the top of the imprinted leaf to the base.

This coin that has been passed down from generations. My mother gifted this to me when she declared me the heir of the coven.

Hot tears prick in my eyes at almost having destroyed it.

This piece of history that holds so much of my ancestors inside. The only object that lets me feel their presence. I almost lost it.

And then I look to the ground. To where it split open, allowing the raw magic to flow into me.

The price of using such magic.

A scream echoes into the night, shattering my heart even more. My feet are moving before I even look. But I know it was Amelia.

Before I can even scan the area to see if she is okay, something stops me. It is cold and unfamiliar. There is a burning sensation from my stomach. Then, numbness.

I look down to see the tip of a blade, coated in blood.

So strange to see it like this.

"Death to the Minuit Coven," a callous, feminine voice says into my ear.

And then that blade is pulled free, and I collapse to the ground.

CHAPTER THIRTY-TWO

THEA

I know that people die during battles. During wars fought for peace. Sometimes I wonder if there is a god-like being who whispers in the ears of lesser beings, inciting their fears and forming a black pit of hatred. They'll choose the malleable ones who have experienced loss in their lives. Where all it will take is a little push, or nudge in the right direction—or wrong direction in this case—and chaos will ensue.

Because for all of my life, I could never fathom how people can hate others so much that they would start deadly wars over it.

Sometimes I hear those wicked whispers. After my parents were killed, and after Valeria. But perhaps it was because I had others in my life who chased those whispers away, that I never truly succumbed to them.

But what happens if those people die, too?

They came from nowhere. It was like they were covered in a cloak that rendered them invisible. A horde of vampires, more wolves, and a witch. I saw it all. It happened within a single blink.

We were winning. I defeated the vampires. Cole finished

the wolves attacking him. And so did Sarah. Amelia, with a thrust of her massive paw and a thrum of her vampire powers, took down the rogue vampire attacking her. And Fenrisulfir was down.

Was.

Now he is standing on all fours again, his jaw around Amelia's bloody snout. Her body is trembling as it slowly falls to the ground, the massive alpha not relenting.

And Cole and Sarah…

Another wolf has its jaw around Cole's throat, a second one clamped onto his calf. Cole's hands are wrapped around the first wolf's jaws, trying to pry them off. Blood runs down his hands and arms, staining his clothing and the grass.

My feet won't move. There is nothing holding on to them or pinning them, yet they do not move.

Sarah is on the ground, her hand clasping at her abdomen. Blood…so much of her blood. It taints the air, wafting all the way to where I am standing. Spiced honey, a tantalizingly sweet and spicy aroma. I blink and the scent is unnoticeable. All I know is my best friend, my sister, bleeding out under the stars.

Standing above her is Alain, the witch who betrayed Sarah and the Minuit Coven. Blood and dirt mar her ivory skin, that small birthmark under her eye just barely visible. A bloody shortsword is grasped in her gloved hands. Blood, Sarah's blood, drips from the sword's point and into the grass. Alain is staring down at Sarah with such disdain.

As if a command was sent to my brain, the only thing my body knows is that it wants to break that witch's neck. My fingers twitch as I rush at the vile witch.

Alain turns when I bellow at her in a grief-filled rage. She stumbles in surprise, but I see her hand raise. And then the stabbing pain in my head threatens to bring me to my knees. I see Natalya's twisted face. The witch who was the first to try and turn me in to the Brais. The first person I killed. I force myself through it, the pain and the memories, my feet moving slower, but still pushing on.

She lifts the bloody shortsword at me, a slight tremble to her stance. Blackness seeps into the outskirts of my vision, and I struggle against the pain in my head. My teeth grind against each other, my fangs tearing into my lips as I snarl.

My body is burning. The magic in my blood boils, radiating to each cell within. It is almost too hot for even me. The heat clears some of the pain and I take a full step toward the witch.

One step. Then another.

Fear drenches her scent, calling to that primal part of me. I can see the vein in her neck pulsing faster and faster from it. The grip she has on my mind recedes. And I use all the vampiric strength and speed I have to lurch at her. I want nothing else than to rip into her throat. To see her blood, to taste it.

But something slams into me while I am in midair, knocking me to the ground. The force of the blow causes me to drop Vitamors. My head collides onto something hard enough that the world spins. Something large and covered in fur stands on my chest. Claws dig into my skin and draw blood.

"Don't kill her," I hear Alain hiss. Her voice is thunder in my ear, though sounds far away at the same time.

I try to blink away some of the fog, but nothing happens. The treetops around me blend with the night sky, the stars swirling in circular motions.

"I've got her. Go finish off the others."

I flinch at Alain's voice. Why is it so loud? The weight on my chest doesn't move. Hot air brushes onto my throat in puffs.

"Fenrisulfir!" Alain yells, making my head feel as though it were splitting in two.

And, finally, that weight lifts itself off of me. I take a

gasping breath, wincing from the sharp agony of filling my lungs. I groan as I tilt my head. Why am I not healing? Vitamors. I need my sword.

Focusing on my sword hand, I flex my fingers.

Nothing happens. Over and over I try and summon the sword, but it doesn't come.

I need to help the others.

I delve into my well of magic. But even that has gone dry. My body is trying desperately to take control of healing. But it is all moving so slow.

Alain enters my vision. I must still be dazed, because though there is only one of her, she now holds two blades. She holds one of them up. "Looking for this?"

Vitamors.

A hateful smile cuts across her face. "I can't kill you, but I also can't have you getting up and ruining everything." She grips Vitamors and plunges it into my stomach. I feel it slicing through tissue and muscle before it imbeds itself into the ground underneath me. A pained gasp escapes my lips, eliciting a sharper curve on hers.

Alain crouches next to me. "I hated you, you know. I always have. Through school and after. You weren't even a part of our coven, and yet, Sarah would always talk about you. Then I met Morwen." The name slices through me, another wave of unending pain. I don't know if it is the name itself or if Vitamors remembers who once wielded it and now it trembles at the thought of her. "I swore to her then that I would aid her until my dying breath."

I grip the blade of my sword, its edges cutting into my palms. With sluggish effort, I try and pull it out of me. To give her that dying breath of hers.

I bite back the pain as Vitamors moves upward, carving at my insides as I pull.

Alain watches my struggle for a moment before putting

her hand on the pommel of Vitamors and pushing it back down.

She leans down and hisses, "You think you have an idea of what she is going to do to you during that ritual? You don't." She straightens, twisting the sword.

I grunt, blood pooling in my mouth.

"And when she's done with you, she'll break your friends. Anyone who would call you an ally. She'll rip—"

Hot blood sprays on my face. Alain's hand releases the sword and rises to her own throat, grasping at something that certainly shouldn't be there. A crossbow bolt. A gurgling sound finishes her sentence. Then, her eyes roll to the back of her head, her fingers still trying to make sense of what happened as she collapses.

I grip the sword again, afraid that whoever did that to her might try and shoot me too. Or one of the others. If they're still alive.

I hear the sounds of frantic shouting as something fiery appears at the top of my vision. No, not fire. A head of vibrant, red hair. Someone pulls Vitamors out from my body and I cry out. A gentle hand presses on the wound from the sword and a familiar warmth tingles from it into me.

The shouting quiets, and soon, I realize that the person kneeling beside me isn't yelling but talking. I blink, my vision steadying, and familiar features come into view.

My lips tremble as I try to make out the word. At the real-ization of who is beside me, not dead.

"Shh," the woman coos. Her soft brown eyes crinkle in relief at the wound she is looking at.

"Riley," I whisper.

She smiles, the sight warming me to the core. "Hello, Thea." She lifts her hand from my stomach, the other releasing a stone dangling loosely from a chain around her neck.

All dizziness gone, I sit up, wincing at the remnants of pain in my head. My body tingles as it stitches itself back together. "You're alive." After finding out about Morwen, I was sure that she had sent Riley somewhere to her death. The grief in my chest at saving Riley from the Brais, just to have Morwen send her through the portal to a new torment was hard to endure.

But then, I remember where we are. What just happened. The forest floor is littered with the bodies of the wolves, the vampires having decayed or turned to ash from my magic. Questions race through my mind, but all I can ask is, "How?"

She wraps her fingers around her necklace. "That portal sent me to upstate New York, like I wanted." She swallows, squeezing the stone harder. "I found my family again. Thanks to you."

I put a hand on hers. "I'm glad. But, Riley, how…why are you *here*?"

Maybe Alain did kill me. Maybe I'm seeing Riley because Morwen killed her and we are reuniting in death. I look to my hand, noting that Merikh's sigil is still there.

"My family and I, we… I am a vampire hunter, Thea. I was returning with a group when we came across some were-wolves who wanted to eat us. We fought them and came across all of you as a result." She glances to our surroundings. "The surviving wolves fled when we arrived. We were able to heal any severe wounds on your allies."

Words have escaped me. I cannot respond to anything that she has told me, too stunned at all of it. *Vampire hunter.* Just like my family.

I follow her gaze and look around. My eyes land on Cole and I am instantly standing. He is shrugging off who I believe is another vampire hunter when our eyes meet. The adren-aline flooding my veins slows as I look him over, noting the lack of injuries with a deep relief. His lips curve slightly into a smile that warms my heart as he looks me over. Something dark crosses his features when his gaze drops to my shirt, to where my blood stains the clothing. But I step toward him and, as if on a tether, he steps moves to me. We run to each other, our bodies melding together as we hold on. Neither of us say anything, we just stand there, pressed against each other with the remains of what happened around us.

After Chaos Comes Nirvana, I would call this painting. Despite what we just went through, I can't help but feel that tiny spark of hope, brought on by something as simple as remembering my love of drawing and painting—something that I haven't done since joining the undead population.

Cole places his hands on my cheeks and brings me into a kiss. A kiss that I relish, absorbing every beautiful moment of.

We break away when more sets of arms wrap around me. Sarah and Amelia hug both of us. We stay like that for a few moments, until one of the hunters steps toward us, clearing their throat.

"We should get to the safety of our manor," he says. "There could be more hiding in the shadows."

CHAPTER THIRTY-THREE

THEA

The vampire hunter's manor is tucked deep in the woods of the mountains within the border of my hometown. It isn't where they usually live, though Isaiah won't give out that information, of course. "We've been tracking the Brais King for years now. This was the first place where his… scent was the strongest," Isaiah says once we all settled into the living room of his manor. Between all the hunters living here, we were all able to find clean clothes that fit.

Cole and I are sitting on the single, brown couch, Riley next to me. Sarah and Amelia are resting on one of the cushioned benches beside the bay window. It looks out upon the forest that stretches far beyond the property. Mica and Alec, who were very worried when we all arrived covered in dirt and blood, stand against the wall opposite the couch, beside a fireplace with a small flame. Isaiah took up a seat in a large chair that faces the entirety of the room.

"It wasn't until I met up with the General that I realized the scent was actually you." Isaiah jerks his chin at me. He rests into his high-backed chair, looking all the part of a man in charge. The fireplace sits behind him, its light causing shadows to dance across his sharp features. They illuminate the scar along the left side of his face. He wears a navy blue t-shirt that shows off his tattooed muscles. Around his neck is a golden medallion with a circle etched into it. The lamplight flashes against it as he repositions himself. "If he and I didn't have a truce, I would have cut down all the Brais who captured you." Behind him, Mica and Alec share a grimace.

I swallow, placing the glass of water down on the small table in front of me. "Amaund had said you were chasing after me."

Isaiah studies me with those chocolate-brown eyes. "We were. But I thought you were someone else."

I almost say her name out loud. "The King," I whisper. Beside me, Riley flinches.

"We realized you were not when we found you captured by the General and his crew."

My gaze flicks slightly upward, to where Mica stands. He is watching me, his expression wholly unreadable. I debate reaching out with my beta ability, but I don't know if vampire hunters can sense that. Sense a vampire using their magic. In fact, I have no idea what hunters are capable of at all. They can heal, as Riley said. And I know that at least Isaiah can create some type of soundproof barrier. And then there is the fact that they have impeccable aim with their crossbows. I shove away the sight of the bolt sticking out of Alain's neck.

"You mentioned knowing my parents. Did you make that connection before or after you saw me that day?" I put my clammy hands on my knees, hoping that no one notices how nervous I am for this man's knowledge.

A door opens down the hall, the click of it closing echoes into the room. Alec glances in that direction briefly before returning his attention to the hunter.

Isaiah doesn't take his eyes off of me as he says, "After." He narrows his eyes. "There is a resemblance, but it wasn't noticeable to me at first. Until we came across you, I felt mostly the same magical signature of the King. But when I was closer, I felt something else. It was so familiar, yet I could not place it."

"When did you?" Cole asks in my stead. His hand finds mine, and I send him a silent plea of gratitude. A log in the fireplace cracks as Sarah places her glass of water on the side table.

Isaiah takes a steady breath. "I visited their house. Your house, Thea."

A coldness seeps into my body. I sense Sarah tensing at the mention of my family's home. To where her mother died and where I burned her body. Cole squeezes my fingers, light enough that I doubt anyone else could take notice.

A light wind howls outside, causing a branch to scrape against the bay window where Sarah and Amelia sit, their bodies so close together.

Isaiah's jaw tightens slightly. He runs a hand over the stubble along his chin, the sound scratching in my ears. "I was…surprised to see it in the state it was in." He watches me, no hint of judgement in his gaze. "But I felt that same signature, and immediately, I knew who you were. I can't believe I didn't recognize it then, and I am deeply ashamed of letting them take you. I fell to my knees at that crumbled house and wept for you. For them." An acknowledging silence rippled through the room. "I used to be good friends with your father, Thea. Him and Juan."

My professor from college. Unlike Mr. Esposito, I never knew Isaiah, though. My father never even talked about him.

"After you were born, your father and mother quit hunting vampires, but I didn't. I respected their decisions and wanted to keep any danger from finding them, so I detached myself from all ties. I tried to get Juan to do the same." Isaiah chuckles, though the sound is anything but joyous. "He was the reason why I believed that some vampires were worth allying with. Worth befriending, even."

Cole exhales a long breath. "Then did you know what

became of him?" he asks gravely. A clock in the corner of the room chimes its hourly song. It sounds sad in this moment, as if time itself was grieving the loss of Mr. Esposito. It is only nine at night yet feels so much later.

Isaiah nods solemnly. "Another piece of information I learned shortly after discovering who you were, Thea. I found out that the General killed one of my oldest friends." A cloud passes over his expression. "I fell into a sadness after I found out. I think," he pauses, "I think if it weren't for you, I might have changed my opinion on vampires.

"But when I was kneeling before your house, I promised to your parents that I would look after you."

I close my eyes for just a breath, letting the silence be a comfort. I can almost feel my parents sitting beside me, as if we were visiting my dad's old friend and having a chat together. When I open my eyes, I lean forward and say, "Then will you help us? Help us defeat the King?"

Isaiah doesn't move, his unwavering gaze fixed on me. There seems to be an endless world moving about in his mind, as if he were taking each second that passes to contemplate his answer. He reaches into the pocket of his jeans and pulls out a circular, amber stone. "This was your father's medallion. All hunters get one eventually." Sadness and nostalgia flash across his aura as he gazes at it momentarily before offering me the necklace. "For as long as you will allow, I would be honored to be your ally."

My heart warms, even as I reach for that necklace with a shaky hand. "And I, yours." The necklace chain seems to pulse in my hands, like my father is reaching out, letting me know that he, too, has my back in this.

But that I will always know.

Both my parents will always be with me.

"So," Cole says, breaking the silence. "Since Thea has vampire hunter blood in her, will she be able to use this like you do?"

"Honestly," Isaiah answers, "I don't know. It's possible that she can get some power from it, but I've only ever known a hunter's medallion to answer to the one it was summoned for."

"Summoned?" I ask, running a finger along the amber stone's smooth edges.

It is Riley who answers this time. She lifts her hand to the stone that hangs from her neck, letting it rest in her palm. "Vampire hunters go through a rite in order to receive our medallions, which is where our true powers come from. During that rite, we face off against our deepest fears. And for those who succeed," she gestures to the stone in her palm. "No one knows where they come from, but our medallions form from nothing."

I wonder what my father went through to receive this stone. Whatever it was, he conquered it. I will take that strength with me wherever life leads. "What happens to the medallion after the hunter is gone?" I loop it around my neck, letting it hang so that that stone rests against my heart.

"They become only keepsakes. Eventually becoming trinkets and then maybe even antiques. The medallions never bond to another hunter," Isaiah says coolly.

"I MOURNED YOU," I whisper into the cool night air. After a few hours of rest, Riley and I stand on a balcony off the main hall of the manor's upper level. When dawn arrives in an hour or two, we will depart, leaving the hunters here in their cavity of safety. When we call for their aid in the fight to come, they will answer.

"I know who it was who helped me escape that night. Aside from you, that is," Riley says in an equally quiet voice. Our arms brush against each other as we lean over the banister. Below us is a garden, the plants mostly transitioning into their slumber for the colder months. A small pond sits in the center, its water quiet like the rest of the night.

I stiffen at her words. Is she saying that she knows that Morwen is the King? I look to her, surveying for that mark that curses her into silence. Into submission, never to fight against the one who imprisoned her. But she shakes her head. "That night I escaped, I know that the woman with the black hair and beautiful face was the King of the Brais. I am not cursed like Isaiah is. Like so many others are." Still, she rubs at her neck, as if she, too, can feel the curses inevitable strangling hold. She lets out a long, pained sigh. "I told you that I was sent to New York. That I found my family."

I nod. "Is Isaiah your family?" A lightness touches me. I'd like to think that she and I are related almost, like Sarah and me are. Not bound in blood, but in the love and friendship of life.

Riley glances at the sky, the colors changing to a blue in the rising sun. "He is my only family now."

And quickly, the lightness is gone. Not because I can't think of her as a relative but because of the implication of her unsaid words. Something happened. Something bad.

"I went through that portal and was sent to New York like I wanted. But it wasn't to my family. I think the King thought you would find me and rescue me. Or that someone would." Her fingers shake as they move to her medallion. I wait for her to continue, if she wants. "I walked through that portal into a familiar room, only to find everyone that I ever knew to be dead."

That cold, numbing dread howls in my ears. My heart breaks for her.

"Isaiah told me that my family never stopped looking for me. And they stumbled on a vampire who knew the King. And then, with the King's orders, that vampire slaughtered everyone. And he let me escape, knowing that I would likely choose to go home, to my parents and siblings. I left them all like that and ran."

I put a hand on hers that grips the wooden banister so hard it's a wonder it isn't cracking under the pressure.

She takes a deep breath. "I think some vampires were following me, because the moment I reached the town's borders, I was surrounded." Her hand loosens its grip on the wood. "But then I remembered you and your kindness. I remembered that you were still fighting in that castle. At least, I hoped you were. I didn't know if you were killed after that night." She turns her attention to me, her gaze teary-eyed but clear. "I channeled your strength and fought them. I fought them with all that I had. That was the night that I received my medallion. Isaiah found me long after they were dead, and I was just sitting there lost and alone."

"I'm sorry." It is all I can think to say right away. But then I add, "You saved me in a way that day, in the castle. Getting you out of there renewed something in me. I just wish that something better was waiting for you on the other side of that portal."

She leans against me, her hair smelling of roses. "I do, too. But I am glad to have met you, and I am grateful for you getting me out of there, despite everything."

"My father used to say, 'no risk, no reward'. I didn't know who the King was that night, didn't know that everything I was doing he was already privy to, but I took the risk that day to get a suffering person out of a desolate, unforgiving dimension. And you risked your life when you decided to put up a fight against those vampires who followed you."

"And our reward is being here, right now, together. I am so grateful for you, Thea," she finishes. Her light brown eyes twinkle in the porchlight.

"Yes," I say, smiling. "You saved me back there. I can't even truly express how grateful I am for you either, Riley."

Riley shrugs, her shoulder brushing against mine. "Now we are even."

We stay quiet for a while, listening to nature as it slowly awakens from a night's rest. Birds start their chirping, the trees waving with their fluttering movements. My father's words ring through my head, over and over and over again.

No risk, no reward.

CHAPTER THIRTY-FOUR

THEA

Time rushes by in a blur of training with the other vampires, researching with Sarah, and bonding with Cole. If an impending doom wasn't hanging over our heads with every day that ticked by, everything might have been a little more pleasant. Every time the sun sets and is replaced with the moon, a little sliver of panic sets into my bones. Three nights ago, it was a half moon, which means tonight's is going to be a waxing crescent. I only have a few more nights until I have to meet Morwen at the ritual site.

We haven't had any luck with even getting a whiff of where Morwen is. No base of operations or attacks that might lead us to her current location. With each failed attempt, more fear wedges its way into my heart. Fear that our final confrontation will indeed be on that ritual ground.

"I'm thinking somewhere like Iceland," Cole says, his voice reverberating into my body. The stars are shining merrily above our heads, the moon having not made an appearance yet.

Every night, after a long day of research and training and tactics, we have come out here and enjoyed each other's company under the stars and away from the others. I tried to get Helios out here with me, but he wanted nothing to do with any part of the dimension other than his room. I don't completely blame him, though. The room that Cole and I moved into is more spacious than the other one, and even has a small fireplace. Helios loves curling up in front of it when there is a fire blazing.

I chuckle, tucking my hand under my chin as I rest on his chest. "You think I would want to go to Iceland after all this is over?"

Most of our conversations have been about what will come after. A part of me knows that Cole does this because he is trying to make it a reality. What will happen in the next day or two freezes me to the core with fear. Talking with Cole about topics like this warms that part of me just a little. At least until I see the moon hovering overhead.

He props his palm under his head, kissing the top of mine in the process. "It's a pretty place," he says, as if I truly need convincing to visit that country. "I went there after revisiting my home in Italy. Have you seen the aurora borealis before?"

"I think most people just call them the Northern lights," I laugh into his chest. "But no, I haven't. I would like to, though."

"It's settled, then."

The stars twinkle, uncaring about the false world they shine for. But then again, maybe they are made from magic as well. The moon must be creeping to a place above our heads, because there is a bit of its glow at the top of my vision.

"But what about you?" I ask. "Where would you like to go?" A light breeze rustles the leaves around us and a corner of the blanket we lie on flaps in its caress.

Cole's hand brushes a lock of hair away from my face that the wind displaced. His fingers on my skin are like lightning. "I've already visited so many places."

I lift my head, looking into the gray of his irises. "Cole…"

"Don't," he whispers, his fingers tracing the curve of my

jawline. I lean into his fiery touch. He rises and props himself on his elbow so that we are eye level. The hair along his chin is a bit longer than it has been. A lock of his dark hair brushes against his forehead in the night's gentle wind. "It'll happen," he says. "After everything that has happened, we will finally get our time together. I can feel it. No immortal soul tethered to ours destined to kill us. No curses."

"But if—"

"Nothing," he interrupts, his thumb pressing against my lips. "It'll just be you and me. For as long as the earth is beneath your feet and the stars above your head, remember?" His thumb tickles my lip as it drops to my chin.

"Yes," I breathe, and then I kiss him.

Our lips crash together in ecstasy. I drink him in like I haven't had a meal in years. If our bodies together were a thunderstorm, his lips are the lightning bolts. Each kiss is revitalizing. His lips part, inviting my tongue to meet his. He cups the sides of my face and slowly repositions us so that he is pressed against me, the ground beneath my back. His head blocks the view of the moon that shines above. And for as long as we lie there together and our limbs entwine in each other, I can't see the moon and its taunting phase.

A VIBRATING pressure on my chest wakes me up. I open my eyes to see little Helios curled on top of me, his purring soothing my heart. The moment I move my hand to pet him, he lifts his head, letting out an adorable little noise. "Good morning, boy," I say, scratching under his chin. He stretches his head, enjoying every moment of his morning scratches.

Cole stirs beside me, lifting his head and kissing my arm. "Good morning."

I smile at his sleepy voice. "I was talking to Helios."

"Oh. Well, I'll just go back to sleep then."

Helios stretches, his paws reaching to Cole's back. "Yes, back to under the covers so you can brood."

"I don't brood," he retorts. Cole grunts as Helios steps off of me and onto his back before jumping off the bed.

"You don't? Because that looks an awful lot like brooding to me." I pull the covers off him, revealing his sculpted back. His muscles flex with each breath. I get the sudden urge to kiss every inch of it. To taste him, kiss after kiss.

Cole snaps his head toward me, only to find me staring at his bare skin. "What were you just thinking about?" His gaze turns hazy.

"About doing this." Ever so gently, I kiss his back, starting at his shoulder blades and moving downward. He hums, almost moaning at each one. "And maybe a bit of this." I let my fangs come out, and I lightly sink them into his skin.

"Hey." He flips over, pulling me with him so that my chest is against his. He presses his lips to mine, running his tongue over one of my fangs. A droplet of his blood lands on my tongue, igniting a fire in my center. My body shivers from the desire, a low gasp leaving my lips. I remember the night we were searching for Sarah and Valeria. When his blood healed poison in my body. It was the first moment that I felt that deep connection to him.

At least in this lifetime.

Reluctantly, I pull away from him. "I promised Sarah I would meet her after sunrise."

"I know," he says with a smirk.

I narrow my eyes at him. "You are a tease."

"It was worth your reaction." His husky voice threatens to undo me. "We'll just have to save it for later," he adds.

Yes, later. I'll tuck that promise into my heart.

Before I cancel plans with Sarah, I huff a breath and get out of bed. Cole remains half under the covers, watching me throw clean clothes onto the floor. "Are you training with Oba this morning?"

"Yeah. I think Alec and Mica are joining, too." He rests his head in his palms, and I look away from how it shows his muscles. The small whorls of his tattoo just barely show on his right arm, hidden by the pillow. "We are trying to see if our magic will combine somehow."

"What do you mean?"

He shrugs and sits up. "I saw three vampires do it once. But they all used fire magic. I don't know if it'll be possible with all of ours."

Satisfied with the jeans and sweater I pulled out from the bottom of my closet, I kick the other clothes back in. "That would be impressive." My father's medallion hangs from my neck as I wrap my hair in a bun. Helios nudges my leg and I reach down to give him a hug, kissing the top of his furry head. "Don't tire yourself out too much," I say over my shoulder. "We can work on your sword skills later."

"I would love to," he says, sketching a bow, though he is still in bed. I toss a clean sock at him and relish in his laugh. In the way that it skitters across my skin. "What?" he asks, a smile still plastered to his face.

"Nothing," I say, walking over to him.

"Liar," he mumbles onto my lips before kissing me deeply. His hand grips my waist, releasing it once I pull away and walk toward the door.

"I love you," he says.

I smile back, my heart equally warming and turning cold. "I love you, too."

"So, why are we out here, in the rain?" Mica asks, holding his hand in the air to stop the droplets from reaching his head. Wouldn't want to get his hair wet. His attitude toward me over the last week and a half has gotten significantly better. I still have no idea why he had suddenly closed off, and when I ask, he denies it all.

I lift a shoulder, tucking my necklace under the rain jacket. "I wanted to take a walk."

He gives me a skeptical look but doesn't say anything. We walk side by side down the main path from the castle. Mica expands his magically-induced umbrella so that the rain doesn't fall on my head. "It's raining," he adds.

"I'm aware."

"I thought you were meeting Sarah this morning." An icy wind rushes between us. I'm not sure if the temperature is natural—well, as *natural* as it can be in a place made from magic—or if Mica is trying to get under my skin. Likely the latter.

I step over a large puddle. "I didn't feel like sticking my nose in any more books."

Mica hums.

I grit my teeth, trying my best to ignore his jabs. After a moment of silence, I say, "Do you think we can win this?"

The temperature drops just a fraction and I know it was because of him. "I'd like to hope that we can." He sighs, a puff of breath clouding around his mouth. "In all the years that I have known the King, there has never been a group as strong as this to oppose him. You made this possible, Thea."

"All these allies would have come together eventually," I suggest, mostly because I don't want to think about my part in it all.

Mica blows out a breath. "I honestly don't think they would have. Sure, each group has been fighting against the King, but never has there ever been a move to do it together. As stupid as that sounds." The rain lightens and Mica releases his magical barrier, resting his arm at his side. "The Essites have always been a force against the Brais, but once Kael killed their King, they figured the war was lost.

"It is obvious that the vampire hunters targeted the King,"

Mica continues as we step over a rather long puddle. Pieces of moss have washed away from a nearby tree and are floating in the water. "And the witches have had their history with Morwen for the longest. The werewolves are newer players, and had it not been for Amelia and Sarah meeting, I doubt the wolves ever would have involved themselves."

A round, tan rock sits in my path and I kick it, watching it skip far down the path, stopping when it reaches the edge of the forest. The portal stands only a few hundred feet away. With time running low, we pulled all our allies to the castle. At least, the ones willing to stay in a vampire-created dimension. The archway on the beach stands unguarded. Morwen wouldn't waste her time trying to get to me now, not with the new moon only a day away. "Too bad Amelia's father didn't hear about everything that happened. Maybe his pack would have fought for her, giving us another ally."

"Allies mean nothing if, in the end, you've always planned on going about things alone."

I look at him, frustration and embarrassment crossing my face. "You knew." I lose a breath and dig my toe into the dirt. "The contract never said I couldn't go early. Figured I might stand a better chance at surprising her. And, at least I know my friends will live."

Mica faces me, his green eyes tinted with so many emotions as usual. I can never quite sense what he is feeling, though. This one time, I want to know. My beta ability stirs in my palm and I let it float to him. It doesn't reach him before he says, "You can just ask, you know. How I'm feeling. What I'm thinking about." He glances to my hands, as if he could see that pulse of energy manipulation. I gawk at him, stunned into silence. "I've lived with the King long enough that I can tell when that ability is coming out to play."

That ability. I reel it back in, more embarrassment creeping up my neck in hot waves. "I'm sorry," I say sheepishly.

"It's okay. I suppose, if I had that ability, I would be doing the same thing." He turns to the portal, to the beach beyond. The waves lap at the shore in a never-ending dance. "Though, to be honest, I think that is how the King lost most of his humanity. He never tried to connect with others, just simply aimed to be commanding over them. But maybe, when you live as long as he does, it is hard to feel that connection."

Focusing on how long Morwen has been on this planet, how much she has experienced, is not a conversation I want to be having at the moment. Still, I say, "Maybe so. But think of all the connections she could have made, if she tried."

He contemplates my words, his gaze landing on the rock I kicked. "True. And that, Thea, is why I haven't told you to turn back and forfeit your quest for solo vengeance. It is because of all the connections that you made, that you are stronger. You fight not just for yourself, but for them. And that is why I truly think you will win in the end."

I narrow my eyes at him. "You aren't mad that I'm going behind everyone's back?" I brace myself, ready for him to haul me back. If he does, I wouldn't be able to fight him on it. I need him to bring me to the ritual site.

He moves his head side to side, weighing his responses. "I can't really judge you on that. It's either admirable, or reckless, but I'm there with you."

It's definitely reckless. A horrible plan, really.

I place a hand on his arm. "Thank you, Mica." I motion to step away but notice that he doesn't follow. "What's wrong?"

He shoves his hands in his pockets. "A long time ago, I made a promise to someone." I stay silent, wondering where this is going. "Well, it's because of that promise that I need to do this." He pulls his hand out of his pocket. A chain dangles from between his fingers. I hear something like glass breaking in his palm, and before I can react, I fall into darkness.

CHAPTER THIRTY-FIVE

The sleeves on this shirt are long and I tug them down, my fists clenched tightly, as I make my way to the ritual site. The heart in my chest beats erratically at what is to come. I can't even remember the last time that I felt it drum so dramatically, and I know it is because of her.

If it weren't for the King waiting for me at the summit of this peak, of the ritual that will undoubtably be cast, I would think it peaceful here. A painter's vision, I would imagine. The stars dot the dark sky in every direction and the leaves sway lazily in light gusts of wind. Most of the branches at this elevation are devoid of their colorful decorations at this point in the season.

The timing for my arrival couldn't have been better. The moon is likely an hour or so from its apex. The new moon is tomorrow, but I know that this moon, so close to what the King wants, will do. I wonder how long it will take the others to realize that two of their comrades are missing.

A gentle breeze glides past me, and I close my eyes. The wind encircles me, almost in greeting. Or in a goodbye. Maybe nature knows of what is to come and is telling me that I will not be alone through it all. It feels sentient here, like a friend who has my back.

The magic in my veins is itching to be summoned, to prepare for the inevitable fight that my heart is screaming about. But there will be no fight here.

At the crest of the hill, where the brightest star shimmers above, black flames burn along a curved line in the shape of a circle. And in that circle stands the King, a pleased grin cutting across his slender, sharp features. In the glow of the flames, the King looks ethereal. His black hair is pulled out of his face, cold blue eyes watching me intently.

"Good evening, Thea," the King says. The outfit he wears is akin to armor. Black, leather armor that devours the glow of his magical flames. There is a nameless sword strapped to his hip. When he notices where my eyes have fallen, he says, "Just in case. I'll admit, I figured you would come here seeking a fight."

I take a few more steps closer to the circle. The heat is suffocating and my magic reels back from its force. "You knew I would come early?" Of course he did. The King is calculated. There is nothing that the King does not prepare for, no path he does not see coming. He knew the ritual would likely happen tonight. Coming here before the actual new moon makes the others safer.

"If you didn't show up, I would have been disappointed in you. Or, rather in myself, for thinking I knew you better."

I shrug and walk forward, stopping just short of the fire barrier.

A frown crosses the King's face for a moment, then he collects himself, plastering that animalistic grin over his face. A predator who has finally caught their prey. He waves a hand and a path opens through the flames. "Not much for talking today, Thea? You were quite chatty the last time we spoke."

The more we talk, the riskier this gets. I just need this to be done with. To say that I have actually done something useful with my life. So that hopefully, wherever there is a next, I can smile, truly smile.

Keeping my expression neutral, I walk to the space between the two posts at the center of the magic circle and hold up my arms. Two heavy chains are tied around the posts.

The King prowls toward me. I'd imagine an inner war happening inside his head. He is likely torn between finishing this ritual and goading me into talking. I know that the former will win out.

With a click of his tongue, the King ties my wrists to the chains, warmed by the infernal fires. For a moment, I worry that my heartbeat will give everything away. That, like usual, the King will see through all falsities. But he doesn't.

After my arms are bound, so tight that I don't think I could break free of them if I wanted to, the King walks to a table a few feet from the posts. "You do know, Thea, that this ritual will erase that which binds our souls. You will die here. And you will not reincarnate."

"I know," I growl.

That provokes a grin. "If there's one thing that's obvious about you, it's that in any life, you are truly selfless. You have always done everything in your power to save those you care about." Now her smile turns poisonous. "And forget anyone who doesn't fit that category."

I open my mouth but snap it closed. Too much talking.

A witch emerges from the flames, as if she used them to teleport here. I've never met her before. She is tall and slender, with dull brown eyes and a thin mouth. Her black hair is cut short and is angled around her jaw. She nods her chin at the King, her gaze then moving to me.

Then, she begins chanting.

The words the witch utters are of a language I have never heard before. It sounds demonic. A sickly green permeates the King's black flames as she continues the ritual spell.

The King unsheathes a dagger and admires it before moving closer. "This dagger was used in so many rituals like this one. My coven," he shoots a hate-filled glare at me. "They used it. Before you betrayed our love. Before you and *him* destroyed them. Turned on them for simply existing."

I want to lash out at his words, to tell him that I know very well what that coven was doing. In the last few months, I've done my fair share of research on them. Most of the coven was killed, but many opted to stop practicing, even relinquish their connection to magic. What happened centuries ago was to stop a coven of witches from their greed for more power.

But still, I remain quiet.

My silence seems to irk the King. I can feel the heat of his flames growing with each angered step. "I have to say, I am a bit disappointed." He flashes the blade, the light of the fire catching in its gleaming metal. "I have killed you more times than I can count, and each time I watched the life leave your eyes was a thrill. But," he says, glancing at the dagger, then at the green and black flames that encircle us. "Everything comes to an end eventually."

I don't point out that he is lying. The only reason for this ritual is to gain the power of a death god. I grind my teeth at his words, my hands gripping the chains. At that, the King smiles.

"I thought that in this life, you would give me the greatest of battles that I have seen." He laughs, a short, forced sound. "I even prepared for it. Me, planning for an encounter that I would stoop to be *nervous* about it." His lips curl, a sneer cutting at me. "But here we are. The last lifetime our souls shall ever meet." A leaf crunches underneath the King's boot just a few feet from where I am chained. His eyes are a deep ruby. "This will be your last evening upon this Earth, dear Thea. With your death, I will become a force my coven could only dream of." His nostrils flare, brows knitting together. "I will finally be able to laugh in the faces of all the gods. When I set foot in their realm, as one of them, they will know my fury." His voice becomes a feral whisper as he says, "Soon, the gods will know pain."

My eyes widen at his declaration. At the realization of what my sacrifice will actually mean. The King meticulously planned this death ritual, all so he can claim Merikh's powers. Only to fail in the end. The King was too arrogant to think that someone might actually outsmart him.

That alone, makes everything worth it. I just wish I could laugh in his face beforehand. But to do so might make him ask questions. And I can't have that.

"Anything left to say?" he asks, angling the dagger to my heart. The witch remains at the boundary of the circle, her chanting increasing in volume. The King inclines his head at the witch. When he notices me staring, he says, "A witch who's bloodline traced back to my family's. She was so eager to see the fall of the Minuit Coven. She was happy to see your death as well."

I look away from the witch's cold gaze. It is then that I notice the sigils etched into the dirt. Familiar ones at that. One calls for summoning. Another banishing. And the last, the sigil of the death god.

The sigil depicting the god glows first. Followed by the summoning one. The witch's chanting slows and she glances to the King.

"The others will be spared," I say, trying as hard as I can to keep my voice steady.

"Valliant to the end," the King replies dryly. "They will be safe for now."

I close my eyes, tired of seeing his face. Tired of hearing his voice.

In the darkness, I see her. Her face is the one thing I see every time I close my eyes. For centuries, it has always been her. *I will find you,* I had told her once. I did, in a way. But it wasn't truly her. And it breaks my heart that I might not ever keep that promise.

But there are other promises to keep. Ones that mean others get to live, another day at least. I know in my soul that the King will fall this time around. There are too many riding on that outcome for it not to be true.

A cold, sharp pain burns a hole in my chest. White covers my vision and is immediately clouded by a suffocating darkness. I can taste my blood that pools in my mouth, can feel it as it pours down my stomach.

I open my eyes and see the dagger sticking into my chest. The King's hand is clutching its grip. My face twists in pain as he pushes it in farther.

I feel the ice in my veins.

My vision darkens.

I will find you.

This was always meant to be. I've questioned my life so many times. Why I had to live and endure after what I did. My part in this wretched curse of the three souls.

The King yanks the dagger out in an unforgiving, cruel tug.

My limbs become heavy. Too heavy, like gravity is greedy to have me.

The magic I cast upon myself earlier shatters away, its fleeting touch like the warmth of a departing lover. The illusions are fading.

The King's eyes widen with confusion then fury. "What the hell?" he hisses, the sound lovely.

"You…" I breathe, painfully pulling air into my lungs. "You should have…asked me to say your…name." Because then, he would have known that I was not who he thought. My vision is clear enough to see that dagger disintegrate in his hands, his fingers curling to try and keep it together. But it's over now.

To kill a god, that dagger could be used but once.

The sigils on the ground flicker before dimming out. The chains that bind me rattle as I lose the ability to hold onto them. The King is frozen in disbelief, his ruby eyes gleaming in hatred.

"You," he seethes, words still escaping him.

The brown of my hair—*her* hair—returns to its pale, almost white color. Just as I'm sure those beautiful hazel eyes have become green again, albeit, probably a dull, lifeless version.

"In…the end, M—" I cough, blood spilling from my lips. The grip that curse holds on me still tears at my throat, despite everything else ravaging my body. "In the end…I got *you*, King." As I speak, the feminine voice spewing from my lips morphs into the roughness of my own.

The King's face twists, reshaping into something absolutely feral. He watches as the dust from my amber sun totem, now broken, is carried away by the gentle breeze. The chain drops to the grass beneath my feet. "Her medallion," the King growls, his eyes moving from the disintegrated stone to the chain. His hands form fists at his side, the ring of fire growing more intense.

The witch is wide-eyed, a state of panic washing over her pale features. She half turns to the flames in which she arrived. "The ritual was started, but not finished. *He* knows." She takes a single foot into her escape route.

But a sword, glorious in every way, soars through the air like something from a story. The blade, gleaming bright despite the lack of true light, spins. And severs the head of the witch.

Vitamors lands in the dirt, the pommel standing into the night. A blast of orange flames breaks apart the black ones like they weren't made from a monster.

I have to blink away the blur from my eyes. Brown hair sways in the firelight that dances in her hazel eyes. Memories of looking into eyes so similar to hers flash through my mind as a comforting peace settles in my chest. Eyes that I will see again soon. Thea enters through the gap in the flames, her furious gaze taking in the scene. She looks at the King for only a second. A *second* she deemed enough to take him in, then she looks to me, her ire melting away.

Her mouth trembles at the sight. "Mica," her voice shakes.

CHAPTER THIRTY-SIX

THEA

 ica is dying.

His skin is so pale, his eyes almost gray. I want to scream at myself. To shout that I should have known better. But I wouldn't have. There is no way that I would have known.

And now, he is dying.

Morwen's wild rage radiates from her body like a tidal wave. Emotions so feral slam into me, threatening to consume any thread of strength I have. But I push my own power outward, shoving hers away. Her eyes flash a vibrant ruby as she moves, not for me, not for Mica, but for Vitamors. I yank at its tether, my palm facing outward. It answers the moment I think it, freeing itself out of the ground and soaring into my grasp.

Morwen slides to a stop when she realizes she isn't fast enough to grab it. Her mouth opens, but I don't want to hear her. Nothing that she has to say is worth listening to.

I charge with Vitamors humming in my hand and my flames pouring from my body like armor.

She dodges the first swipe as it swings down on top of her.

The second, she jumps to the side to avoid being decapitated.

The third strikes down like the first and she moves cleanly to her left to avoid it, where a sword of red hot flame awaits her.

She barks in pain as it slides across her back in her attempt to duck under it. Burnt cloth and flesh fill my nose.

I don't relent. With Vitamors in one hand and my flame sword in the other, I throw swipes and jabs, arching and stabbing. She doesn't counter, only evades. I don't give her a moment to unsheathe the sword at her hip.

Her nails become her weapon, elongating to a lethal point as she slashes at me. Nail scrapes against metal as I block attack after attack, her movements becoming quicker, steadier.

Mica watches from where he is bound, his head bobbing as if it were heavy. It looks like he is struggling to not succumb to his wound, which looks like it is right where his heart is.

I didn't notice the ground she was gaining on me until she was far enough away that with a single jump, she was out of melee range. And that is dangerous.

Flames, black and menacing, erupt from her. My flame sword becomes a shield, blocking the majority of her attack from turning me to ash.

But then the fear devours me. I shrink away, my magic completely withdrawing. I try to call upon my beta ability, but nothing answers.

A knee to the head sends me flying backward, landing just shy of her ring of fire. She is on top of me a moment later, a fistful of black flames aimed at my head.

My beta ability flares to life, clearing the rest of the fear that latched onto me. I have just enough time to react as her fist plummets for my face. I strike at her side with Vitamors in a jabbing motion. She jumps back, her flames diminishing.

We stand at opposite poles of the circle. Mica is still tied to the posts, unmoving. I listen for any sign of a rhythm in his chest, dread filling my body when I don't hear anything.

Morwen only laughs.

I lunge for her, jumping across the space of the circle and creating my second weapon again. She dodges both with ease, her speed increasing still. I see her fist before it can collide with my jaw and turn just in time.

At every attempt to gain distance, I close it. I can't risk her using her flames like that again. I need my fire to shield against hers, but I can't defend against her energy manipulation without my own. And I have no idea how to use both at the same time.

She jumps back when I arch Vitamors down for her head. My conjured, flaming sword morphs into a dagger that I throw, which she also evades. But instead of moving farther away, she closes the gap. Her speed is inconceivable. She advances in blurred movements, too hard for my eyes to keep up with.

I feel a blow to my stomach as the air is knocked out of me. Another to my chest, something cracking with the impact. And the last one in between the two, sends me to the ground.

I don't even have time to register the throbbing before she kicks at my side. Pain lances across my entire body in sharp tendrils. But Vitamors warms in my hand, healing the injuries she inflicted. The sword knows that all my magic needs to focus on attacking and defending instead of healing.

Again she stands above me. Her flames engulf her hand, growing and growing as the temperature skyrockets. There is so much of her fire that I think it might disintegrate me. It hovers over her head for only a moment before she sends it barreling to the ground.

I have no time to react. Can my magic even block this?

Vitamors, held above me, takes my flame, devouring it in a flash. Then, it spreads it out like a disk. The shield knocks Morwen down, though doesn't stop the fireball hurtling toward me. With my sword covered in my fire, I summon my beta ability. It comes, eagerly awaiting its use. And I throw a mental shield around my orange flames.

The heat is unbearable. I want to scream, to cry as it explodes around me.

And then it disappears. The fireball of black flames. The heat. All of it.

I blink, my energy manipulation simmering.

Her flames reappear like a torpedo. Gone is the giant fireball. Instead, a straight, powerful attack strikes.

Its target isn't me.

It strikes Vitamors, the sword trembling as if it realizes its fate too. The gem in the pommel explodes with the force of Morwen's magic. I watch as it shatters into hundreds of pieces, disappearing into the grass.

"No," I cry, barely a whisper, as I move to get to my feet.

Only I can't. It feels like my body was struck by a vehicle. I gasp, my vision blurring around the edges, as pain shatters into my body. I clutch at the ground, at my chest, at anything to stop the throbs.

Every part of me hurts, and I can hardly get enough breaths down. Panic sets in, my fingers grasping at the ground. I will my magic to heal, to soothe, but it is slow. It reaches for parts of me that are on fire but can't quite get a hold of them.

Morwen exhales loudly. "That felt good," she admits. I hear her footsteps on the leaves as she makes her way to me. I flinch at each sound. She grips my hair and pulls my head up so I am looking at her cruel face. "That which you are feeling right now? That is all the injuries Vitamors healed for you, coming back tenfold."

One of my ribs snaps, and I gasp a pained breath.

She shoves my head away, leaving me panting as she takes a few steps toward Mica. "When I saw you holding my sword that day, I was furious. It evaded me for so long, but then it showed itself to you. Of all people." She spits the last few words. "But I knew that the time would come for me to carry out what I intended to do. So I let you take it with you."

Cuts and scrapes form out of nowhere along my body. All places where Vitamors healed me after a training session.

Morwen places a finger on her chin, tapping it in rhythm with my throbbing headache. "Hey, didn't you heal Cole after he was about to die? That wound is going to hurt again."

I did. The stake in his chest was made from a plant that wasn't quite dead. And a living plant's toxin is deadly. I healed him. Vitamors healed me. And now, Vitamors is dead.

My eyes widen with that realization. At the implication of it all.

If I was going to die today, I thought that it would be directly at Morwen's hand. Not because Vitamors was destroyed. And all that it did to save me over the last month is being undone.

She laughs in that cold, detached tone, as she turns to Mica again.

"Leave…him," I seethe.

"Oh, I don't think so. He is still alive, barely. I want him to watch you die." A feral smile. "Again. And then I'll put him out of his misery." She grabs him by the chin.

I snarl at her to get away, yet the words don't make it out.

But the sound of a wolf howling does.

CHAPTER THIRTY-SEVEN

COLE

The moment we crest the hill, my heart stops in my chest. Thea is on the ground, clearly in agony. And Mica is…

"Gods," Oba curses.

"No," Alec murmurs, his mouth forming a snarl.

If it weren't for the note that Mica left for us in the castle, would we have been too late? Are we still? It had only been an hour after Thea ditched Sarah, the latter coming to me with worry. We found the note in the foyer after frantically searching for Thea. It took us only a half hour to gather our allies and come up with a strategy.

The note said we might find Thea unconscious at the base of the hill where the ritual site is located. When she wasn't there, I feared for the worst. And now, my heart thunders in my chest.

On the upper ridge, Amelia's howl cuts through the chilly air. It sends a shiver down my spine even though I know her warning is not for us. It is for the vampire who killed her. Who stands at the center of that ring of black fire, staring up at the ridge like the fact that a wolf is there is a minor inconvenience.

She let's go of Mica, his chin dropping like it is a lead weight. Oba curses again.

Morwen raises a hand and sparks jump from her fingertips. She looks from Amelia to the three of us, her eyes a blazing volcano.

There are more howls from the other side of the pass. Those howls are meant for us. I see Amelia dip her head in a snarl as she sniffs the air. Whatever she smelled made her change plans and dart down the hill to the north.

"Don't think I didn't bring friends for all of you," Morwen says. I sense them the moment before she finishes the sentence. Brais vampires emerge from the dip of terrain, masked by some magic that prevented me from knowing their presence.

"We can handle them," Oba says, pulling one of his daggers from his bandolier. "You get the King and rescue Thea and Mica." He and Alec move cautiously toward the Brais. With them fighting the rest of the Brais, I can focus on the King.

"Thea!" I exclaim, shifting my attention to her for a moment before returning it to Morwen. The barrier of black flame prevents me from moving forward.

Morwen snickers at me. "Now you get to watch her die as well, Nicolai."

"Thea, please," I plead, ignoring the vampire.

Thea wavers but tries to sit up. She presses a hand to her chest, blood staining her clothes. Her eyes are pained as she says, "Save him." I want to gape at her as she points feebly at Mica. As if she weren't also on the brink of death. Why isn't she healing?

Morwen only watches the interaction like it were a movie.

I look around for Vitamors. My temper rises when I can't find it and I step back from the ring. Angling myself away from Thea, I form a pocket of churning air and hurl it at the barrier. The moment my magic slams against hers, it feels like my heart is being torn from my chest. I see memories of Thea, dead and bleeding. Of the others beaten and torn apart.

My magic doesn't even make a dent in Morwen's.

"You'll have to try harder than that, Tempest," she calls out with a bored expression. She glances to her left, where Oba and Alec are fending off the other vampires. They are fighting together, as if they have been for eons. Where one falters, the other appears.

I force myself to stand, pushing through the aching fear that grips my body. Touching her magic with my own leaves me open for her beta ability to strike. I could pull the air from her lungs, but that hardly affected her before. And it still wouldn't help me get through her flames.

I form more pockets of violently churning air. My hair sways in the wind, my shirt rippling. The flames dance, swirling to the intensity of my air. Morwen's smile falters, her eyes widening just slightly when mine lift from the fire to meet hers.

The two air pockets fly from my hands like bullets. Morwen braces herself, but the impact is delayed and she drops her arms just as it hits her square in the chest. She is knocked to the ground and rolling from the hit. I'm already readying to release more air bullets when she snarls and gets to her feet. The magic I send to her, more intense than the previous hits, misses by a few inches. They tear a chunk of the earth as they hit.

If Thea and Mica weren't on the inside of the circle, I could unleash everything on the King. As it is, I need to do something to get on the inside of this ring of fire. Nothing I can do outside of it will help her.

"Cole…" Thea mumbles.

"Thea just stay with me," I say frantically, attempting another blast of my magic at Morwen's black fire. The leader of the Brais hurls her magic at me. I dodge the blast of fire, not looking to where it lands, as I shoot air at her.

"Wait," Thea says, her voice so low that I hardly hear her. "Cole, wait."

My hands itch for the wooden stake tucked in my belt. But I know Morwen would just catch it. She'd likely use it on one of them or throw it back at me. Somewhere behind the ritual site, I hear wolves colliding.

Amelia and her wolves are fighting off whichever pack was foolish enough to ally themselves with Morwen. No doubt she offered them some sort of power exchange. I look to the upper ridge, hoping to see our promised allies. But they are nowhere to be found.

Movement catches my eyes. Thea is forcing herself to stand. Even as she grasps her stomach, even as there is agony etched into her features. She faces Morwen, who looks almost impressed. "Vitamors is gone."

Gone? How can a sword be gone? I have so many questions but refrain from asking them as Thea lifts her bloody hands. A small spark forms in each of her palms, the fire bright despite its size.

I hear Morwen chuckle at the display. Still, she shifts into a defensive position. Morwen removes her stare from Thea and looks to Mica, whose skin is incredibly pale. "See, Mica? This is the fight I wanted."

Thea roars as she unleashes herself, her magic. She lets it take over, succumbing to the intensity of her emotions. Her arms move outward, palms pressed against the night air. I don't even notice any flames projecting from her hands. I just see the orange fire that engulfs the ring of black flames.

Inch by inch, Thea's flames swallow Morwen's. I see the tremble in her arms as she continues holding them out, allowing her magic to keep going. And they do, until not a wisp of black flame remains.

With Morwen distracted by Thea's magic, my own whirs in my palms, forming those wind scythes. My psychic ability flares and latches onto a wooden stake, keeping it hovering beside me.

And then the ring is extinguished.

Morwen snarls, her gaze instantly moving to me, but I am already moving. My scythes are in my hands, my beta ability holding that stake. I feel her own telekinesis trying to grasp a hold over mine in an attempt to seize control of the stake.

I swipe with one of the scythes. She isn't sure what shape my magic has taken, and when she jumps out of the way to dodge, she doesn't move far enough. The curved air blade catches her in the arm. With expert movements and years of experience, she twists and dislodges it from her body before I can yank it back. It could have taken her entire arm off if I had moved quick enough.

She spins on her heels, trying to grab the stake that quivers beneath our magics. But I still hold the most control over it and I move it out of her grasp.

"Enough of this," she growls. And an unbearable sharpness shatters in my mind.

I double over, clutching at my head. It feels as though it were being split open, cracked at from the inside. I hear Thea's pained cries over mine.

"Did I forget to mention that with Vitamors destroyed, all of my witch powers returned to me?" Words spill from her mouth, spoken in a dark language. Nothing like that of what Sarah utters in her spells.

The ground beneath us rumbles as cracks form. It starts to open like the maw of a monster ready to devour its dinner.

All I can think about is rushing to Thea, to wrap my arms around her or to toss her out of the way, I don't know. Morwen's magic is vast. I can feel it digging its poisoned roots into the earth.

There is a blinding flash of light from Thea's direction and I turn, ready to try and save her. But what I see erases all thoughts in my mind.

CHAPTER THIRTY-EIGHT

THEA

The pain in my head was too much. Too great when mixed with that of the repercussion of Vitamors' destruction. And when Morwen chants in a witch's language, terror floods my body. It blocks everything out. The pain, the anger.

All I see is Cole falling to her hate, her power. She is going to kill him. Right in front of my eyes, I'll have to watch him die.

Again.

Whispers echo in my ears. Whispers of defiance. *Not again.* They fill my body with a renewed strength. All the voices of my past souls. Of my ancestors who watch over me. And of those Morwen has killed.

My parents. And Valeria. They place their loving hands on my shoulders. That final nudge forward.

All the souls whispering to me place their remaining energies into one object.

My father's medallion burns against my chest.

I pull it out from under my shirt, the light emanating from it blinding. Their instructions come to me, clear as the stars overhead. A rock juts out of the ground in front of me, pushed upward by Morwen's chanting.

And I smash my father's amber stone against it.

It shatters into tiny pieces before my eyes, the light intensifying. Morwen's chanting stops and I hear her grunt. A pulsing, warm energy explodes from the stone. It floods my body, scouring every inch and soothing anything that aches. I feel the cloud of darkness from Vitamors' death being chased away.

With renewed vigor, I stand. My legs are shaky, but I manage to get to my feet. Morwen gapes at me, an expression of fury and disbelief crossing her sharp features. Dirt is smudged along her brow, blood drying on her arm.

Something cold forms in my palm. I open my closed fist to find a new medallion, formed from the warm energy of the old one. Seven small, amber stones fused together to form the shape of a flower. In each one, a different-colored stone is tucked safely within. Attached to it all is a chain to hang around my neck.

"A hunter's medallion? But how?" I hear Morwen's rage-filled question.

I glance up at her, black flames pouring from her arms. Her irises are a bright crimson. I slip the necklace over my head, my hand wrapping around the stones. "Because I am the daughter of Connor and Evelyn Knight." A thrumming sensation pulses from the stone to my hand, filling me with so much power.

Her eyes widen a fraction, but she manages to school her features. "And you will die like them. Like all the vampire hunters before you whose blood I spilled."

I feel the ghost of a friendly hand on my shoulder. It slips away, returning to where Mica is. I don't know if his heart still beats. And that alone sends me into a frenzy.

Morwen raises her hand, aiming at me with a prepared fireball.

But the medallion lends me its power. And I feel myself rush through the air at a speed I never knew possible. I am beside Morwen a heartbeat later. Even she couldn't monitor my movement.

Flames form around my fist as I land a blow against her chest. She grunts, flying backward and crashing against the ground. She recovers fast, getting up and charging at me with a feral wildness. With the hand that once held Vitamors, I clasp my medallion. Its power pillows from me, creating an invisible barrier.

Morwen slams right into it and stumbles back in a daze. I lunge at her, throwing fist after fist. The first few land, but she regains her senses enough and blocks the rest.

Morwen jumps back and hurls a wall of fire at me. I block it with my own surrounded by my beta ability. Her manipulation does not sink its claws into me. The fire magics dissipate, and I notice her attention flicking behind me. To where I sense Cole as he attempts to free Mica.

Morwen starts chanting. I throw a fist at her, but she blocks it, not breaking her concentration on the two behind me.

Cole curses as a fire erupts around him. One of normal flames, not black ones, created with her witch powers. He picks up Mica, limp in his arms, and staggers, trying to avoid the creeping flames.

"You think that you have won?" Morwen hisses. "I've only just tapped into all the power I have." Her irises change from red to a molten orange, her fangs becoming even longer. "I am the first vampire," she says. "Without me, you all would have died a long time ago."

I snort. "Are we supposed to say thank you?"

Her lips pull back from her teeth. "You should worship me."

"I think you spent too much time with your friend Merikh."

Morwen flinches at the name casually spewed from my

lips. I take advantage of that and throw a right hook at her jaw. She catches my wrist, pushing it up and out of the way as her other hand wraps around my throat. Claws dig into my skin and blood flows down my throat, making it even harder to breathe.

She brings her lips to my ear. "If you did worship me, perhaps all those you cared for would still be alive. *We* would be together still. And we would be the strongest vampires to ever exist. Our enemies would cower beneath our love."

With a strained voice, I say, "I may have loved you once, but you have proved over and over that I will never again."

She snarls and snaps my wrist, throwing me onto the ground.

I'm writhing from the broken bone when the faint click of a crossbow reaches my ear. In almost the same moment, there is a thud and Morwen grunts. A wooden bolt, smooth and sharp, missed her heart by only a few inches. She pulls it free and throws it with incredible strength and speed back toward the ridge. I don't see whether or not she made her mark. "I was wondering when you would join us, hunters." Her brow rises as she draws a vial from her pocket. A thick, red liquid sloshes inside. "And coven leader, I thought you would be hiding with your tail between your legs," she adds, raising her voice so those on the ridge can hear. She drinks whatever solution was stored inside the vial before chucking it to the ground.

She rubs at the wound where the stake had imbedded itself in her. "Even I am not immune to the effects of a tree's poison," she says as she glances to the empty discarded vial. "I made sure to take plenty of that wolf's blood after I turned her." Only the blood of a vampire who she last turned could heal her of that poison. As Morwen's would heal Amelia. Morwen tilts her head back, gazing out to where the werewolves are fighting. "How is she doing by the way? She got such an upgrade when she became a vampire werewolf. A werevamp? A vampwolf?"

"Sounds like you took your time on her like you used to with me," I grit out.

An unreadable gleam flashes across Morwen's features. "You were quite the taker."

I lift a brow, ignoring the sharp pain in my wrist. My bones grind against each other as they heal. I need to move away from her so the hunters can make another shot. I also need to distract her so she won't deflect or dodge the crossbow bolts. "I think the reason I ended our relationship was because you are insane." At her growing ire, I add, "It is definitely a because-of-you-not-me, situation."

Morwen's nostrils flare, her face turning red with anger. She moves so quickly, her feet gliding across the grassy terrain. I see her reaching for my head, but I dodge out of the way, spinning so that I can see Cole.

Black flames encroach on him and Mica. I watch as he tries to snuff them out with his magic, to no avail. He looks worried, trying to decide whether or not he can make the jump across the fires while holding our friend. I need to help him.

I jump back, Morwen's fist missing my face by an inch. My evasion must allow one of the hunters to gain a shot. One of the bolts cuts through the air and pins Morwen's foot to the ground. She gasps, dropping to the ground to pull it out.

I see all the hunters on the ridge, and the ones who have followed Sarah down to our elevation, aiming their crossbows directly at Morwen. All except for Isaiah. He is running toward us, a stake in his hand.

Morwen is struggling to remove the bolt, which I have realized has barbs at the end of it. They are preventing her from lifting her foot through the bolt. And with that, I dart out of the hunters' way.

I watch as black flames engulf her, growing so that they

cover her entirely. And still, they grow. A ball of menacing black fire. Sweat beads along my skin at the intensity of it.

She's going to take out this entire forest with that blast.

"Thea, can you get rid of these flames," Cole yells frantically. The fire is forcing his back against the cliff of the ridge, and Mica is a weight in his arms.

I rush to him and drop to the ground, one palm pressing against the grass, the other gripping my medallion. Flames sprout from my fingertips, small at first, but they grow.

Morwen's fire is the size of a house. If she lets it explode, it will make a crater of us all, likely even igniting a landslide. The results could be catastrophic.

So I pour more of myself into the magic that flows to the ground. A soothing heat blooms from my chest, down to my feet and arms. Orange flames simmer along the grass, moving gently toward Cole and Mica. They swallow the ones that Morwen created and retreat back to me, back to the fires that are slowly encrusting the black flames.

My magic hisses against Morwen's. It isn't so much the intensity of her magic but the endless darkness of it. Like all the hatred she has ever carried in her lifetime is expended through that fire. They smell of rot and promises of death. But my magic pushes harder. Her fireball stops growing the more it becomes covered. And when her black flames are fully engulfed in my orange ones, I let it shrink.

I can feel her screaming inside the ball of flames, her terror increasing with each push of my magic against hers. "Get ready to shoot," I shout to the hunters through tired breaths. Out of my peripherals, I see them aim their bows.

My fist closes, and so does the flaming sphere.

A volley of bolts fly through the air. Morwen cries out as a dozen sink into her flesh. She is crouched, her foot still pinned to the ground. I blow out a breath as Isaiah runs toward her, the stake in his hand ready for the finishing blow.

It is about to be over. Finally.

A part of me wants to stop the hunter from being the one who finishes her off. After everything she has done, to me and all the past lives I have lived, a piece of my soul wants to be the one to claim that. To watch as she takes her last breath.

Something catches my eye. A flicker of light where she is crouched, reminiscent of a projector screen.

Or of a spell similar to what the hunters did at the marsh.

A deep breath tells me that there is no scent of blood. The air should be heavy with the scent of her blood.

"Isaiah, stop!" I yell but am too late.

Morwen's body disappears, then she is on top of the hunter. It was an illusion, her crouched there. The scream-ing…everything. She made us all believe that she was beaten.

There is a sickening crunch and Isaiah screams as Morwen tears off his right arm. Her molten irises burn bright in the night. She looks to me before sinking her teeth into Isaiah's neck.

So much blood.

It undoubtably is rejuvenating her, replenishing all the magic she burned through.

A numbing wave washes over me. I am vaguely aware of my own body, as if I were watching myself through another's eyes. The longer I watch, the foggier my control becomes.

Someone mumbles something close by, but I don't hear it. I can't distinguish the voice. Not over all that entrancing blood.

Isaiah's honeyed blood wafts to my nose, igniting the ravishing hunger inside. My mouth waters, and I take a step to him. To where Morwen has lifted her head to watch me, golden eyes bright. The hunter's blood coats her chin, glis-tening in the dancing flames around us.

I'm so, so hungry.

Other vampires emerge from the hill, their hungry pres-ence like insects. They want this blood, too. But it isn't theirs to have.

It is mine.

Someone calls to me again. Still, I don't hear them. Not over the roaring in my ears. I didn't realize how famished I was until now.

All I see, all I know, is that delicious, honeyed drink. Morwen beckons me over to her, to join and drink until there is nothing left.

Someone steps in front of me, blocking my vision of that wonderful, enchanting scene. For the briefest moment, I am furious at not being able to see. But then a soft hand touches my cheek and I blink. A heaviness washes away from me.

Cole. He placed himself in front of me, blocked my view all the blood, of Morwen's magic.

The haze lifts from my mind, and my thoughts come clearer now.

"Thea," he says softly. His gray eyes are sparkling, both with worry and protectiveness. "You're safe. You're in control."

I blink at him, my mind free of the manipulation as I lean into his touch. "Thank you."

I feel Morwen's energy rush toward us. She probably planned to take advantage of his back to her, but it seems that we were both still ready. Cole turns to face her but I push him away, positioning myself between him and her. But as soon as I do, she vanishes from my sight.

There is the sound of bone crunching behind me, followed by a gurgling sound that churns my stomach. I turn and look down and the world stops spinning. Noises stop reaching my ears. The wind no longer touches my cheek. Everything is replaced with an icy numbness.

Cole's hand moves to my face for just a moment before it slips away, his skin becoming pale and cold. Morwen stands behind him, a satisfied grin on her bloody, dirty face.

"No," I whisper, though am not sure if any noise comes out. Cole falls and I reach to catch him. "No." He stares, unseeing at the dark expanse of the night sky. At the stars that shine even though they shouldn't.

"No." I ball his shirt in my fist. The stake in his chest, in his *heart*, is stained with his blood. "Please, Cole."

But he doesn't move.

Because Cole is dead.

CHAPTER THIRTY-NINE

THEA

Cole stepped in front of me to break the spell Morwen cast. A spell to entrance me. He knew that I wouldn't want to hurt Isaiah. He took a gamble, that his touch would destroy Morwen's hold on me. And he knew taking his eyes off of her would be a risk.

But he did it all anyway. To rescue me.

No risk, no reward.

But there is no reward in this.

I press my forehead onto his chest and scream. I cry out, cursing all the vampires and gods and witches and whatevers in the world.

All of this, everything, it was for us. So we could finally live, together. But now…

Cole is dead.

And Morwen is standing over the both of us.

I reach for her, hardly moving at any significant speed to do anything. I expected her to be smug, to grin at her work of killing Cole. But her expression is solemn. Even still, as her hand hits the inside of my wrist to deflect my attack. She grabs me by the throat and slams me against the ridge wall.

"That ritual would have prevented your reincarnation. But

I guess you will have the next life to try harder, Thea," she says, pulling her arm back. With nails like claws, she digs them into my chest. They wrap around my heart.

An obliterating pain shreds into me. Darkness seeps in from every side. Beyond us, the battle still rages. The hunters and Sarah are fighting off the vampires. None of them seem to notice that half the reason why I was fighting is dead. And soon I will be, too.

Will they stop fighting then?

Will I reincarnate as soon as I take my last breath, or is there some sort of limbo that my soul will linger in? Maybe another dimension.

A dimension of death.

Like the death god's domain.

As if my thoughts awakened it, the symbol on my palm burns cold. Only a breath has passed since Morwen's claws dug into my chest. And in that breath, I saw everything. I saw how this will play out.

My left hand grips her arm, the symbol scorching into her flesh. At the same time, darkness erupts around us. There is everything and nothing inside this sphere of darkness. It is just like the place Cole and I were plunged into when talking with Merikh.

Morwen bellows from the contact. She releases all of me and staggers back. It is only us in this void, and Cole's lifeless body. He came, too. I can feel the death that has kissed him, claimed him for its own.

I feel all the deaths that occurred tonight. The vampires and wolves. Some of the hunters, too. Mica's life hangs on a thread, teetering between this place of death and that of the living.

Mists swirl around the black, endless depths of the ground. I flex my hands, my magic roaring within my veins. It feels like Merikh's power flows through my body, mingling with that of my own. Like a supercharged battery.

"You," Morwen breathes, her terror flooding my thoughts. She trembles with each step backward. "You took his power?" Her words echo into the void.

I lift my chin and let my vampiric powers push past their limits. It only adds to her fear. I let power flood me. Mine and that of the death god's. It is like pure adrenaline. A violent waterfall that rushes over a cliff, or an inferno churning in a storm. Flames pour out of me. They are bronze-colored, though black at the base, and swirl around my limbs. The mists at our feet eddy with my magic.

She shakes her head and opens her mouth, though no noise comes out. "It isn't possible." I show her my palm and the symbol etched on it, glowing in this darkness. "No," she breathes. Her fear turns to anger, fuel no doubt, for what she is about to do.

I take one step forward as Morwen swings a punch at me. Surprise crosses her face with the swipe of her arm, likely as she realizes her lack of magic here. With a sidestep, her attack misses. My fingers dig into her chin, and I haul her off her feet. "You have no magic here. You did not deserve the power you wield. All your life, you destroyed when you could have helped. You sought power, greedily taking it no matter who you hurt in the process. And that, Morwen, was your down-fall." She grunts as I throw her, her body landing hard on the invisible surface. The mists part, disrupted by her body.

I blur over to her, my speed catching her off-guard. She inhales sharply at my sudden reappearance. "You will die here, Morwen, for good. Alone and hated. Your soul will never see life again."

The darkness moves. It writhes and slithers, hungrily wrapping itself around her limbs, keeping her pinned. Morwen screams.

I stand beside her prone, shivering body. A sword of fire emerges, clasped by both of my hands, and I hold it above her chest. "Goodbye, Morwen."

There is a shimmer in her eye as she looks at me. Her voice is low and hoarse as she says, "I just wanted to love you again."

As she closes her eyes, embracing the darkness, I drive my fire sword through her heart. I feel her tired, ancient soul leave her body. The writhing wisps of the death god's magic consume what is left of her.

And then the last bit of the witch who became a vampire vanishes.

I feel the joy of those who had fallen by her hand as the last of her soul, her essence leaves the world, forever bound in this dimension of death. I feel their joy, but also their sorrow and relief. At their exhaustion and readiness to finally depart into that eternal rest.

But I am not done here.

I turn. My face crumples at the sight of his body. I kneel beside him, tears falling from my cheek. I tuck some of his hair behind his ear, its softness like a stab to the heart. Every part of him, now so lifeless, is like a thousand cuts. My soul is mourning.

"Come back, Cole. Please," I plead, debating whether or not to invoke the death god himself. "Come back."

It is just me here. And the darkness.

I kiss him on the lips, already cold. "We were supposed to travel and see the aurora borealis together. I wanted to take you back to Italy, to see where you once called home." I sob into his chest. Something that was once so warm and loving, now cold and distant.

"I know a place," I whisper with trembling lips. "I saw it in a book. A place so isolated from the rest of the world that you could live an entire lifetime thinking you were the only ones alive. There is a meadow there." I remember the dream sanctuary he created. How every detail was perfect, everything that I would want in a place to retreat to.

"Please, Cole. I don't want to do this without you." I

hardly get the last words out through the sobs that wrack my body. I wish the darkness would engulf me, too.

The mark on my palm burns then pulses with each beat of my heart. The endless void that we are in hums, the air becoming electrified. I look at Cole's pale, lifeless face, then to the black sky. I feel the wisp of another's life slipping into the void.

Mica.

"Please." My voice quivers. I look to my shaking hand, to the sigil of death etched upon my skin. I ball my hand in a fist before slamming my palm down onto the murky, depthless ground. A gray, shadowy light explodes from the force. It is blinding, so I close my burning eyes. My heart races and I feel like I am tumbling through space. I fumble through nothingness, trying to grasp Cole's fleeting soul. His body moves far away, becoming a speck of light in the dark distance. Like a star in the night.

Everything stops spinning, but I keep my eyes closed, my chest heaving from exhaustion. A throbbing pain bounces in my skull as tears prick my eyes.

"Thea." I hold my breath, unsure if the voice I heard was inside my head. "Thea." His voice startles my aching heart. Cole is faintly smiling up at me.

"Cole?" I say his name through a sob.

"You don't have to do anything alone. I told you that, remember?"

I don't know if I should cry or laugh or scream at him. "You're here." I clutch at his shirt, at his hair. Color returns to his skin, to his beautiful smokey eyes. "You're here," I say again. Merikh's magic brought him back. Cole is alive.

Cole's hands slide to the sides of my face. "Always." And he kisses me, both of us kneeling in the grass of the field.

I kiss him back again and again and again.

. . .

MORWEN'S VAMPIRES fled the moment the dark veil exploded over the ritual site. It is instinctive, I suppose, to fear a power like the death god. That power created vampires, after all.

The mark on my palm is nothing but a scar, the only remnants of having ever met Merikh.

Cole was the only one who Merikh's magic brought back. As the power of the death god left me, I felt it giving thanks for me holding my end of the bargain. Merikh's powers took Morwen's life and gave back Cole's. If I ever see the death god again, I will have to thank him. Though conversing with a god again is not on my list of things to do.

A few hunters died when the Brais attacked. And Amelia lost two wolves. Oba and Alec survived, though were badly hurt.

But Mica…

"There is nothing that any magic can do," Riley says gravely. "The blade that Morwen used was ancient, its strike absolute. And the ritual needed to be paid once it was started." She leans back and removes her hands from his body. "I honestly have no idea how he has even made it this long."

I kneel at Mica's side, opposite of the hunter, still on the hill where the battle took place, but far enough away that we cannot see its remnants. Mica's breathing is shallow and pained, but he smiles weakly when he sees me. "Hey, Kindria." His eyes, usually bright like an emerald jewel, are now dull and clouded with death.

I laugh as tears stream down my cheeks. "I told you not to call me that."

He chuckles hoarsely. "I knew you would do it." There is a speck of blood that pools at the corner of his pale lips. "From the moment I saw you, I knew you would."

"You shouldn't lie on your deathbed," I jest, though there is more sadness to the words than humor.

Mica's hand finds mine and he swallows roughly. "I'd do this again." His words are labored and between breaths. "I knew you in one of your past lives." My heart shatters at those words, but he keeps talking. "Did you know? I kept that promise." His eyes flutter from mine, scanning our allies who have gathered around. It doesn't seem like he can see their faces, though. "Alec?" he calls out, even as his gaze passes over the vampire who is standing at his feet.

Alec kneels beside Riley with tear-rimmed eyes. "I'm here."

"I kept that promise," he repeats.

Alec forces a smile. "I know. I hope you can forgive yourself now."

"Yes," he whispers ever so quietly. "I think I do."

"Thank you for saving me, Mica," I say in his ear, his hair tickling my lips.

"No," he says, his fingers just barely flexing around mine. "*You* saved *me*, Thea." He murmurs another word, but I can't hear it.

Nor do I hear the weak drum of his heart.

CHAPTER FORTY

THEA

The sun greeted us with its warmth only a few hours later. The autumn air is crisp but offers a gentle warm wind as we carry our comrades down the mountain. There is a heavy silence between all of us, even with the light that was sure to follow.

We were free.

All of us, free.

"Thea, a moment?" I turn to see Isaiah walking a few steps behind me. His shoulder is wrapped in a bloody bandage. Though his comrades managed to stop the bleeding, each movement seems to be pained. He winces as he gestures for me to follow him. We stop at a copse of birch trees, their golden leaves shimmering like the sun.

"How are you doing?" I ask gingerly.

His expression is solemn, eyes red from mourning his friends. "I was prepared to be the one who died during that fight. None of the others," he pauses, "they were supposed to make it through."

"I'm sorry for your losses." My beta ability, though tired, stirs in my chest. It floats to him, an energy of peace mixing with his grief.

"As I am sorry for yours."

We stand in companionable silence for a few breaths. I listen to the rustle of the leaves above our heads and the sounds of our comrades as they continue moving down the mountain at a slow pace.

"We are setting out to a sacred burial site, open only to vampire hunters. Would you care to join us?" Riley walks by as he asks, her gaze fixed on the ground before her. A spark of hope blooms in my chest at her survival.

I look to Isaiah and offer a gentle smile. "I would love to visit this place and pay my respects. But first," my gaze lands on Cole who stepped to the side, waiting for me. "I need to bury my own comrade."

Isaiah nods in understanding. "Of course. My door is always open to you, Thea Knight," his attention drops to my medallion briefly, a spark of pride flashing in his brown eyes, "should you ever want to learn more about your parents or your heritage as a vampire hunter." He offers his left hand to me.

"Thank you, Isaiah." We shake hands to a new friendship.

Cole slips his fingers into mine as we join the descent down the mountain. I can't help but touch the stones of my medallion. Something that brings me a little closer to my parents.

Sarah went with Amelia and her pack. The members they lost were wolves that Amelia had known for a while. The alpha would be sure to need comfort.

ALEC KNEW where Mica would have liked to be laid to rest. So here we are, burying our friend underneath a large weeping willow tree. It sits in the center of a spacious open field, far from any prying human eyes. The forest stills in our presence like it, too, were mourning the loss of a kind soul.

I can't help the tears that fall. Nor can anyone else for that matter.

Under the sweeping branches of the willow, we share our favorite stories of the pale-haired vampire who equally enjoyed irritating those he cared for as well as helping them. Mica was truly a kind soul, stuck in the life that was cruelly dealt to him.

I knew you in one of your past lives.

The pain of losing him cuts deep into my heart. I mourn for him, but it feels like that past life is, too. Someday, I will ask Alec if he knows the story of Mica and my past self.

For now, I will only say goodbye.

Oba and Cole stepped back, leaving Alec and me to gaze upon the turned dirt. Where, next season, there will be grass and flowers and all sorts of life seeking shelter under the tree's protection.

"Mica once told me," Alec starts. He takes a breath, collecting himself. "He told me once he knew he wouldn't be able to see the woman he loved in the afterlife. Not unless he forgave himself for all the things he blamed himself for." Alec swipes at a few tears. "I'm glad he did, in the end."

A goldfinch chirps from one of the branches above. It offers us a song, quiet and sad.

"Me too."

Alec turns his red-rimmed eyes to me. "Don't blame your-self for what happened."

I look to Cole and Oba, who are walking slowly back to the path through the woods. "I brought Cole back. He was dead, but I used the power of a death god to bring him back. I tried to help Mica, too, but I didn't have enough power."

He considers but ultimately shakes his head. "I don't think it would have worked. And besides, Mica went to that site knowing the inevitable outcome. And he knew what would have happened if it was you who died instead." He makes his way down to where the other two are waiting, giving Mica's resting place a final glance. I follow suit, saying goodbye.

"He did it mostly for you. For you and all the past reincarnations of yours whose lives ended because of the King."

I run a hand through my hair. "It doesn't make it easier."

"No," Alec agrees. "But now you can make it up to him by having that life you never could."

"ARE you sure you don't want to stay here?" Oba asks as we make our way to the portal for the last time.

Helios meows in his carrier, unhappy about moving again. "Yes, I'm sure."

"It could be cool, you know. Living in a castle." He shrugs, turning away from the enormous, stone building.

"I've *been* living in this one. I don't want to for another minute." We pass the statue of Morwen, the only thing that is keeping this dimension together. Well, the statue and the portal, I suppose. I look at it, no longer gripped by fear as I do so.

Morwen is gone.

And Cole and I can be at peace.

Sarah is certain that Morwen will not be reincarnating back into this world. Having been the one who started this vicious cycle of death and rebirth between Cole and me, her death ended it. She became the focal point for that curse responsible for bringing our souls back over and over again.

With that information, we are sure that if either Cole or I die, then we will not reincarnate again. These are our last lives, and we plan to live them together, to the fullest.

We owe it to our past lives and to those who helped us get here.

To Mica.

Oba laughs and Cole groans. "Whatever it is you are

about to say Oba, we don't want to hear it." Cole winks at me and readjusts the grip he has on the boxes of all the stuff we couldn't bear to let be destroyed with the dimension.

"Oye, you're rude. I was just going to say that I've heard other vampires talking about the two of you as if you were in charge."

I lift a brow. "In charge of what?"

Cole groans again.

"Of vampires." He snorts when my jaw drops. "You'll need a castle for that."

"No," Cole and I echo.

Beyond the portal, the ocean still dances with the shore. The trees sway and the sun shines. I feel, in a way, that we will be freeing the magic that has created this dimension. For centuries, it has been stuck in this endless place, only witnessing violence and hatred. But after today, it will return to the earth.

Everyone has joined us to watch as the last piece of our nightmares crumbles. Sarah used her magic to keep the portal open. Now, she and Amelia lean against the porch to Cole's small cabin, their hands intertwined. Alec and Oba stand shoulder to shoulder, a new friendship formed, the latter quiet for once. Cole and I watch from just beyond the disintegrating portal.

I will forever bear the mark of the Brais on my skin, and the sigil of the god of death. The memories of what I endured will also be etched into my soul for as long as I live.

And as the last of the dimension crumbles, Cole leans into my ear, and whispers three words that will forever melt my heart.

ACKNOWLEDGMENTS

Writing this series has been a decade long journey. When I started, I was an undergrad student learning about geology. I never thought that I would be here, at the end of the road, thanking people for helping me get to this point.

With that, I want to say my unending gratitude to the friends and fellow writers who pushed me all those years ago. Brittany, you inspired me to pursue my dream of creating worlds. Even when I doubted my writing capabilities, you were there to encourage me to keep going. Thank you for agreeing to be my proofreader again as well, you truly are the best! Sienna, your kind words made my ego self step back so that my creative, inner child could do what she always wanted to do. You encouraged me to reach out to Tara, another absolutely gifted person, who helped me take those initial steps toward publication. Thank you, Tara, for everything that you have done while I was a baby author, unsure of my footing. All three of you deserve the best and I can never fully express how grateful I am for you.

And of course, thank you for my family and friends. You all are a main reason why I continue to write. I am deeply grateful for the bottomless cauldron of your support and love.

Thank you, Nicolette, the best editor in the galaxy. You have such a kind soul and the best cheerleader ever. You always know how to engage my creative side so that my stories can be their best and fullest. My writing improves daily because of your support and guidance.

To Natália, a mastermind of art. You have absolutely blown my mind with each piece of art for the covers of this series. Do I stare at the covers sometimes to just admire your work? Guilty. You perfectly capture the essence of each book when you create the design and I think that is magic. I will be forever grateful for you and what you have done for me.

Franziska, thank you for creating the title font for the cover. You are so talented and I am grateful for your work. Even creating the font, you captured the vibes of what I wanted perfectly.

And of course, thank you to each person who has picked up this book. If you're here, then you have stuck around for all three books and I could cry just thinking about that. YOU give me the strength I need when I am stuck. Thank you for reading and loving Thea, Cole, and the others as much as I have. This was my first story to come alive and I am am grateful that someone likes it.

For my undying gratitude, thank you all.

ABOUT THE AUTHOR

Arleta Rae is a first time author living in the beautiful hills of
New England. Her debut novel, RISING EMBER, came
from her love of writing, the supernatural, and nature. She
has a BS in environmental studies and a MA in ecopsychology
and she hopes to open a nature retreat in the future. Arleta
weaves her enthusiasm for fantasy and nature into her books.
When she isn't writing, she can be found hiking, working in a
greenhouse, sipping a latte, or reading.

instagram.com/authorarletarae

threads.net/authorlarletarae

facebook.com/araebooks

tiktok.com/@authorarletarae